3FTx

Timed Terror

by

Robert Wright

Bob Wrighh

This is a work of fiction. Names, characters, businesses, institutions, organizations, places, events, occurrences and incidents are either the products of the author's imagination or are used in a fictitious manner. Any resemblance to actual businesses, institutions, organizations, places, events, occurrences and incidents, and persons living or dead, is coincidental.

Cover Design: Robert Philip Wright
Snake Graphic:©www.gograph.com/imgvector

ISBN: 978-0-578-61580-6
Library of Congress Control Number: 2019919461

Published in the United States of America
by Robert Philip Wright

Acknowledgements

Sincere thanks are extended to Greg Bundy, Ian Griffiths, Bill Washington and cousin Dave Skelton for their reviews and advice. A very special thanks for Janice, my dear literary wife of 54 years, for her strict no-nonsense editing. And a nice stroking pet goes out to Luci, our yellow-eyed, long-haired black cat who sat next to the keyboard of my computer in the wee hours of the morning, giving comfort and motivation.

Prologue

Clouds slid slowly by far below under a crystal
clear blue sky. Cauliflower towers of white dotted
the horizon. The air was as smooth as silk despite
the billowing convection near the ground. Captain
and first officer monitored engine and navigation
systems. Auto pilot controlled the aircraft. Tedium
was interrupted by radio calls with control
centers. Flight attendants pushed carts picking up
the refuse of the in-flight meal. Passengers dozed.
Some by the windows gazed down. A baby cried.
Someone pushed the call button for a tiny bottle
of wine. Soon they would land, but the expected
descent had not yet started. Flights over the same
daily route had become routine. In a few hours,
with anticipation, some passengers would be at
home with husbands, wives and kids, others with
friends at their favorite bar or in a hotel room to
rest for the next day's business meeting.

Preparing for periods of boredom, the first

officer had picked up an interesting magazine at the concourse newsstand. The cover had grabbed his attention – "Ancient Mesopotamia." He had flown combat aircraft over that ancient land.

In flight, he again rechecked position, heading, altitude, air speed and exhaust gas temperatures of the pair of big turbofan engines, then fished the magazine from his black leather flight valise and thumbed to the feature article. Skimming the introductory paragraph, he read how archeologists had discovered fragments and artifacts near an ancient city. Carbon-dating had confirmed that the environ of Baghdad was the earliest known clustering of human beings for mutual benefit, the origin of cities, and civilization, on the banks of the Tigris River.

He keyed the flight-deck intercom, "Hey, Jen, you ought to read this. Interesting stuff. Jen ... are you alright? Jen?"

Tigris

Husayn went to see his brother about a very important decision. Mustafa was sitting with his wife who held their first child, Akmal. "Marwa and I are leaving Iraq forever. She is pregnant. I will not bring up my child in a place such as this. With the catastrophe in New York City, the Americans will be back with misdirected vengeance. Mark my words. Hellfire will fall from the sky, again!"

"My brother, my brother. You must do as you wish. Have you spoken to Father?"

"No, not yet. I will tell him, but I know he will not understand. His head is as thick as yours."

"Where will you go?"

"First to Turkey, maybe Jordan, to prepare and apply to live in America."

"Husayn! Really? That is a Christian nation. Their believers look down upon us. Have you forgotten the Crusades?!"

"Dear brother, the Crusades were long ago. The invading infidels came from Western Europe, not America. Much later, the Treaty of Tripoli, signed by a president of the young United States of America, confirmed that the nation was not founded on the Christian religion and that it had no hostility with the believers of Islam."

"I do not know of this treaty. You are the eldest, Father's favorite. You had your head buried in books at the university while I worked long hours in the market stall."

"Marwa and I will take our chances. I have heard that people in America can speak their thoughts without fear of torture or death."

"What of the market stall?"

"It is yours, if Father so wishes."

Husayn stood and turned to leave; Mustafa stood also. Despite the political fracture between them, they still shared the same blood. They stared at each other as little Akmal began to cry. Both placed their right hands over their hearts. Mustafa spoke first, "*Saalam Aleikum* (Peace be with you)."

Husayn replied, "May the peace of *Allah* be with you."

They touched their cheeks lightly together, side to side, as air kisses were being exchanged, then hugged each other, not close, but with hands pressed firmly on shoulders. As Husayn walked away down the street, Mustafa stood at the doorway and called out, "You have my address."

Husayn walked with his thoughts, his decision, along the banks of the wide Tigris that flowed gently. From high mountains in the north, its greenish murky waters had given life to the arid region: transportation, commerce and irrigation had nurtured the cradle of civilization. Cultures – their beliefs, their leaders, their armies – had vied for the area. Bodies and blood had been sacrificed on this altar of human development. But out of the turbulence had arisen agriculture, the planting of cereal crops, the invention of the wheel for transport to evolving villages and cities where cursive script, mathematics and astronomy had been developed. Clusters of people had settled on the banks of the meandering river which grew into a sprawling city. They bestowed the name "God given" – Baghdad.

As if this divine gift came with a curse, conflict still embraced the city. Foreign armies with modern engineering and their supporting mathematics were now bringing devastation to the ancient city; some destruction came from the air, guided with precision. Husayn paused, gazed across the calm water at the mirrored reflection of the earthen bank and buildings on the other side, knowing it would be the last time he would walk along the river of his youth. He picked up a stone and pitched it far out, as he and Mustafa had done as boys. As the ripples spread out in widening circles, Husayn turned away and walked to the apartment where Marwa waited.

†

Mustafa walked through the rubble-strewn labyrinth in the predawn morning. Bricks, cinder blocks and gray concrete chunks had once been privacy walls and the faces of buildings before the aerial bombings. Apartments that had housed families were now open to public view framed by their supporting structures, hollow gray shells with reinforcing rods laid bare, twisted and bent by raw explosive force. His two young sons, Akmal and Ramza, ran ahead of him, playing tag, laughing as they raced to see who got there first. They stopped and waited at a wide, familiar hinged metal face. Mustafa unlocked and rolled up the security door and they all set to work to open the market stall for business. Varieties of dried fruits, nuts and dates were scooped from lidded barrels into shallow woven baskets. Spices were poured into copper bowls. Mustafa set them all out on a wooden rack that slanted towards the narrow street. It became his work of art: a spectrum of browns and tans, accented with yellow, orange and deep reds. Akmal and Ramza knew exactly where to place the small paper signs with hand-written names and prices.

Small metal scoops were set out. Mustafa hung the scale and set out a stack of paper sacks. He drew money from his pocket and filled the cash box hidden under the rear of the rack. Akmal and Ramza swept the stall and the street in front. They were ready for business, before the morning call to prayer.

Mustafa had learned the business from his father, and his father from his; buying in bulk from farmers and wholesale merchants, selling at retail prices, leaving profit in their wakes. The family lineage was deep, now held in aging memories. The rental arrangement for the space, sealed with handshakes over the years, had parallel roots. The rent was modest, affordable with the meager profits from the family business. The location was not ideal, but near the very long Souk al-Safafeer where sheets of copper and brass had been transformed by hand into beautiful pots and bowls for centuries on al-Rasheed, the oldest street in ancient Baghdad. This *souk*, an ancient Arab marketplace, drew throngs of customers and visitors to the sounds of hammers striking metal. Many walked the narrow street and passed right by Mustafa's edible offerings.

Mustafa's market stall had another benefit, discussed and emphasized over recent generations. Its front faced Mecca. A small vertical line had been accurately etched with a chisel on the stone wall across the street by Mustafa's grandfather. When standing, or kneeling, in front of the center of the stall, Mustafa knew that if he faced that line, he would be facing in the direction to the *Kaaba*, the holiest site in all of Islam, the center of the Great Mosque of Mecca, the center of the *Hajj* pilgrimage that all believers must struggle to complete once in their lives. As the family lore went, one learned in Islamic sacred law and theology, a *mullah*, had not been so sure if this was appropriate and had come to see this attempt to recreate the *mihrab*, a niche within a mosque which enabled the same directional accuracy. The *mullah* had come with an adviser holding maps and charts of the day. Since all Muslims everywhere were required to know the sacred direction, the *mullah* had approved and had asked *Allah* to bless Mustafa's grandfather, and by implication the etching, according to family legend. This was often repeated to customers at the stall. Some came down the narrow street just to see the mark on the wall. It was good for believers, good for prayer, good for business.

In the early days, before modern plumbing had been installed, jugs of water had been carried into the back of the stall for the ritual ablution before each of the five daily prayers. Now a single faucet and sink with a special white towel were used for the required purification ritual, the

Wudu, before spiritually facing *Allah* in prayer, and the *Kaaba*. Akmal and Ramza would gather at the sink at the strong behest of their father for the *Wudu*, somewhat shortened. Water from the slowly streaming faucet filled their cupped hands. Following their father, they wet and washed their faces, washed both arms up to their elbows, wet their heads and hair, removed their sandals and washed their feet by rubbing their wet hands over them. For drying, the shared towel was used. But that almost was not needed in the dry desert air that drifted across the city.

The clear sky started to lighten from the sun just below the horizon. Akmal and Ramza knew what was coming. Mustafa pulled out three small rolled-up rugs from under the wooden rack, handed one to each child, kept one for himself as they stood in front of the open stall. The call to morning prayer filled the street. Mustafa rolled out his rug first with its woven likeness of a *mirhab*. He aligned it with the etching on the wall, knelt and bowed down, touching his head to the rug at the top, open palms on the rug out to the side. Akmal and Ramza followed quickly, aligning themselves with their father as *Allahu Akbar* (God is the greatest) was heard twice and filled their minds. They believed, all around them believed. The faith was taught them by Mustafa, taught in their school, their *madrasa*, taught in the mosque. They had not yet reached their teen years; Akmal and Ramza believed.

†

Over a decade earlier, Mustafa had huddled with his family in the basement of their apartment building near the Tigris River as the bombs fell, deafening, violent. Shaking with fear, they had fervently huddled and prayed to *Allah* for deliverance from the wrath of the coalition of forces from the West, acting to liberate a tiny country far to the south from its Iraqi invaders. But bombs fell far to the north of Kuwait exploding near Mustafa, his father, mother, and his older brother, Husayn. Among the aerial targets had been radar installations, command and control centers, air bases and air defense systems. The family unfortunately lived not too far south of one of them: the Iraqi Republican Guard base and airfield of al-Taji. While bombs were released and guided with modern precision, laser spot location errors had been made by pilots and by intelligence officers. But the will of a merciful *Allah* had been upon them, and upon the leader of Iraq who survived with forces that ensured his continued survival in power.

Mustafa and Husayn had had their beliefs about the Prophet and power of Islam in their daily lives, but more private beliefs about the Arab Socialist Ba'ath party. They knew about Kuwait's complex, troubled history, exacerbated by British influence and the fall of the self-appointed *caliphate*, the Ottoman Empire. The British and the Ottomans had agreed on a border separating Iraq from Kuwait. Following a world war, the British high commissioner in Baghdad approved of the proposed border which was included in a broad application to the League of Nations concerning all of Iraq's borders. The discovery of reserves of oil within the borders of an independent, sovereign nation very close to land-locked Iraq's vulnerable and only access to the Persian Gulf was too much for Saddam. He had thought that crossing the border to annex or control Kuwait was Iraq's latter-day manifest destiny.

Mustafa and Husayn had heated but very private arguments about all of this. They were used to arguing as rival siblings as they grew up and began to understand what was being taught in their *madrasa*. Mustafa believed that Islam had been spread by the holy word; Husayn believed it had been politically spread by the killing sword. This fundamental family schism was still with them as they discussed politics and power. Mustafa felt that Kuwait belonged, or should belong, to Iraq. Husayn felt that the case for this was not as strong, and that Saddam and his followers had underestimated the West's interest in Kuwait, greatly underestimated their combined military capabilities, and had brought down rains of bombs around their family that had huddled in the basement.

The sibling rivalry between Mustafa and Husayn was not helped at all by the market stall. Their aging father had wanted Husayn to take it over, as the eldest son. But Husayn would have none of it; he had his sights set higher. He wanted to become educated beyond the *madrasa*. Husayn attended classes at the University of Baghdad, increasing his knowledge of life and the world. He helped at the market stall when he could, which was not often. Their father was distraught.

With no-fly zones imposed by Western powers to help protect independent-minded Kurds in the north and Shiite Muslims in the south from air strikes directed by the Ba'ath Party, and with Saddam still in control of powerful ground forces, Husayn had had too much. He had just married when he learned that Arab militants from their country had associated themselves with a group of Islamic extremists, *al-Qaeda*. They had commandeered and flown passenger airliners into two tall buildings in

New York City, bringing them down and killing thousands. Husayn saw them as innocents,

Mustafa had a different opinion. The terrorist pilots and their accomplices, too, had believed, but with blinding light reflected from a different extreme facet of the faith.

Husayn had been right. Bombs did again rain from the sky, but this time they were followed by the mass invasion of Western infidels. Akmal and Ramza were raised in a country occupied by Americans bent on forming an Iraqi government in the image of American democracy. Saddam had been found and later dispatched by the new government, with some members seeking revenge and justice on the ousted dictator. But peace was slow in coming. Shiite leaders from the south had slightly different views of how power and oil wealth should be shared, as did the Kurds in the north. In the turbulence, others with more ancient beliefs arose from the rubble of war. Large cities, not far west of Baghdad, al-Fallujah and Ramadi, fell under a new banner. They had a strong leader. His fiery, impassioned speeches proffered something very fundamental – the *caliphate*. He spoke to the very core of the faith.

After they prayed in front of the market stall, Akmal and Ramza ran through the same labyrinth of streets back to their home. Along the way they briefly slowed when patrolling American soldiers saw them. They laughed and waved, then ran on.

But their bright faces hid the growing hatred in their hearts. Their mother had breakfast waiting for them. They wolfed it down, then picked up a soccer ball, a gift from their father, and ran to the door. They heard the command from their mother, "Only for a time, then to the *madrasa*. Don't be late, do you hear me?"

"Yes, Mother." They made their way to al-Zawraa park, just northwest of the heavily-fortified, so-called Green Zone, the International Zone where the interim Iraqi government was being formed. They had also practiced the art of soccer in the side streets. After some pick-up soccer games at the park, they made their way to their *madrasa* on the banks of the Tigris. There they had learned to read and write the beautiful Arabic script, numbers and their arithmetic, their Arabic history and something more: the *Qur'an*. This further cemented them in the faith of their father, during morning prayers and at evening prayers, after dates, nuts, dried fruit and spices were stowed away and the stall locked up for the night. The call to prayers from the *minaret* became an integral part of their lives. As if it were a verbal bell tower, a holy man at the top of the mosque's tall *minaret*, the *muezzin*, gave the time of day as accurately as they needed, enfolding their daily lives with a guided spiritual dimension.

    As they grew from boys into men, they tried

to find other work outside of the market stall. As they had often done after classes in the *madrasa*, they often sat in the shade of a palm tree on the bank of the Tigris, throwing stones, watching the ripples spread outward. Work was very hard to find. The fighting had decimated the economy and it was slow to recover. The wholesale price of dates, nuts, dried fruit and spices rose as the number of customers fell. They felt the frustration of their father. Akmal and Ramza had come of age and talked about life, girls and their futures, as pebbles splashed in the greenish water. They spoke more heatedly about the Americans, especially after Ramadi had been retaken by Iraqi forces with the help of the Americans.

They prayed daily, frequently in the mosque, especially on Fridays. They willingly, without question, fasted with their parents during the holiest month on the Islamic calendar: *Ramadan*. Their local mosque had been visited on occasion by a *mullah* from somewhere else. He seemed different, a little more intense, with purpose in his eyes and a deep scar on his cheek. After the *Isha'a* one evening, he pulled Akmal and Ramza aside and spoke directly. Their eyes widened as the *mullah* said he had been making special prayers to *Allah*, and that *Allah* had revealed to him special plans for their lives. Running a market stall would not be in their futures, but

Syria and the *caliphate* would. A truck would be there next week to take them for basic military training somewhere in a remote desert before joining forces in and around a besieged city. He described how an Islamic state was being formed with the intent of establishing the long-awaited *caliphate*. He pointed to the water in the Tigris that was flowing past the mosque and said that ar-Raqqah was also on a river, the Euphrates. As if it was also a revealed truth, he said that the two rivers joined far to the south at al-Qurnah, where their combined water then flowed into the Persian Gulf near Kuwait, the land that really belonged to Iraq. He added that *Allah* had placed his human creation in the area between the Tigris and Euphrates. To cement his words, and the motivation of Akmal and Ramza, the *mullah* asked rhetorically, "What could be holier than that?"

Akmal and Ramza placed their right hands over their hearts as the *mullah* departed from them, his black robes flowing. Later that evening, over dinner, they told their parents of their decision to join the fight for the *caliphate*. Their mother broke into tears and covered her face. Mustafa stood firm, stoic, and wished aloud for *Allah* to be with them.

Flight

Jennifer Grissom had been raised on the cornfields of Kansas, a freckled-faced, sun-touched farm girl. An only child, she grew up playing and hiding in long rows of ripening corn on towering stalks, or fantasizing while prancing among their snow-covered stubble. But Kansas was a special place in more ways than its flat, fertile land, humid summers, and wind-drifted snow. The broad central area of the country had a natural target on its back: tornadoes, more than any other place on earth. She had huddled with her frightened parents in the cellar as tightly-twisted funnels danced over those same fields of corn. Regardless, she loved the place. Jen grew into a hard-working member of her small farm family. Before she was a teenager she drove the big grain truck in the fields, or the huge John Deere combine that filled it with tons of corn.

As a reward for her hard work, her thrifty father took her to an air show at the nearby Salina airport. They had watched their own private air shows as hired crop dusters skimmed low over their fields. Those flights had impressed Jen, but just as a part of modern farming. At the airport, they were watching with awe as small, nimble aircraft were put through rolls, loops, twists and turns.

A vintage B-17 Flying Fortress from a bygone age came to life with belched smoke and deep-throated fury from 9-cylinder, Pratt and Whitney engines, started one after the other. It took off and returned for a low pass down the runway. They could not only hear, but feel, the low deep, rhythmic throbbing of its four radial engines. When parked, they walked under its wide riveted wings and crawled through the cramped fuselage, bomb bay and cockpit, trying to imagine what it must have been like to be on a daylight mission over Germany surrounded by flak and fighters. The magic of flight was still seeping out of the old aircraft. Jen felt it.

They strolled among the crowds and down the tarmac by all sorts of aircraft, some owned by local operators at the airport. A handsome young man stood by a little red and white Cessna 172 in the shade of its wing, smiling, holding a strut. Jen noticed the plane, and the pilot who winked at her. A sign advertised that rides in the little aircraft were available for a reasonable price. Her father saw the glint in Jen's eye and pulled out his wallet, "Alright honey. Let's go."

He climbed in first and took a rear seat. Jen took the seat on the right with the pilot's help and special attention. With her tousled short reddish-blond hair, freckles and broad smile, she was a ringer for Amelia Earhart, and he said so. Jen just shrugged. She had heard that name before when studying history in high school, but that was it. She had forgotten that Amelia not only set flight records, but broke barriers for women in early aviation.

As the wheels left the runway, the city of Salina, grain silos and corn fields to the horizon spread out beneath her. Jen became addicted to the magic right then and there, somehow suspended in clear space over the neat rows of summer corn and fields of golden ripening wheat.

She became fully focused in that new direction, with a little financial assistance from her somewhat-worried parents. She took flying lessons from the young man on the tarmac. Before long, she soloed. A private pilot license followed. Then she was legally equipped to take others for a ride, including her father and mother into the Kansas skies to circle low over the family farm. With clenched, white-knuckled fists, they knew small-plane flight was not for them, but that flying was now their only child's dream. Someone else, maybe her cousin, would have to take over the family farm as they aged.

After graduating from high school, as money would allow from jobs in town and outright family contributions from work on the farm, she moved up in the government-approved ranks of aviation. With ground training and instructed flight using only the on-board instruments to navigate, and keep the aircraft from unwittingly rolling over, her license showed that she was qualified to fly in poor weather conditions under government Instrument Flight Rules, IFR in aviator parlance. More training, flight hours and tests followed. Jen earned her commercial pilot rating and became a certified flight instructor with the coveted Certified Flight Instructor endorsement on her license. She checked out in the twin piston-engine Cessna 340. With its wings below her, not above, to her it just looked more like a real airplane. This aircraft was faster and made the magic of flight a little more comforting as even modern engines had been known to fail; having two was better than one.

Jen went to work for the fixed-base operator at the Salina airport from whom she had rented aircraft and had paid for instruction. She now taught others to fly over Kansas fields. She also had redone her history homework and purchased a leather jacket like the one seen in old photographs of Amelia Earhart, also a daughter of Kansas.

She leveraged that persona at Salina air shows, holding the strut of a Cessna 172, or standing by a Cessna 340, netting more students. Jen's logbook filled with flight hours paid for by those she was teaching to fly. She also flew charter flights for wealthy people who knew how to farm.

Jen had briefly considered logging hours as a crop duster. She had seen them, in rather ugly aircraft, swooping down very close to the ground, wheels brushing the tassels of the family's corn. One duster had told her that it was only there that he felt the sensation of speed in flight, different than being suspended in apparent slow motion higher up. But Jen's brief allure with that faded when balanced with what she was told that could happen, and had, flying very low over fields of corn: mostly-missed power lines and startled pheasants that flew up into wings, spinning props and windscreens.

During her student pilot time and when later instructing others, she had often flown cross-country to Kansas City International Airport for practice in its highly-controlled airspace, landing and taking off amid large commercial jet aircraft. Radio communications with the control tower were constant and confusing, but that training was also needed if your sights were set higher than the Salina airport. The big behemoths of the air caught her attention: Boeing 777s and Airbus

330s, all headed to distant and exotic places. That was for her. She set her sights.

Jen loved Kansas and its corn fields and wanted to fly over them with more than a student or a few passengers. Living with her parents, working out of the Salina airport, she was still able to comment on the corn harvest and drive the combine and grain truck. But like all pilots everywhere in the country, she had to work her way up, logging flight hours and birthdays before any airline would even talk to her. Jen finally passed the thresholds of age and flight time, nearly 2,000 hours as pilot-in-command. Jen applied to a number of regional carriers, so-called feeder airlines that flew in and condensed passengers at the hubs of the major carriers at large cities, or dispersed them back out from these centers. But an airline far to the west caught her attention, and she caught theirs; Caldera Air with its fleet of sleek Canadian Bombardier CRJ200s powered by twin jets mounted on the rear of the fuselage near the tail. Its wings were clean and it could carry 50 passengers cruising at three-fourths the speed of sound.

Fittingly, Caldera Air's hub was at Portland International Airport, known in shorthand as PDX, the official three-letter code assigned by the International Civil Aviation Organization. Close to the east, the Cascade Mountain Range was dotted north-south with beautiful, snow-covered peaks of hopefully-dormant volcanoes. The eruption of Mount St. Helens not far north of Portland had announced that the range was very much alive and could be awakened. Its volcanic crater, its caldera, was still in formation. But stunningly beautiful Mount Hood was still in a deep sleep, as confirmed and forecast by geologists so the people of Portland could sleep at night. Portland itself had a volcanic past, lower mounts that had been volcanic vents, spewing cinders that settled out and collected as cones, one with blackened rock still visible as a reminder.

Caldera paid for her flight to PDX for an interview. Wearing her attitude and motivation on her sleeve and her captivating smile, she carried her logbook, documentation of a passed flight physical, and the papers for all the required flight ratings. Hiring Jen was a no-brainer. Caldera Air nabbed her. She excitedly called her parents, who were not so excited; aviation was taking their daughter away from them and the corn fields of Kansas. She flew back to pack and take care of her move to Portland. She looked out of her passenger window as the plane climbed out east, over the Columbia River Gorge. Looking at majestic Mount Hood, and the verdant, forest-covered rolling landscape, she knew she had made the right decision.

After hugs and kisses on the porch of the family farmhouse, Jen returned to Portland and completed Caldera's training program for the Bombardier CRJ200 and for her Airline Transport Pilot certification. She had managed to make the down payment and moved into a modest two-bedroom house on the shoulder of Mount Tabor in Southeast Portland, not far from the small dead volcanic vent above her. From the rear deck, Jen could see aircraft flying into and out of PDX, feeling even more connected to her new career path. Nearby, she discovered a thoroughly British place, the Horse Brass Pub. Jen often went there for relaxation and companionship, and a pint of good craft beer for which her adopted city was famous.

Jen soon found herself in the right seat as co-pilot, or more elegantly, first officer, flying to and from such exotic places as Salem, Eugene, Bend, Ashland and Richland. A city larger than Portland was also in the mix, Seattle. As hours and experience accumulated, Jen was promoted over to the left seat as pilot-in-command, but she preferred to be called the proper title, captain. She enjoyed every flight hour. With weather and moisture from the Pacific Ocean to the west, her instrument experience increased, a lot. Fog, rain and low clouds were dreary to some, but the winters were warmer than those of Kansas. But the magic of flight was still very much there, and Jen still had her eye on the larger birds of modern aviation that she saw fly into and out of PDX.

Flying out of Seattle one September morning, Caldera Flight 496 was directed by Air Route Traffic Control to return and land at the airport, and stay landed. There was much confusion in the concourse packed with passengers, their eyes glued to television monitors and the column of cancellations. Jen and her first officer looked into a bar on the concourse, its televisions screens ablaze with a horrifying reality. Jen stood in a trance watching black smoke billowing out from the twin towers of the World Trade Center in New York City. This was followed by recorded video showing commercial passenger jets being flown into the towering buildings, then their collapse. Her aviation world changed forever. But Jen continued to fly, in front of reinforced doors, logging hours and opportunity.

✝

Two hundred miles south of Salina, and a few years after Jen had first soloed a Cessna 172, Christopher McDonald started down a different aviation path. Chris was an Oklahoma boy through and through, but not a farm boy. Born and raised in Enid, he helped out at his father's hardware store when not delivering newspapers, mowing lawns or shoveling snow. In high school, Chris had an interest in flight, but more from a nerdy, technical perspective. When not in the basement with a tornado siren wailing outside, he wondered – just how did a wing generate lift? He did well in high school math and physics classes and wrote a paper that described that the relatively lower pressure on a wing's top side was not magic, just fluid dynamics in action.

Meteorology, tornadoes in particular, also fascinated young Chris, and terrified his parents. One had swept away the detached garage and tore off part of their house. But there was another motivator near Enid, a subliminal one. Chris often looked up and saw young officers from the nearby base being trained to be military aviators. With some satisfaction, he knew that the wings on their training aircraft played by the same laws of physics.

With good high school grades, Chris was accepted at the University of Oklahoma, another two hundred miles south in the city of Norman. He majored in meteorology. In his junior year, he netted an internship at the National Severe Storms Laboratory just a couple miles from the campus. In classes and at the laboratory, he found that tornado formation and its forecasting were a little more complex and elusive than a wing generating lift, but he stuck with it. Both involved the fluid atmosphere. He was motivated by the fact that a national network of Doppler weather radars had helped increase warning times and decrease false alarms, saving lives.

With degree in hand, he took advantage of a government job opportunity at NSSL. He would start the following October. While he had lived on campus during the school year, he had often driven home to see his parents on holidays, often dropping a big plastic bag full of dirty clothes in the laundry room. While his mother complied, he went to hang out with his high school chums. When of age, that included the Land Rush bar in downtown Enid. With a gap summer now ahead of him, he moved back into his room, refilling the empty nest. Unwinding at the Land Rush bar, lifting a pint with friends and flirting with waitresses and girls he had known in high school were in his summer plans.

Since Chris was old enough to legally drink anything with alcohol, he felt a kinship with the Land Rush. Its decor included enlarged, framed reprints of photographs and paintings of clusters of overeager men on horseback or driving covered wagons, all bent on claiming free land that had been wrested from the Native Americans. From his father he learned that he was a descendant of a Tennessee man who had staked his claim, but had found that farming the rich soil was not for him. A city had sprung up as a result of the rapid influx of people: Enid. There he had opened a dry goods and seed store now linked by generational ownership to his father's hardware store.

Chris still had a few weeks to go before moving to Norman and starting work at NSSL. He had helped his father open the hardware store one September morning and was stocking and dusting some shelves, writing down inventory. His father turned a radio on, trying to find some music to lighten the load of their work. As he turned through the stations, all he heard were excited announcers covering something of importance. He stopped the dial on one station. He and Chris listened as they learned that a commercial aircraft had flown into one of the towers of the World Trade Center, on a clear blue-sky day. Then, like an ice pick to the heart, the announcer, almost screaming, described that another plane had flown into the adjacent tower.

The mood in the Land Rush that evening was muted; recorded music had been turned off. Chris sat with two of his equally-shocked friends at the bar, holding cold beers. Roger said he was going to enlist in the Marines, Gary in the Army. They looked at Chris and asked what he was going to do. Was he still going to work in the safety of the NSSL? Or, was he going to "take it to 'em!"

He paused for a moment. He had been thinking about this all day at the store. Chris set his beer on the bar with a loud bang and announced that he would go into the Air Force. They raised and touched their glasses in unison, binding their announced commitments. In the following days, Chris applied and was accepted for their Officer Training School. A college degree was required, and he had one. Soon, Chris left for a few months of education, rigor and needed discipline in Alabama. Commissioned as a second lieutenant, he returned for Undergraduate Pilot Training at the same base he had known since he was a kid, Vance Air Force Base. He did not move in with his parents, even though his mother had encouraged him to do so. Chris settled into Bachelor Officer Quarters and began the stressful grind to become a military pilot.

Over those same flat fields of corn and wheat, he checked out in a twin-jet, side-by-side trainer, the T-37, then in a very-sleek, supersonic tandem-seated one, the T-38. He did exceptionally well in the weather course and helped others to understand the complexities of the atmosphere in which they flew. On Friday afternoons, after an intense week of training in the air and in the classroom, Chris went to the Officer's Club bar to hang out with one of his instructors who had flown fighters in actual combat. Influenced by him, and other seasoned military aviators, he set his sights on fighters to bring it to 'em; air-to-ground. In these bar-side discussions, his perspective of flight morphed from nerdy and technical to lethal and macho. Chris fantasized on becoming a fighter pilot, hoping to elicit envious looks from men and admiring glances from women when not ending enemy lives and destroying things.

Follow-on aircraft type assignments from Vance were partially-based on class standing at graduation, balanced with Air Force needs at the time. Top students were generally given their choices, which were most often fighters. Chris received orders for training in the venerable C-130, a four-engine, turbo-prop aircraft. Its looks were more akin to the clunky planes used to dust corn fields than the supersonic trainer. Primarily, the stout and husky C-130 carried cargo, but also passengers. He had requested fighters, but his middle-of-the class ranking got in the way.

After graduating and upgrading into the C-130, Chris spent the next few years in the right seat, flying cargo and passengers in theaters of operation all over the world, including Afghanistan. He took special interest in the weather briefings, as weather could bring a plane down as well as automatic rifles or shoulder-fired missiles. Some passengers were special and actually decided to leave his perfectly good aircraft while in flight: the elite airborne troops of the US Army and sometimes smaller cadres of very special forces, delivered in the dark of night from very high altitudes. With more hours, most of them in combat, Chris started logging time in the left seat as pilot-in-command. With his squadron commander's recommendation, and very good Officer Evaluation Reports on file, he transferred to a very different aircraft and received special training. With ultra-close, flight-deck aircrew coordination, Chris flew the MC-130 Combat Talon very close to the ground in nap-of-the-earth operations to avoid detection, or delivered lethality from somewhat higher altitudes in the cloak of night. Infrared, low-light-level, laser-guided, 105 mm Howitzer and Gatling gun became a routine part of his mission planning vernacular. That soon drew him back into the skies of Afghanistan and then Iraq.

While very proud of his service, Chris realized that the Air Force was just not for him, that he had cheated death more than once, and was probably using up his quota. He walked into his commander's office, saluted and respectfully placed his signed papers on the desk, his request for separation. The weathered, lined face of the colonel was stern and unsmiling. Chris saluted and wound up back in Enid, honorably discharged.

Pleased parents gave him his old bedroom back, if only for a time. Chris helped his parents overcome their lingering empty nest feelings and even helped out at the hardware store, like in the old days. Maybe being a hardware merchant was for him as suggested by his father who spoke of retirement. Maybe he could re-apply to the NSSL in Norman. While he contemplated his future, he just knocked about, unwinding from the stress of flight in general, and flight in combat in particular, trying to figure out what to do with his life. What better place to come to terms with all of it than at the Land Rush. As luck, or rather fate, would have it, he met his two friends there. Roger was still in the Marines, on leave, and Gary, having honorably separated from the Army, was now learning to fly at the Enid regional airport. After hearty man-hugs, firm handshakes and slaps on the back, they sat at the bar. It had been a long time since Chris had left for Officer's Training School and when Roger and Gary had gone to basic training and ground-combat assignments in Afghanistan. Beers were poured and war stories flowed. They had all seen or caused death and mayhem on the ground in Afghanistan. As stories were elaborated and dates confirmed, Chris found that he had actually supported them with airdropped supplies or with dense rains of Gatling gun slugs that pulverized their attackers in the Hindu Kush.

The bar finally closed, but the long-time bartender let them stay while he cleaned up. He had overheard their conversation and had slid their beers across the bar, on the house, his way of thanking them for their service. Finally, he unlocked and let them out the rear door. As they walked to their cars, they asked Chris what his plans were. He just turned, shoulders shrugged, palms turned up.

†

Little Nina Taylor was thrilled to walk down the aisles, handing out packets of chewing gum before descending to land, to help passengers clear their ears as cabin pressure increased. At five years of age, she was drawn into aviation long before Jennifer Grissom's first flight out of the Salina airport and Chris McDonald's military training flights over the fields around Enid. The daughter of divorced parents of some means, she often flew alone between Los Angeles and Portland, in First Class, under carefully-chaperoned care in that upper-class section. With starry eyes, she looked with awe at glamorous stewardesses in their sharp military-styled uniforms and envelope-shaped hats.

Living in the West Hills of Portland, Nina

grew into a smart, sophisticated young woman and entered Portland State University. With her refined upbringing, she appreciated the finer things of life, including the elegance of flight as a passenger, if not the magic of flight itself. Some of her friends became stewardesses. With both university and flight-scheduling flexibility, they managed to juggle hours and continue their educations. With vivid memories of her flights to Los Angles and Portland, that was for her. She carried packs of chewing gum in her purse and usually offered some to classmates before a big exam to help relieve a different kind of pressure. Nina made a run at the airlines while a freshman at the university.

She interviewed with the major carriers, but the competition was tight. A mere three pounds above stewardess weight standards kept her from serving coffee or tea at 35,000 feet, if not packets of gum. With a stiff upper lip, Nina pressed on and continued her education at the university in the arts, theater and languages, knowing the latter could be a requirement for becoming an airline stewardess on international flights. Nina received her diploma and continued her graduate studies, included a summer course at the University of Madrid; there were a lot of Spanish speaking countries with international airports, she had reasoned.

Nina still pursued elegance. She worked in high-end retail for women's clothes, makeup and perfumes while still watching for flight stewardess opportunities. But, as the years added up, her age put her on the wrong side of an airline hiring decision.

Even though those three pounds still nagged her, she sat straight up when her stewardess friends told her that one airline had changed their age requirements. She applied again, and looked very good doing it; those three pounds somehow vanished during the interview.

Glorious years followed in a dream-come-true job based out of PDX, living in Portland, serving others in flight, and selling the best French perfumes and latest Paris fashions to ladies in the upper-crust of Portland society. Now she was on the other end of a young-girls' eyes, gorgeous and sharp in her crisp, professional uniform. Along the way, she rose to the level of Purser, in charge of everything in the back of the aircraft, and for preparing her crew for flight. Nina did not marry, but she was beautiful and life was good. Handsome pilots helped balance her life, but the Association of Flight Attendants, her union, soon got in the way. On overnight layovers, no longer could flight attendants, and pilots behind the door to the flight deck, stay in the same hotels. But there were ways that could be managed.

International flights were still crowded by flight attendants with more seniority, but Nina logged hours with that career target in mind. Then the punch, straight to the gut: two aircraft had been flown into the twin towers of the World Trade Center in lower Manhattan; another into the Pentagon; and yet another into a Pennsylvania field. Nina was serving passengers when her aircraft, and all other aircraft flying above the United States, were ordered to land. In the concourse of the San Francisco terminal, she crowded around a TV screen, watching with disbelieving horror. From there, things slowed down in commercial aviation. Armed air marshals were added to the passenger list. Nina served them as well. Undeterred, Nina stayed with it; it was still her dream career.

Smithy

A steel hammer brought down hard on red-hot iron echoed through the Maryland pines. A husky boy had watched his father wrought the iron for a gate ordered by someone in Baltimore. The work cooled and was thrust back into the fire of the forge. With growing arms, young John pumped the big bellows. Nearly white hot, the square iron rod was pulled out to further fashion it with strength, skill and sweat. The old brick building, just outside of Whiton, had been around since the Irish had arrived. Driven out by the potato famine and the heavy hand of England, Eamon Kelly had brought his Irish Catholic roots and the knowledge of hand-working iron. His descendants had carried on the family tradition as an occupation. Young John Kelly had chosen that heritage with pride, as had his father, even though it was a dying artisanal niche. Modern, computer-driven machinery could make gates, railings and other things of iron that looked intentionally old, but real character had not been pounded in by hand. The family blacksmith shop had that character: anvils, tongs, a forge, hammers, bellows, calloused hands and leather aprons. John felt that tradition. He paid close attention to his father's seasoned words and also became a traditional blacksmith, eventually to take over the small family business as the only child.

John was a big man, over 10 pounds at birth, now over 220 pounds and over 6 feet tall. Irish, with red hair and piercing blue eyes, he was impressive. His arms competed in size and strength with the limbs of the big walnut tree that shaded the blacksmith shop. John had been forged by his strict parents, sermons in the town's Catholic church, priests in the confessional and strict nuns in the classroom. The tolling of bells in the tall white steeple reached the Kelly house and their blacksmith shop three times a day, summoning them to stop what they were doing, bow their heads as they recited the words that Eamon Kelly had learned in Ireland, the Angelus prayer: *And the word was made flesh and dwelt among us.*

On Mondays, Sister Mary Joseph would ask each of her students to stand and tell the class what they had done over the weekend. She felt it was good oration practice and required thinking on your feet. It had better include attending Mass and taking Communion. She called on John. He said nothing about what he had done at the forge or in the woods, but stood and started to recite, from memory, Henry Wadsworth Longfellow's famous poem, *The Village Blacksmith*, "Under a spreading chestnut tree, the village smithy stands ... and the muscles of his brawny arms are strong as iron bands ..." He flexed his biceps as a visual aid.

She cut him off, "That's enough John. Now, tell us what you did this weekend."

"Yes, Sister."

Sister Mary Joseph thought she should bring John down a notch, thinking she would help keep the sin of pride from befalling him. He was easily the strongest person in her high school class, if not the entire school. He was proud of his strength, but had only used it to keep bullies at bay, or to defend himself. She had assigned the class to read the story of Samson and Delilah from the Old Testament of the Bible. She asked a shy girl to stand and tell the story. When she told of Samson bringing down the pillars in the Philistine temple of Dagon, Sister Mary Joseph noticed John flexing his biceps, looking at them, as she knew he would. John was likely thinking he could do the same thing if given the chance. He tugged on his hair; it had not been cut for a while. Sister asked, "John, did you know that George Washington could break a dried walnut between his thumb and forefinger?"

John stood, out of respect, as required. "No, Sister, I didn't."

"Well, he could. Can you?"

John didn't answer and sat back down, slightly humiliated, wondering.

On the family property were two huge Black Walnut trees, one next to the blacksmith shop. His mother gathered walnuts in the fall, removed their husks and let them dry in the house by the fireplace. She would set a basket of dried walnuts by the anvil in the shop for John and his father to munch on while they labored. They tossed the nutmeats in their mouths and their shells into the forge. They were cracked open with a simple tap of a big hammer against their hard shells set on the anvil. After school that day, he went into the shop where his father was making a section of wrought iron fence. He picked a walnut out of the basket and held it between the thumb and the middle knuckle of his curved forefinger of his right hand. His father watched as John squeezed and squeezed, holding his breath as his face turned red. He let his breath out and set the walnut on the anvil, whereupon his father lightly taped it with a hammer and tossed the nutmeats to John. From then on, John would try and try to break a walnut with thumb and forefinger, but to no avail. He thought his reputation may be at stake. George Washington had lived not too far away in Mount Vernon. His father was quite proud that he had made a special iron piece ordered by the curator of George Washington's historic plantation mansion.

It wasn't until his senior year that a walnut finally gave way. It almost surprised him. He did it again and found that there was a little trick to it. First, he knew he had to have the strength, but rather than slowly adding force, as if in a vice, he did it with a quick pinching snap, like a small pile driver. His father's eyes opened wide when he demonstrated his strength and skill against a walnut. He shouldn't have, but John just had to visit Sister Mary Joseph right during her class. He walked in the classroom and up to her desk, "Good afternoon, Sister."

In front of the class, he held up a walnut between his thumb and forefinger, to make sure she saw it. Then, with a quick snap, crushed it like an egg and laid the shell fragments and the nutmeats on her desk, then walked out. A bit of pride had befallen him.

Surprisingly to some, despite his size and strength, John also had a light, precise touch. Coupled with his keen mind and eagle vision, his hunting skills were on a par with those used to forge iron. John had often hunted with his father in the Maryland woods to add to the family larder. Eamon Kelly had also done so to help his family just survive in their humble cabin in the Maryland woods. America had welcomed immigrants, but social safety nets were scarce back then. It was a free country, free to worship, free to speak, free to succeed and free to fail. John learned how to hold a rifle, align its sights, gently squeeze the trigger and put a round right on target.

When not forging iron, John practiced shooting, as he had done with the walnuts, but on a more limited basis due to the cost of bullets. Soon, he amazed even his father. One day, in a large clearing, he set tin cans on a fallen log and paced away from it, measuring distance with steps. They reached a point where his father missed, but John didn't. He paced farther out. John's bullets still found the tiny targets, flipping them into the woods. He was able to do so even farther out when he had lain down, prone, with his left elbow planted in the grass. The finger of John's beefy hand barely fit in the trigger guard. With controlled breathing and feeling the beat of his heart, watching the wind brush the grass, the rifle kicked back, almost as if by surprise, and a rusty can jumped off the log.

John was working in the blacksmith shop. He had been doing so full time over the summer vacation months, but was due to start high school classes next week for his senior year. His father came running from the house, "John! Come quickly. Something horrible has happened. It's on the news right now!" He dropped the hammer, tongs and a hot iron rod and followed his father into the house where his mother was glued to the small television set. John came just in time to see video of a plane crashing into a very tall New York City building with black smoke coming from the one next to it. That changed everything, including John's plans to become a blacksmith.

In the following days he watched as terrible news unfolded in the immediate aftermath of 9/11. John decided that he wanted to join the military, to serve his country, but he was too young. His father wisely said that he would have plenty of opportunity, that his country would need him in the coming years, but that he had to first finish high school and reach his 18th birthday.

That day came. He drove the family pickup truck into Baltimore and found the recruiting station. He came back and announced that he had enlisted in the United States Marine Corps with orders to report for training at the Marine Corps Recruiting Depot Parris Island in South Carolina. The Marines were always looking for a few good men. And they had certainly found one.

He didn't buckle when drill instructors

shouted at him, nose to nose in the barracks, on the parade ground or on a forced march. His strength in the obstacle course stood out. When his buddies had learned of his past, his intended occupation and strength, they hung a distinctive handle on him: Smithy. At follow-on training at the School of Infantry East next to Camp Lejeune, his marksmanship skills stood out. But he would impress others – with walnuts.

Off base, when on a weekend pass, he had won a few bar bets that he could break a walnut in his bare hand. He took to carrying a few in his pocket in case the bartender did not have any unshelled ones handy. He'd let other Marines at the local bar give it a try. Then he casually held it up as he had done for Sister Mary Joseph, crushed it with a snap, then gave them the nutmeats in exchange for a beer. An unsuspecting local lad walked into the bar one weekend evening. With bib coveralls and a big pickup truck parked outside, he looked to be a farm boy, big and strong, about the size of Smithy. The farm boy intentionally took a stool right next to him. The locals did not always appreciate young virile Marines spreading through their town and chasing their women. One thing led to another and soon 20 dollars changed hands, from the farm boy to Smithy. Unable to crack the walnut, he was none too pleased to be embarrassed in front of the entire bar when

Smithy did so. He extended his hand for apparent congratulations for Smithy having won the bet. When he had a firm grip on Smithy's hand, he started squeezing harder and harder. Smithy calmly advised him that this was not a good idea. His answer was not good, "Yeah, not good for you, Gyrene."

The crackle and snapping sounds were covered by his blood-curdling scream. With one vice-like clench, bones in the local boy's hand had been broken, to the amazement of those in the hospital emergency room. No charges were brought; just a Marine defending himself.

Upon graduation as a Marine infantryman, with orders in hand, he had a few days to visit his parents back in Whiton before deployment. In his razor sharp uniform, he walked around in the old blacksmith shop, giving it a farewell, just in case. He stopped by to see the parish priest and Sister Mary Joseph. They had been following the news and knew, despite their best prayers for him, that John Kelly might not return. With hugs from his father, kisses and tears from his mother, he was off to Afghanistan to bring it to 'em, those that had brought down the twin towers in New York City, or who had anything at all to do with it.

†

In Afghanistan Smithy distinguished himself as a soldier, an infantryman, a Marine. He was assigned as an automatic rifleman on one of the fire teams of his squad. Whether on the desolate plains, in urban streets or in the rugged Hindu Kush mountains, Lance Corporal John Kelly's skill, courage and leadership stood out on patrol and in fierce firefights. After casualties, he was moved up to team leader. He did not often fire his assault rifle in 3-round automatic burst mode. He preferred to use the optical reflex sight or aligned laser pointer and carefully squeeze off precise rounds, one at a time, taking out enemy combatants who had thought they were hidden among mountain rocks or behind the window curtains of an urban building. Smithy sometimes used the old iron sight with equivalent accuracy, as he had done hunting with his father in the woods of Maryland.

His strength was starkly applied when two Taliban insurgents leapt down from a rocky outcropping above a cliff ledge as he was bringing up the rear of a patrol. The ledge curved to the left and he was briefly out of sight of his team. A thrust knife glanced off his helmet as the attacker tumbled to the ground. Smithy literally picked the man up and threw him, screaming, off the high cliff just in time to react to a second one that stood up in front of him, knife drawn.

A squad rifleman in front of Smithy heard the scream, turned around and came back just in time to see Smithy put the man's neck in a vice-like, one-armed headlock, then with a quick twist of the insurgent's head with his other hand, snapped his neck. It was all over in a few seconds. Smithy tossed the limp body over the cliff.

In the ninth month of his tour, death had brushed close. Another rifleman in his team had been shot as he sprinted across an open street intersection in an urban fire fight with the Taliban. He lay wounded, unable to move as the insurgents fired down on him from the roof of a building. Fortunately, their training was not nearly as good as Marine training at Camp Lejeune. Some held rifles above their heads from behind the edge of the roof spraying rounds indiscriminately as if watering a garden with a spray hose. A few took more careful aim. Smithy did not hesitate. He sprang from cover, ran to his stricken buddy, grabbed a handful of battle uniform and dragged him back to cover. As he did, a round pierced his left shoulder. These two wounded Marines were taken back to the nearest field hospital where a Navy corpsman treated them. The bullets had caused major tissue damage to Smithy, and bone and lung damage to his fellow rifleman. They were both airlifted to a regional military hospital in Germany, then back to the United States.

His initially shocked but later relieved parents had been notified. But it was still a surprise when John Kelly walked into the family blacksmith shop and tapped his father on the shoulder from behind; he turned, dropped his hammer and wrapped his arms around his only child. The same welcome greeted him in the kitchen. During his extended leave back home to recover, his changing world swirled around him. On his Marine dress blues, combat medals hung from his chest: the Purple Heart for his battlefield wound and the Bronze Star for heroic service while engaged in action against the enemy.

Without him ever wanting it, Smithy became the proud talk of the town, their local hero. Sister Mary Joseph invited him to speak to her class. He looked very sharp and squared away as he walked in and set a paper bag on her desk. Then he spoke and answered their questions, emphasizing that he had graduated from their school and that Sister Mary Joseph was tougher than the drill sergeants in basic training. One student saw something in Smithy's hand and asked what he was holding. He held up a walnut from the tree over the blacksmith shop, looked at Sister Mary Joseph, then crushed it with only thumb and forefinger. Young boys' eyes widened. He picked up the paper bag and walked down the desk aisles handing out one walnut to each student, boys and girls.

With his laptop computer tied to the Internet, and phone calls, Smithy set about taking a new path in the Marines, a career path. He applied for the very tough Marine Corps Scout Sniper School. He had been recommended by his battalion commander. Certified mail arrived at the Kelly home in Whiton. Inside were orders for Corporal John Kelly to report to the sniper school in Quantico, Virginia; he would not be too far from home. At least until his next deployment – Iraq.

al-Falluja

In full battle gear a Marine automatic rifle team stood by their armored tactical combat vehicle, the ubiquitous Humvee, at their base camp near the western edge of Baghdad. After massive aerial bombing by the Western Coalition, the city had fallen and had been occupied by ground forces. Months later, Humvees were lined up to head a few miles west to an ancient Babylonian city on the other river of civilization's cradle: the Euphrates. From the start of the conflict, al-Fallujah had been bombed as well, but resistance there was fierce and motivated. US Army elements had been sent in earlier, and now Marines were being dispatched to the beleaguered city as part of a combined operation. A Marine manned the .50-caliber machine gun mounted on top of the Humvee. Another Marine, from the battalion's scout sniper platoon, stood among them with a very special rifle; it had a precision scope. He was accompanied by another sniper that would be his spotter.

Rumors of the sniper preceded his arrival: a

combat veteran in Afghanistan with battlefield awards and the top graduate at the Marine sniper school in Quantico. They shook hands with Smithy, a welcome addition to their team. The team members were well-qualified marksmen. But Smithy would deliver precise fire on selected targets at much longer distances. Over the radio the command was heard. They climbed aboard and headed out towards the hell of al-Fallujah.

†

He ran across the hard-scrabble land with his friends to play on the banks of the Tigris. Hadi had grown up in the small town of al-Mahzam a few miles north of Tikrit; Baghdad was 100 miles south. The faith of Islam had enveloped him and his young friends. At their humble *madrasa* they learned the roots of their faith, but they were still boys at heart, like boys everywhere. On the river bank they took turns throwing rocks. The splash farthest out determined the winner. Hadi's rock landed nearest the shore, as it always did. He was taunted by the others as they ran back to their homes for evening dinner and sunset prayers. Hadi had been teased often about his lack of rock-throwing prowess.

Hadi dug around on a kitchen shelf and found some twine and a swatch of cloth. Frequently, before bedtime, his parents had later found him practicing, flinging rocks with his home-made sling. It fit neatly in his pants pocket. Laughing, he and his friends gathered on the bank of the Tigris examining and picking up the best rocks for the contest. The rock-throwing champion flung a stone; its *sploosh* was at a considerable distance. Finally, it was Hadi's turn. He placed his smooth round rock in the cloth pouch, placed a finger through the loop at one end of the twine and with the same hand held a short stick tied to the other. With a raised hand, his small frame rocking back and forth, the circular speed increased until the twine sang in the air. He let go of the stick at just the right, practiced moment. The rock's splash out distanced all the others by at least double. His friends moaned, accusing him of cheating. He explained that getting a rock to land the farthest from the shore involved more than the strength of his arm, it included the strength of his mind. Soon, all of Hadi's friends were slinging stones into the greenish water. But he retained his championship with more practice and slings of different designs, all copied by his companions.

At the *madrasa,* in addition to the *Qur'an* and the daily prayers, they also learned of the Christian Crusades and of Salah al-Din who finally defeated them in an epic battle over eight centuries earlier. The *mullah* made special explanation of Salah al-Din and his military victories as he was born in nearby Tikrit. The *mullah's* words had been sharpened by the massive bombings by infidel Americans who had labeled their aerial atrocities Desert Storm, suggesting that a modern day Salah al-Din was needed.

Hadi and his friends talked about Salah al-Din from Tikrit on the banks of the same river that flowed past them. Soon, as a game, they divided into two groups, one representing the Crusaders, the other the forces of Salah al-Din. With branches and sticks as pretend swords they had pretend battles, each trying to out maneuver the other, but never doing any actual harm as they fenced with their sticks. The leader of the pretend Crusaders was not given a name, but Hadi's group would be led by a pretend Salah al-Din. Since first slinging a winning rock into the Tigris, Hadi had spoken with natural authority. For some reason, his words carried reasoned weight. The playtime defenders of Islam voted for Hadi to be their Salah al-Din. After pretend battles, the combatants came home with nothing more than scrapes and minor cuts on legs and arms. Parents cautioned restraint, but boys remained boys.

A few days later, both sides arrived at the battlefield on the edge of town, not far from the river. Hadi's troops were unarmed; no sticks. The other side had theirs at the ready. Hadi was asked if he had surrendered already, afraid to challenge them. He calmly told both sides to go to their positions, from there to charge towards each other as foot soldiers when he shouted the command. Hadi and his defenseless soldiers charged, hollering at the top of their young lungs. Just before the two sides came together, Hadi's side turned around and retreated towards the river, the latter-day Crusaders in hot pursuit. Hidden on the sloping bank of the river was a bundle of sticks, each much longer than the stick swords of their attackers. As Hadi had planned, they picked up their pretend spears and charged back across the field. With their parents' cautions in their minds, the longer sticks were just waved back and forth, scratching ankles, beyond the reach of their opponents.

A decade after Desert Storm, the Americans had returned as invaders. Hadi had hardened his beliefs that only a holy struggle, a *jihad*, could rid the land of these detested vermin. He read of the defeat of Iraqi tanks in the open desert. The main gun of the American tanks had a longer range, like his stealthily hidden sticks on the river bank. He joined the fight for the *caliphate* using his considerable leadership skills, relying on the will of *Allah* and the *Qur'an* to guide him. The leaders of the Islamic State soon promoted him

to lead the descendants of Salah al-Din's army
in the streets of al-Fallujah. In a darkened back
room, Hadi met Muhammed Talib, a middle-aged
man with a black beard. They probed each other's
backgrounds. Hadi found that Muhammed Talib
was very knowledgeable of Islamic tradition,
Islamic law and had essentially memorized the
Qur'an and the meaning of these revealed words
of *Allah*; he was a *mullah*.

†

Laser guided bombs had leveled buildings.
Rubble filled the streets and barricades blocked
their advance. They started taking fire from a
tall building; a mass of .50-caliber rounds from
their Humvee's machine gun were returned
towards its roof and windows. With enemy fire
temporarily suppressed, they dismounted and
entered the ground floor and the lone stairwell.
They encountered urban fighting at its worst: an
unfamiliar building, confusing close quarters,
combatants springing from hidden alcoves and
rooms. At the top of the stairwell they were met
with a locked metal door. An automatic rifle burst
failed to unlock it. A plastic charge was set against
the bullet-riddled lock. The deafening explosion
blew the door open as Marines bolted through the
door and smoke. The sources of the rooftop gun

fire, caught out in the open, turned to face M16s. They fell where they had stood. The Marines quickly swarmed over them to check if they had been killed; they had. Over a hand-held tactical radio they reported that the roof was secure.

Smithy and his spotter took up a position on the roof facing towards the center of the city and set up shop. The legs of his sniper rifle were set on a firm stack of empty wooden boxes, ammunition and binoculars were set close, radio communications were established, backpacks were set alongside with water, field rations and other items essential for a deployed infantryman. As the dead bodies were dragged down off the roof, Smithy noted that each head had been covered with a wrap of cloth to prevent facial identification. He thought that this insurgency had taken on a different dimension, guerrilla warfare, enemy combatants melding, unmasked, with the civilian population when not trying to end his life.

Smithy and his spotter maintained their position overnight. With night vision goggles they watched fire fights, but the running targets were random, illusive. But one had momentarily stood still in the night thinking that he was hidden behind the corner of a building. Smithy's thermal night vision scope removed the cover of darkness. A round was squeezed off and what remained of the insurgent flew back across the alleyway against a brick wall. Word spread at the far end of the street that a sniper was watching them. Some were ordered by an unseen commander to spread out and find the sniper's location.

Morning twilight revealed the long street in their line of sight with some closer Humvees parked on either side, roof-mounted machine guns dispensing bursts of death. Other Marines were in concealed positions, advancing, while their Humvees followed, machine guns firing at building doors and windows to give them cover.

Smithy saw a man with an open, bearded face dash across the street and into a doorway. The man had not been carrying a weapon and wore a black turban and dark clothes. He took a position in an exposed doorway and motioned with a waving hand for others to follow him. On the other side of the street, Smithy and his spotter saw somebody pointing and directing, an apparent tactical leader. As he did, men with faces covered, dashed here and there, firing as they ran, then taking up concealed positions on the street or in buildings. Then, in an instant, Hadi ran across the street, too fast for Smithy to carefully aim and fire. Smithy knew that a sniper could do serious physical harm, and do harm to morale as well, greatly hindering enemy operations from afar. Combatants shot, from out of apparently nowhere, stopped or slowed things way down. If a leader, a commander, could be taken out, the effect was more than magnified.

With more hand waves, another ran across the far street and into an open doorway exposed to Smithy's view. The three men could barely be seen, but sufficiently to align the telescopic sight and make adjustments. Smithy's spotter called out the unfolding scene. They discussed the best target. The last man to run into the doorway was momentarily out in the open looking around, checking things out on the street. The two others, including the one with the black turban, stepped back into the building, out of sight. After a deep breath, Smithy slowly exhaled, stopped breathing and felt the beats of his heart during his controlled respiratory pause. For a fraction of a second he was back in the woods of Maryland and on the rifle range at Quantico. It all came together between the beats of his heart. The rifle kicked, almost as if it had a mind of its own. The unleashed round crossed the distance at nearly 3,000 feet for each tick of the second hand on Smithy's wrist watch. The exposed man's chest blew apart. Flesh, bone and blood splattered on the interior wall by the doorway and onto the two others standing close. The next round was chambered as Smithy's spotter confirmed the hit. Hadi exposed himself as he reflexively reached out and down to the falling body right next to him. Another round was sent on its way just as Muhammed Talib yanked Hadi back into the doorway, leaving Hadi's left arm exposed for just an instant. The bullet struck the elbow, taking the forearm completely off as if severed by a knife. The energy of the round was not completely spent. Concrete exploded off the wall and the ricocheted bullet struck Muhammed Talib, deeply gashing his cheek.

Smithy could not hear the screams of pain as blood flowed from cheek and arm stump. The doorway was now empty. Inside, the bleeding battlefield *mullah* took off his turban and quickly made a tourniquet on Hadi's upper arm to stop the pulsing red flow. He wrapped the remainder around the bloody stump, then held his hand to his own torn face. Others were called to rush to their aid. The now one-armed Hadi was writhing in pain, in shock, as he was carried off down an alley, then into the basement of a house some distance away. Muhammed Talib followed, holding a blood-soaked, wadded shirt to the side of his face. That night, they were evacuated west to a small building on the outskirts of Ramadi on the Euphrates. There, they received care and recovered in the following months. Muhammed Talib stood by Hadi, continuing to offer advice and strength from *Allah* as he quoted from the *Qur'an*. Their bravery and leadership had been proved in hard combat against the infidels. Both would still be needed, not to fight, but to train, lead and motivate, and maybe to plan; Hadi was good at that.

†

Following the retaking of al-Fallujah, Smithy rejoined his sniper platoon and deployed to areas farther west, in and around Ramadi, engaging the enemy at considerable but lethal distances. He and his spotter helped swing the tide in close firefights, saving lives, ending other's. While not injured, he had another close call. Smithy's concealed position behind a low stone wall had been discovered and overrun. His close battlefield buddy and friend, his spotter, had been killed in the action. Smithy managed to barely escape under the withering, covering fire from Marine reinforcements.

The worst was yet to come in Ramadi, but Smithy had survived. He completed his tour of duty in Iraq and returned home, a well-seasoned Marine, a seasoned sniper. His after-action reports were impressive with a considerable number of combatant hits recorded, many of them confirmed as kills by his spotter or by others that had been involved in the actions he had supported.

Letters from Smithy made it to Whiton

with estimates of when he would walk through the door. He arrived quietly, let off by a taxi driver some distance from the family home and blacksmith shop. Smithy quietly crept up from behind his father working at the anvil, as if he were still in al-Fallujah. The hammer was lifted high for the next strike on the glowing, orange-red metal bar, but a big strong hand grabbed it, by surprise. Before he could turn around, Smithy's father knew who was there; soon his mother did also. Word spread through the town and down the pews at the Catholic church. There was another class to educate, another invitation by Sister Mary Joseph and more walnuts to crush. This time, a further-decorated Marine corporal would do the honors.

†

Those in the assignment system and combat commanders had reviewed Smithy's record closely, and his signed application. The Marines needed excellent snipers in the field, in combat, but they needed excellent instructors even more. Smithy's father laid another certified envelope on the kitchen table and called for his son to get out of bed and shed the morning cobwebs. Hunting all day in the Maryland woods the day before could have been tiring, his father thought. The smell of his mother's bacon and eggs filled the room as Smithy opened the envelope. Corporal John Kelly was again to report to the Marine sniper school in Quantico, as an instructor. He would spend more than a few years at the school, turning out skilled, lethal snipers, before his next assignment to the roiling Mideast cauldron, a special assignment.

†

Taking and holding ground, at great human cost, had been one thing; capturing the hearts and minds of a different culture quite another. Planners had underestimated the influence of a spin-off terrorist organization, *al-Qaeda* in Iraq. Their consistent objective had been to remove all Western influence from the land and replace it with Sunni Islamic governance. With the catalyst of al-Fallujah, that metastasized into the Islamic State, which capitalized on centuries of *caliphates* since the founding and spread of the faith by Muhammad. Many hearts and minds were more than open to this ancient direction. If not, brutal application of "The Way" would follow, Islamic religious law that encompassed all corners of life: *Shari'ah*.

Ad Astra

The flight from Ashland in Southern Oregon to PDX had been easy, the landing difficult. Jen had flown the sleek Bombardier CRJ200 proudly from the left seat for Caldera Flight 213. They had moved her up to captain. Weather for the flight at altitude had been clear, too clear. Moist air was not uncommon in the Willamette Valley, but at PDX it was very moist that night. The wide Columbia River flowed by closely and added water vapor to what had drifted in from the huge evaporator to the west: the Pacific Ocean. The wet blanket of air was not moving; the winds were dead calm. The forecast had been for reduced visibility at the estimated time of arrival, but above landing minimums. The ground had cooled as its infrared heat radiation escaped into space. There were no intervening clouds to absorb and re-radiate energy back down: the notorious green-house effect. The cooling ground was in direct contact with the damp air above, cooling it to where air temperature matched dew point temperature. At 100 percent relative humidity, the previously-evaporated water vapor re-appeared as uncountable, very tiny, very slowly falling droplets: fog.

On letdown into PDX, Jen requested the latest observation from the control tower. Visibility had been dropping fast to near where Jen was allowed to land. Having to land at her planned alternate became a real possibility. She rechecked remaining fuel load as her first officer checked weather at the alternate. Passengers, and Caldera Air, would not be particularly happy about this. But there was time, and fuel, for two landing attempts. Reported surface visibility and instrument-determined Runway Visual Range mandated an instrument approach with glide slope and runway alignment readout in the cockpit using PDX's Instrument Landing System, the ILS.

Her first officer was new to Caldera Air, having just completed required training. This was their first flight together. Before hiring on, he had logged hours in Southern California. He had flown instrument approaches in foggy conditions before, but this was much different. Nothing at all on the ground could be seen. The dense shroud of fog around them was lit by the landing lights and the hypnotic flashing of the wing-tip strobe lights. He was assisting Jen as best he could but was obviously stressed. Jen not only had to fly the approach, but she had to help him help her. She just chalked it up to training. Finally, they reached decision height but could not sufficiently see the runway or its lights, or even the sequential strobe lights on the ground leading to the approach end. Jen calmly executed a missed approach as her first officer not so calmly handled communications with the control tower. Over the cabin's speakers, he kept the passengers informed, but his rapid verbosity only made them anxious. For everyone, especially the first officer, it seemed like an eternity before they were again lined up on the ILS. On this second attempt, a very light southerly surface wind had arisen, just enough to barely turn the small blades on the airport's wind measuring system, the anemometers next to the runways. The densest part of the fog moved towards the river, just enough. At decision height, Jen claimed to have seen enough runway lights tapering off into the fog and set the Bombardier down as smooth as silk. She made the announcement of their safe arrival; relieved passengers applauded.

It was getting late as she drove up the driveway to her house on the shoulder of Mount Tabor. The fog had also slowed her on the ground. She opened the front door and Tiger, her tabby cat, came to greet her with purring meows.

Jen gave Tiger's arched back a good welcoming scratch, took off her jacket and tossed her black leather flight satchel on the couch. With a touch on a remote, classical music surrounded her from Bose speakers. Tiger jumped up on her lap as she leaned back in the recliner and sipped the stiff, extra dry vodka martini she had thrown together in the kitchen. She had misplaced the vermouth, but just an olive would do.

As she relaxed from the day's flying and stressful landing, she reached into her satchel and took out the latest copy of *Aviation Week and Space Technology* that she had purchased that morning in the PDX concourse. She set the martini down and leafed through the informative magazine, skimming and speed reading. She stopped at an article that caught her attention. Below the "Astra Airlines" title, words leapt off the page: "Portland International Airport" – "Hub" – "Boeing 737" – "Caldera."

†

It had been weeks since Chris's reunion with his two high school buddies at the Land Rush. Roger had since been assigned with his Marine unit to another Mideast location. Gary was still busy taking flying lessons at the local airport while working as a UPS driver. Chris had helped close up the hardware store. He told his father to not wait dinner on him; he was headed to the Land Rush. Chris sat down at the bar watching the evening news, munching bar peanuts between sips of beer from a can. Just then, somebody slapped him on the back, "Mind if I join you?"

Chris immediately recognized that voice, "No problem, Gary. Have a seat."

Gary sat down and waved for his standard order of craft beer in a pint. He pulled a magazine from his jacket and tossed it on the bar. Chris looked down at an issue of *Aviation Week and Space Technology,* "What the hell do you want me to do with this?"

"Well, if you're going to be like that, I know of a place where you can shove it. Seriously, I saw this in the flight lounge where I'm taking lessons. There's something about a new airline that may interest you."

"A new airline? What's it called?"

"Astra."

"What the hell does that mean?"

"Hell, Chris, you've got the college degree. That's *Latin* for stars. Some billionaire nerds in Silicon Valley are starting up another airline to crowd the skies."

"What do they fly?"

"All the latest variants of the Boeing737: 700s, 800s and 900s."

"Where's their hub going to be?"

"Portland, Oregon. The FAA has given them their Air Operator Certificate. Flights are scheduled to begin later this year."

Chris put down his beer and read the article, then looked up, "These are some of the same techies that started a successful space launch business. Wow! Well, who would have thought that Microsoft, Google and Amazon would be what they are today?"

Chris tried to digest it all, "Hmmm. Astra Airlines. Stars Airlines. Has a certain ring to it."

Gary replied, "I think it ties in with the space launch business. Their motto is *Ad Astra* – To the Stars. They could have used *Stellae*, but that doesn't roll off the tongue as well."

"OK, OK. Don't rub it in. I studied real science, not that liberal arts crap."

Chris was drawn to a photo of one of Astra's modern Boeing 737s in the front of a maintenance hangar at PDX. Graceful Split Scimitar winglets, that reduce lift-induced drag in flight, added to the aircraft's beauty. On the white fuselage above the row of passenger windows was the name *Astra Air* with its logo, the constellation of Orion, the hunter, with his belt and bow of stars as black dots connected by thin black lines against a white background, all in a black-lined circle. Below the cockpit window was painted *Ad Astra*. The solid black tail also had the constellation of Orion, each silver dot connected by a thin silver line.

"Hey, Gary, it says here that they've bought out a regional carrier, Caldera Air, to provide connections from smaller airports in the Pacific Northwest. Caldera, that's a strange name for an airline. But the folks out west are different, especially in Portland; weird, some would say."

"Well, Chris, what do you think?"

"I'm spinning my wheels here. I think I'll send them an application. With all my flight hours and turbine engine experience, I should be able to jump right into the 737, at least the right seat."

Gary finished his pint, gave Chris a high five, "See ya in the air."

☦

Jen re-read the article, made another martini, flopped back down on the recliner, deep in thought. Tiger fell asleep on her lap. At first Jen was pissed off. She had been moved up to captain and Caldera management didn't have the decency to let her know about the merger, and with a start-up airline, no less. But she had a wry smile thinking this just may be the opportunity to move up to a larger aircraft, the Boeing 737. She vowed to make an appointment with Astra management, or at least find out where their office was. Visions of a 737 with upward-curved wingtips with a downward-angled fin floated through her head as she joined Tiger in sleeping through the night.

In Caldera's flight planning room the next morning, she asked the first officer how he was feeling after last night's final approaches. He just nodded, "OK, I guess," then looked away and set about planning for the flight to Richland while Jen checked the weather. She walked over to the matrix of cubbyhole mail boxes. In hers she found a plain envelope with her name on it, hand written. With her forefinger, she ripped it open and unfolded the hand-written letter. It was from the president of Astra Airlines, without any letterhead or logo, just a plain sheet of paper. She flipped it over, thinking that the circled constellation of Orion could be on the back. It wasn't. She shook her head thinking that nerds think in a different dimension, in a parallel technological universe. Her eyes widened as she read: "Please come see me about checking out to fly our 737s." At the bottom of the letter was penned a phone number and the address of an office in downtown Portland, at the top of a very tall building.

†

In Portland, across the desk from Chris was a middle-aged man wearing low-quarter canvas boat shoes, no socks, jeans, an open-collar white shirt under a slim-fit sport jacket. Successful techies from California dressed differently than an old bank president back in Enid, or a hardware store merchant. He stood and extended his hand, "Welcome to Astra. Take a seat. Coffee? Diet Coke?"

"Coffee, black, thanks."

"We like your record and expect you to start our 737 training and check-out program as soon as you can, after you sort things out back home in Oklahoma. We'll start you in the right seat. Others have more seniority, more commercial hours."

Chris stood, "No problem. I'll be here next week. I'll live out of a hotel near the airport until I find a place. I'm very used to no-notice overnight bag drags to who knows where."

A business card was slid across the desk. "Shouldn't have to live like that for long. I've already contacted a real estate woman; here's her card. She's identified some downtown high-rise apartments. You're a bachelor, aren't you? That's what I told her."

"Yes, I'm single, just haven't found the right one yet, but haven't really been looking."

"OK, but be careful. She's … well … you'll see."

Chris walked out of Astra's office just as

somebody from the elevator lobby around the corner was coming briskly in the other direction. He was in a hurry and so was she. He walked right into her. She stumbled. Male instinct kicked in. Chris reached out and grabbed her shoulders to keep her from falling, "Oh! I'm so sorry. I didn't see you."

She steadied herself, smoothed her short hair and bluntly replied, "Obviously. Your situational awareness needs some tuning." As their eyes made contact, close up, she lightened a little, "...maybe mine as well. I was in a hurry for an appointment. I think their office is just down the hall."

Chris glanced back at the only office in the short hallway and asked, "Astra Air?"

"Why, yes. How did ....?"

He couldn't help but strut right on the spot, "I'm an ex-Air Force pilot, C-130 type. I thought I'd give them a shot. Are you applying to be a stewardess? I think they've relaxed the age requirements."

Her brow knotted tight as contempt slowly oozed out, "It's flight attendant now. And, by the way, I sit left seat, Bombardier CRJ200, but I'll be moving up to the 737. That's why I'm here."

With just a bit of attitude, he reached out his hand, "I flew left seat over Afghanistan and Iraq, low and lethal or high and quiet. I'm Chris, Chris

McDonald."

"Well, I guess I'm pleased to meet you. I'm Jennifer Grissom, but you can call me Jen, or captain if we fly together."

"Good luck. I'm coming aboard as a first officer, we used to call them co-pilots. Shouldn't take long to move over. I've got a lot of C-130 time – in the stress of combat."

Jen attributed that statement to male vanity and forced a smile, "I look forward to seeing you on the flight deck."

†

It was the end of another long day in the air after the flight from San Francisco. Nina was headed to the taxi queue at PDX, but stopped and picked up a magazine from a concourse newsstand; *Aviation Week and Space Technology*. She was well-versed in the liberal arts, but she tried to keep up with things that happened on the other side of the door to the flight deck, to speak their language. At her home in the West Hills, she poured herself a glass of Glenfiddich, neat, kicked off her shoes and sat back in the big cushy chair by the bay window overlooking the lights of her beautiful city. Relaxation enveloped her as she casually leafed through the technical and policy sides of aviation. She hesitated on one page, noting that a brand new airline would be operating out of PDX. Nina took a sip and savored her fine Scotch. She had not been selected for international flights, despite her repeated requests. Maybe it was time for a change.

Driven

They spoke quietly. Wise old men cautioned the young ones agitated by recent events up north. The undulating call to prayer had spread over them. Each had knelt and faced northwest, recited the *Fajr* then made his own way down the alley to the almost-sacred morning gathering. In the small space, companionship and a divine aroma greeted them. The roasted beans had come from terraced trees in the central mountains. Water boiled in a copper pot in a small back room. Grounds had been added and married with dashes of spice once carried by camels on ancient trade routes: cardamom, cloves, ginger and saffron. A tray of small cups of strong coffee was set in the center of the group as they sat or knelt on cushions and a thick hand-woven rug. Masoud and Dabir raised their cups to the others and to their lips amid the industrial sounds from the nearby docks where the others worked, or had worked before their beards had turned white.

A fishing settlement had taken root on the southern shore of the vast Arabian Peninsula.

At the center of the intersection of water-borne commerce between India and Africa, and overland trade-route communication to the north, the village had grown into a vibrant commercial seaport: al-Mukalla. Dabir and the others often had friendly arguments about the birthplace of coffee, if not its bean, its brew; Ethiopia or Yemen, or both.

Conversation turned serious with visceral anger as Masoud read accounts from the newspaper about the vicious fight for a modern *caliphate* in Iraq and Syria. A true believer in Islam, Masoud knew regional histories dating back centuries, and certainly knew the depths of his faith. It drove him beyond rational thinking. The elders were more cautious. Yemen had been wrought with war. Operative cells of *al-Qaeda* and Shia Houthi rebels had struck cities and targets across Yemen; al-Mukalla had suffered terrorist attacks. Saudi Arabian air strikes, supported by military equipment and intelligence from the United States, had considerably stirred up and divided the population. Dabir's father, a humble career truck driver, had stood too close to a teenager strapped with explosives; both were taken away in a blinding blast. There was not much left to find and bury before sunset. Masoud and Dabir spoke with the passion of youth. The elders spoke with the compassion of wisdom.

Despite the turmoil, the docks of al-Makalla teemed with trade, as was its birthright. The whistles and horns of ships mixed with the metallic *clunks* and *clanks* of containers and the *whir* of the huge gantry cranes that unloaded and loaded them. Big trucks came and went, the sounds of diesel engines changed as gears were shifted.

Masoud and Dabir were brought back to the reality of their jobs: truck drivers. They stood and bade their older coffee-drinking brethren farewell. They walked to the docks and climbed aboard two large loaded trucks of a Yemeni transport company and set to distributing once-seaborne goods throughout Yemen. Next week, they returned to the coffee shop. They had had more time to think on the road, and decide.

As rich coffee was served, Masoud and Dabir spoke with renewed passion. The elders certainly knew, but Masoud took it upon himself to remind them of the *caliphates* since the days of the Prophet. He lectured the group about the need for a state under a steward of the Islamic faith, a *caliph*. The self-appointed Ottoman c*aliphate* had been shred apart by European alliances and the First World War. Dabir expressed his frustration with the festering arguments following the death of the Prophet as to the rightful successor and the great Sunni-Shia divide. Masoud stood up and spoke with fervor, spreading his arms out as if he were a great orator, to emphasize how far and wide Islam had spread. To bind believers of many nations and shepherd the faith, the need for a *caliphate* had never been greater, he argued. Masoud announced that he and Dabir had heard the call and would be leaving to join the fight near Baghdad.

Dabir admitted that the downing of the twin towers of the World Trade Center in New York City may have had something to do with Americans desecrating the land with their very presence. He also inserted that the greedy Americans had arrived decades earlier in the quest for oil. Dabir had heard, at the mosque on good authority, of an exceptionally fervent man who was commanding forces along the lines of the very first *caliph*. Word had been received that believers were needed in the fight. Following rather extreme interpretations of the *Qur'an*, beheadings had been used to quell and control any opposition. The Prophet and his followers had had swords and had used them in their struggle to bring Islam to the region: the first *jihad*.

With the morning newspaper rolled up in his fist, Masoud waved it around like a sword, speaking of American air strikes, cruise missile attacks, encirclements by Kurdish and Iraqi forces, all with the help of the Americans.

More than newspapers had motivated Masoud and Dabir. The man who led them in prayer at their mosque, the *imam*, strictly followed the fundamentalist teachings and writings of one Muhammad ibn Abd-al-Wahhab some 300 years earlier. That morning they left the coffee shop and walked away from their loaded trucks at the dock. A rusty, green van picked them up behind the mosque.

After an arduous trip with others, crossing remote borders, Masoud and Dabir arrived in Ramadi in the dark of night. They tumbled out to shouted directions, down an alley, into a building, down a flight of stairs to join a group of newly-arrived recruits. They had to be sorted out by age and skills. They milled around meeting fellow fighters nervously waiting.

A door opened. A command for silence announced his arrival. He walked in and paced around the men, looking them over. He was not much older, but had been steeled by combat in al-Fallujah. Following the carnage, he had been given a battlefield promotion. He was a natural leader, now with only one arm to prove the point. A *mullah* came in and stood nearby as this young commander gave the recruits a motivating speech. They were to fight, and die if necessary, for the *caliphate*. They all knew this abstractly, but to hear it from a battlefield commander in the dark basement was stark and sobering. This was the real thing, more than a newspaper article in a coffee shop near the docks of al-Mukalla. The *mullah* began to speak words of spiritual encouragement and what awaited them in the afterlife if they bravely died for the *caliphate*. The deep scar on his cheek punctuated his words.

A deep rumble interrupted Muhammad Tabil. It shook the building and the floor, followed by another, then another. Guided 2,000-pound bombs, built in America, were being delivered by American pilots; their infrared systems removed the veil of night, their lasers sliced through clear desert air to put guiding spots on targets.

Then silence. In a corner of the room were two large wooden boxes. Two fighters came in with automatic rifles slung over their shoulders, Russian Kalashnikovs. One opened the box; it held more Kalashnikovs, the other box held full clips of ammunition for them. Hadi announced that all would be given basic training; how to clean and operate the weapon and aim it with reasonable accuracy in the close quarters of urban combat. If they had other skills, those could determine their assignments. Another form of precision guided munition was not mentioned: suicide bombing.

Hadi came up to Masoud and Dabir, "Where

are you from?"

Masoud answered, "Sir, Yemen; al-Mukalla."

"What was your work?"

Pointing to Dabir, Masoud explained, "My brother and I were professional truck drivers, as was our father. We drove the big ones that pull large trailers filled with things from the docks."

"Can you fix a broken truck?"

"We can fix tires, change wheels, change oil, and do things to engines to get them running when on the road far from a city and mechanics. We have been truck drivers for over ten years."

"Excellent! In the face of our warriors, Iraqi forces fled Mosul leaving behind many war-fighting vehicles, American Humvees and armored personnel carriers. You will drive them in combat."

Masoud straightened with pride, "Sir, we are ready to drive for you and your soldiers and to serve *Allah* to bring death to our enemies."

†

The tide of battle in Ramadi had shifted. Rain had come to the city, not water, but bullets from Gatling guns on low-flying aircraft in the dark of night. The armor piercing rounds made short work of vehicles and those in them. Infrared images of fighters dashing from building to building caught the attention of those in the air. Sprays of bullets minced them into unidentifiable scraps of flesh and bones. As death came from the sky, the noose tightened around the city. Hadi weighed his options, including retreat and evacuation to the west. His scouts reported the disposition of the advancing forces around the city. He saw a weakness and directed a counter attack. Captured Humvees, machine guns blazing, would be integrated into the advance of ground combatants to break through the perimeter of Iraqi security forces. When through, they would turn and attack their flanks from the rear, cutting off reinforcements. It just might work, if it was the will of *Allah*.

Masoud and Dabir each sat in a Humvee with their assigned Kalishnikovs alongside, and with fighters inside that would dismount in the heat of combat. They had not seen action since their arrival, but had demonstrated that they could fire a Kalishnikov and actually hit things at close range. They also showed their prowess behind the wheel and had trained other, younger ones to operate the vehicles. Some of them had been selected to lead the offensive. Masoud and Dabir had seen that these vehicles did not hold soldiers. They had been loaded with explosives. Protective armor plating protected the drivers until they were within their enemy, whereupon they would detonate the vehicle. Insurgent forces would follow through the breach. The suicide drivers would soon know if the promise of the *mullah* were true.

Black flags had been mounted to their vehicles. Masoud and Dabir read the words they held: Muhammad is the messenger of Allah - Muhammad is the messenger of God. The vehicles were not gathered into a clump that could easily be targeted from the sky. They were distributed, including the suicide Humvees, down alleys and streets, some in garages and under cover in passageways. Upon Hadi's command, they would be driven to the common axis of attack and follow the lead Humvees, the rolling bombs. Masoud looked over at his brother who sat in another Humvee. They nodded in the mutual understanding that this is what they had been called to do in the name of *Allah*. There was no higher motivation. Soon, bullets were glancing off of sides and windshields as they weaved down the street, taking fire from the ground and from rooftops and windows. Their machine gunners returned fire, but from a moving vehicle their accuracy waned. Slumped over, a machine gunner had been instantly killed, half his skull missing as blood flowed down on Dabir. Then came an immense explosion, followed by another. Masoud's ears rang and the sounds of

battle were muffled until they cleared. In amongst
their enemy, Masoud and Dabir stopped to let
soldiers disembark. The fighting was fierce. The
initial shock of the suicide bombs had passed and
Iraqi forces flowed in from the flanks to fill the
gap. The attack was failing. Gripped by fear and
confusion, other drivers froze in their vehicles,
but not Masoud and Dabir. They got out and
joined the fight, some hand-to-hand with knives.
Masoud looked around and quickly realized the
immediate situation. He began shouting orders,
firing his Kalishnikov as he ran for cover. Others
followed, but it was too late. Hadi had spread the
order to retreat back into the maze of the city.
He realized that he had to husband his forces to
fight another day, in a different city. But in the
melee, he had seen the bravery and intelligence
under stress of Masoud and Dabir. These would
be given special assignments in the weeks and
months that lay ahead.

As Iraqi forces flowed in, supported by
American-led air power and surveillance, *Allah's*
forces filtered out in the dark of night into the vast
surrounding desert to make their way west to the
capital of the *caliphate*: ar-Raqqah.

Boredom and Stark Terror

Jen and Chris frequently found themselves on the same Aster flight, she as captain in the left seat, he as first officer in the right seat of a Boeing 737-700. Aster Airlines had become hip, especially among millennials. The folks from Silicon Valley knew how to market a basically old service to the next generation, wrapped in a different cloak. Young minds in marketing went into warp speed and fantasized that an Aster aircraft was the real-life equivalent of the Starship Enterprise of early TV's Star Trek fame. From the digital revolution, their pockets were deep. Aircraft interior colors were changed in an attempt to match that of the studio starship. Even pocket sliding doors had been installed to separate the different classes of passenger flight, opened and closed with the push of a button. Their *thwip* sound had been engineered to be close to that heard when crew members on the Starship Enterprise went from chamber to chamber. Some in Aster management went so far as to consider having flight attendants wear base-colored uniforms like the crew on the Enterprise, as if they had been lifted from the wardrobe of Stage 9 of Paramount Studios in Hollywood.

†

Chris walked with Jen down the concourse at Portland International Airport, past the gate desk then down the jet bridge to Aster Air Flight 2123 to Salt Lake City. Jen entered the flight deck while he stopped and spoke to the flight service manager that they had come to know, "Hi Nina. Getting things set up back here?"

"You bet. How's it looking, weather guy?"

"Not too bad. We'll pick up some light turbulence over Boise. Maybe moderate. Let your crew know. I see you haven't gone Trekkie yet, like we have."

Nina slid her hands down the sides of her hips, "Hell no! We're pushing back. We're not all as trim and svelte as those Star Trek actors. The union's involved."

He entered the flight deck and greeted his captain, "Morning, Jen. Get enough rest? The flight from San Francisco dragged on, didn't it? Being stacked up waiting for landing clearance was a bummer. Those Guard F-15s were involved in an exercise.

"I'm fine. Hit the sack right off, skipped the bar, as you know. Let's get this show on the road."

After confirming with Nina that all safety and medical equipment was on board, Chris settled into the right seat and began the preflight system checks, calling out switch positions, some echoed by Jen. Chris carefully checked fuel load and cross-checked the final weight and balance of the aircraft against that planned. Chris continued as Jen entered flight plan information into a keypad, the data maw for the powerful Flight Management Computer that could safely fly the plane without human intervention. At altitude, Jen and Chris would still be there, monitoring automatic flight *en route* just to make sure. They would disengage autopilot during ascent and descent, out of and into terminal controlled airspace, with unpredictable deviations, to avoid other aircraft.

As Jen and Chris tended to preflight duties, the cabin had filled with passengers. Nina shut the reinforced door to the flight deck with a comforting *thud* and locking *clunk*. Now, even a well-placed hand grenade or bullets from a .45-caliber pistol could not open or penetrate that door, even if such things could get past airport security. The 9/11 downing of the Twin Towers at the World Trade Center in New York City had changed everything, including the flight deck doors of commercial aircraft. Nobody could get past the door by force.

Before long, they were winging their way across Idaho towards the Great Salt Lake. With autopilot disengaged, Jen and Chris guided the big Boeing 737 safely down into the control zone for the Salt Lake City airport. The turbulence over Idaho had been moderate, to the discomfort and concern of those in back.

At the gate, Jen stayed in the left seat, carefully watching all the hurried activities surrounding her aircraft. Chris stoically stood in the open door to the flight deck, like an icon, making eye contact with departing passengers. He felt he was helping Aster, and Nina who maintained a wide plastic smile as she nodded and robotically repeated, "G'by ...Have a nice day ... G'by ... Have a nice day." With equal, practiced sincerity, she welcomed new passengers on board, all headed to San Francisco. Chris remained by her side, exuding his best male, toothy-grinned, pilot *élan*.

The turn-around was quick and efficient. Soon the City by the Bay and the Golden Gate Bridge came into view with a streak of the setting sun glinting over the ocean to the west. The descent was beautiful and the final approach smooth and steady with a long wide, empty runway before them.

Jen's attention was focused on the runway.

Through the windscreen, Chris scanned the crowded terminal airspace side-to-side, as he always did for any airport while coming down final. His head suddenly snapped left. He pointed and shouted over the intercom, "There! Nine o'clock! Nine o'clock!!"

The small plane, now seen by Jen, was on an apparent path that would intersect theirs in a few seconds. They both knew that an object on a constant relative bearing and decreasing distance had always been a concern for ships at sea, but much more so for aircraft with their much greater speeds and much shorter pilot reaction times. The position of the plane on the wind screen did not move, but it grew larger. If nothing was done soon, the paths would intersect.

"Got it! Call go around!" Jen banked the aircraft steeply to the right and pulled up hard, spooling the engines up to full thrust at the same time, just barely passing over the Cessna 172 that had stumbled right across their final approach. Chris looked down and saw it cross below them, close, not at all changing its flight, its pilot oblivious to the near tragedy. The control tower rapidly communicated with them and the other aircraft in the busy terminal control area, clearing the way for Aster Flight 2123 to climb out and safely merge with a re-shuffled landing and takeoff order.

Things were handled well in the back by Nina and her crew, keeping things as calm as possible. But it took all four of them, which included a husky male flight attendant, to hold, wrestle and subdue a bearded man. He had unbuckled his seat belt, sprung up and had run back and forth in the aisle, arms waving above his head, shouting repeatedly, "Come to Jesus!"

At the gate, the well-intentioned man who had been religiously stimulated by apparent imminent death was summarily escorted off the aircraft by airport security. Jen and Chris did not come to Jesus, but Jesus came to them disguised as a local Federal Aviation Administration official who questioned them and left with their signed statements for his near-miss report.

After another quick turn, after the visit by the official-looking Jesus, they reached Portland having been in the air for over six hours that day. To that was added the unexpected stress of the landing at San Francisco International. Before heading to their respective homes, they joined Nina and her three flight attendants at an airport bar. One needed a stiff one after the mayhem on final approach at SFO. For Nina, it was Glenfiddich, neat. Jen tapped an empty glass on the bar with her pen to get everyone's attention and dramatized an old aviation maxim. She stood, raised her glass high and solemnly gave a toast, "To flight – hours of boredom punctuated by moments of stark terror."

A first-time flight attendant for Aster replied, "Amen to that," and tossed back his shot glass of whiskey. The others tipped their glasses, bottoms up, then all chatted and relived their near-death experience that day, and for some of the older ones, including Nina, on other days. To put things in perspective, Nina described a quiet descent into Denver, both engines having quit in severe icing conditions. Keeping passengers calm, she had internally made her peace, but a few thousand feet above the ground, the engines, and she, were brought back to life.

The bar thinned out as Nina and her crew left to get their rest for tomorrow's flight over the same route. Jen and Chris lingered a bit longer to review and discuss their roles in aviation, a nostalgia trip, of sorts. They were pilots and the go around had put things in a more-sober point of view. Chris philosophized a bit, "Jen. When was the last time you felt the magic of flight, like when you first soloed out of the Salina airport?"

"Well, Chris, outside of that final approach today, it's been a long time. I guess a little of the magic has worn off. But the pay is good and we're providing a safe service, flying complex machines of the air, something only dreamed of since cavemen first watched the birds."

They left the bar together, Jen heading for her parked car, Chris for the MAX light rail line to downtown Portland. Chris stopped at the top of the escalator and looked at Jen. They stared awkwardly at each other for more than a few seconds. They knew each other, but not that well, plus they were professionals. They both understood that intimacy, real or perceived, between co-workers was always a risky thing: clouding judgments, tainting appearances, risking perceived favoritism. Yet, Chris was thinking: 'That damn Cessna could have taken away any future opportunities, let alone their lives. We have only so many minutes on the clock of life.'

Chris did not speak what he was thinking but Jen could read it on his face. He exhaled slowly, then stepped on the downward moving escalator to the MAX Line to downtown; Jen continued across the sky bridge to her parked car, "See you in the morning – 0-dark-thirty. After we file our flight plan and check weather, let's go to that new restaurant on the concourse."

Camp

They met again on a rocky bank of the Tigris, in the dark this time. An hour earlier they had prayed the *'Isha* with the local *mullah*. He gave Akmal and Ramza the time and location of their pickup and two words. He said them again and asked them to repeat everything, to make sure they remembered. Arrangements had been made. They had been told what to bring, and not. Their cloth carry bags, old pillow cases, held their clothes. Their mother had thrown in bags of dates and nuts from their market stall and small plastic bottles of water. They did not know what to expect following the will of *Allah*.

They stood alone at the edge of al-Zawraa park under the cover of night. They knew it well from kicking soccer balls around with their friends. A pair of soldiers walked by on patrol. Akmal crouched quietly behind some bushes near a bridge by the lake and pulled Ramza down with him. The soldiers passed. Then they heard it, coming slowly over the bridge; stopping, waiting. They came out from their cover. The driver of the pickup truck spoke in a hushed tone, almost whispering, "*Sayf* (sword)."

Akmal answered, "*Rayiys* (head)." Without realizing it, with those two words their training had started. The driver, not much older, motioned for them to climb in the bed of the truck and to lie flat. They did and the truck sped off into the night. They looked up with their heads resting on their bags, each alone with their thoughts of what lay ahead. The lights of Baghdad fell behind. As they rumbled and lurched along, they stared at the clear night sky, stars ablaze. They felt the truck slow to a stop and heard the voices of soldiers that had waved the driver over. Akmal and Ramza looked up into the blinding glare of a flashlight as a soldier pushed their bags of clothes around, looking for weapons. Finding none, they heard the driver describe that he was taking the boys to work in the olive groves, but did not say where. The truck accelerated and headed west. Hours passed. The driver turned off onto rough, unpaved secondary roads, then no road at all. Akmal and Ramza bounced up and down over ruts and bumps. They dozed off a few times, but finally awoke to the light of the rising sun. With eyes filled with fear and excitement, they just stared at each other, saying nothing. The truck screeched to a stop and their trance was shattered by a loud shout commanding them to get out and run to where others were standing. Volunteer enthusiasm was not enough for what was to come. Training was needed. Religious fervor was needed.

✝

The camp was remote, somewhere in northern Syria, miles from the nearest road. A black flag with white Arabic writing and an ancient symbol of the Prophet fluttered in the wind. Akmal and Ramza were commanded to stand in line, abreast with others, not to speak, to look straight ahead and to be attentive. They set their bulging pillow cases at their feet, in the shade of a steep rocky hillside at their backs. Low scrub trees followed low, narrow ravines. Temperatures climbed as did the sun. It soon beat directly down on the young recruits, but they did not waver. Soon, other trucks and small vans arrived. Amid directions and commands, teenagers and mere boys jumped out and joined the line to be trained to fight for the *caliphate*. They stood for over an hour. A few of the younger ones started to speak quietly among themselves. This was followed by a loud directive from behind them. "Silence!!"

Eventually, a man stepped out from a cave opening in the cliff. He had an AK-47 Kalashnikov automatic rifle slung over his shoulder, wore a satchel vest and had a ski mask pulled down over his head. He welcomed them and directed that they look at him as he dramatically lifted off the mask, showing his face, as if this were a demonstration of bravery. The apparent camp commander went on that they would receive instruction and training before being sent out to join others battling the infidels. Then he lifted his hand signaling another who walked out of the cave then down the line, pulling some to stand forward. The ones sorted out were very young or of slight stature, probably unable to carry and effectively fire an AK-47, but not too small to wear an explosive vest in a crowded market, or a mosque. They were herded into a waiting truck, driven off, never to be seen again. The remaining group was led into the cave which expanded into a huge interior. Inside, they were given further instructions on absolute compliance with the five daily calls to prayer, where to eat, how to help prepare their food, and where to dig septic trenches outside beneath the low tree canopies lest overhead satellites, piloted aircraft or drones disclose the camp.

In the following weeks, Akmal and Ramza found themselves listening to stern lectures on the *Qur'an*, *Shari'ah* law and what it meant to be part of the *jihad*. These were interspersed with military instruction on how to clean and operate a Kalashnikov including live fire on a hidden target range on the other side of the hill. In the heat of the day, they had been forced to run up and down the hill, only two at a time, carrying a backpack filled with rocks until they stumbled from exhaustion. Inside, a long, narrow extension of the cave was used for an obstacle course which included overhead bars, barriers to climb over and a low layer of barbed wire to crawl under. Shouts of instructed encouragement echoed off the cave walls. It was dreamlike in the dim light, a nightmare to test resolve.

One evening, a large screen and a projector was set up with a cable leading to a small generator running outside. Akmal and Ramza watched videos of street fighting in ar-Raqqah while the instructor emphasized that this was the capital of the *caliphate* and that their fighting was needed to cast out infidels, to kill them, behead them, torture and crucify them. With that, the next scenes were of actual beheadings, some done with a large knife while the head was held, some with the fall of a sharp, curved scimitar, across the neck of a bound, kneeling prisoner. At the sight of pulsing, gushing blood and a rolling head, a young boy vomited on Akmal. The instructor ran over, chastised the shaking boy and forced his head up to watch the next beheading on the big screen. He was singled out for more training; there was no turning back.

On the target range, Akmal's skill and that of Ramza were of modest accuracy. With an AK-47, they proved themselves effective only at close range. At longer ranges, only a few rounds from a spray of bullets fired on automatic setting had struck the target: the full-scale, cardboard outline of a person. They would not be trained as snipers, but were judged that they could be effective in a door-to-door urban street fight. But it was Akmal who stood out some weeks later.

A van pulled up outside. Two prisoners from ar-Raqqah were hauled out and brought into the cave. Their hands were tied behind their backs; they wore orange jump suits, the color selected in revenge for how those captured from their ranks had been clothed while being abused in the Abu Ghraib prison, seen on television news programs worldwide. The prisoners were forced to kneel; one was quivering and praying to *Allah*, as if in a trance. The other just had a blank look and stared off into space, as if this was not happening, as if this were a dream. The young trainees were told not to avert their eyes, lest the same fate befall them. The man who had lectured them since they had arrived held one condemned man's head and severed it from his neck with three well-placed, deep cuts, the last severing between spinal bones. He let the twitching body fall forward. The kneeling man next to the body closed his eyes; his prayers became more fervent as he bent his head forward. A scimitar was drawn. But before it could be used, a hand was raised. It was Akmal. He asked if he could dispatch the poor man, just a village merchant who had spoken too loudly against the *jihad*. He was being used as an example to others. Another instructor pointed a video camera at Akmal. The instructor smiled; his lectures had been effective. This trainee would be a good soldier. Akmal came up to the kneeling man and spat upon him. The scimitar was handed to Akmal. He set his feet apart, as he had seen, to steady himself and the arc of the blade. Holding with both hands, he lowered it over the back of the man's neck, then raised it until both arms pointed vertically. Akmal hesitated, looked up to the ceiling while saying a silent internal prayer for strength, then brought the scimitar down accurately. The head rolled forward, the bound body fell sideways, landing on Akmal's foot, covering it with blood. He did not attempt to withdraw his foot, but used his other one to kick the body away with disdain, as if it were just useless trash. The instructor shouted for everyone in the cave to hear, "*Allahu Akbar! Allahu Akbar!*"

The true value of prisoners in the *jihad* was starkly revealed. An especially high-ranking one could be used as barter for a prisoner exchange, or even more value, brought to a grisly end on a recruiting website. For the *caliph*, and those in the fight, the Geneva Convention on the treatment of prisoners may just as well have been in a different universe.

†

The weeks wore on. More young boys and teenagers arrived. The camp swelled. There were no older men in the ranks, men in middle age. In other remote areas their training was being done, brutal and demanding, physically and religiously. Akmal and Ramza had proved themselves among the clutch of younger *jihadists*. They and a few of their comrades were ready for deployment to join the fight in and around ar-Raqqah. The entire camp was rounded up into the cave's meeting area. The head instructor told them that they had the honor of being visited by a battlefield commander and a combat-hardened *mullah*. As Hadi and *mullah* Muhammad Talib walked into the cave, all were ordered to stand, to give the visitors the respect they deserved. Akmal and Ramza had been intentionally seated at the front with others selected for deployment, or for suicide duty. Akmal did a double take at Hadi and the missing forearm. The instructor introduced Hadi who just stood erect, a strong, silent sentinel. His battlefield wound spoke loudly about the future of the boys in the front row. Muhammad Talib stood beside Hadi, then spoke with an authoritative, motivating voice, about *jihad* for the *caliphate*, for the capital of the Islamic State under the leadership of one Abu Bakr al-Baghdadi, a self-declared *caliph*. He invited those seated before him to come forward and line up. Hadi placed his remaining hand on the shoulder of each graduate saying, "*Allahu Akbar.*" He had been told of Akmal's beheading of a prisoner and peered deeply into his eyes. Hadi then looked at the instructor, "This one will ride to battle with me."

Akmal pointed to Ramza, "Sir, my brother?"

"If he believes, he may ride with us."

"Sir, he is a believer, as is my entire family in Baghdad."

They clambered into the van with Hadi and Muhammad Talib. The driver turned around, "I am Masoud. I will drive you to battle." He pointed to the right seat. There sat a stern-looking man with an automatic rifle set between his legs amid a stack of cartridge magazines on the floor. "This is my dear brother, Dabir. The route can be dangerous. The night will cover us."

✝

Mustafa and his wife said nothing as he drank his strong morning coffee. Months had passed since their sons had left to fight for the *caliphate*. They had not heard from them or anything about them. When a few friends had asked at the market stall, Mustafa proudly described what Akmal and Ramza had done, and were likely doing. He emphasized that their work was much more important than selling dates and nuts. But he secretly hoped that they would not be called upon to sacrifice themselves with explosives strapped to their chests.

Mustafa stood, about to leave the breakfast table for his trek to open the market stall. His wife returned from the front door where she had gone to check their mail box and now held an envelope, postmarked in America. Mustafa sat down, looked at the name on the return address, then ripped the envelope open and unfolded a handwritten letter. It was from Husayn. It had been years since they had separated. Husayn had indeed made it to America. Mustafa read the letter aloud. It described Husayn and his wife's journey through mindless bureaucracies and helpful people. Husayn wrote how they had made it to a refugee camp in Jordan near Amman and eventually to the United States Embassy there where he had applied for entry into the United States. He wrote that the approval process had been exceedingly slow, but that a church group had intervened and had sponsored them, and that his wife's pregnancy had helped move them up on the priority list.

Mustafa's eyes welled up as he read, "My dear brother, we have a son and have named him Mustafa, after you. I have not forgotten that we are of the same blood."

The long letter went on to explain that a Christian church group, based in Hillsboro, Oregon, somewhere in the Western United States, had found them an inexpensive apartment, that church members had helped them fold into the very welcoming community of the city, including learning English and finding a job. Husayn wrote that he now worked in an automotive parts warehouse and that his son could read, write and speak English like an American, as well as being fluent in the Arabic he and his wife had taught him, that he was doing very well in school, and liked technical things and computers.

Mustafa finished the letter then reread it quietly. In finishing, Husayn had written, "Please give this letter to Father. We hope he is well."

He then looked up at his wife, still standing at the other side of the table. She could see the question in his eyes, about Akmal and Ramza.

Route 66 Routine

With the weather checked and their flight plan filed, they walked towards their gate down a PDX concourse to the new restaurant. The entrance had been covered by sheets of plywood during its construction. The previous business, a sports bar with large TV screens, had succumbed to the unplanned vagaries of cost and clientele in the competitive concourse environment. The name of the restaurant was now displayed by a large white sign over the entrance in the shape of a shield with a black outline and black letters: ROUTE US 66. They stepped in and back in time to the sounds of "Wake Up Little Susie." Chris chuckled, "Well, that fits. You should download that to your cell phone alarm."

They continued past the "Please Seat Yourself" sign to a booth by one of the windows that framed the ramp and their docked aircraft being prepared for flight. They easily spotted it with its distinctive black tail with the constellation of Orion. They looked around the place and soaked it all in. The floor had a black and white checkerboard pattern in large squares; a swath with smaller black and white checkerboard squares was on the front of a long eating counter with round, swivel stools on an elevated platform. The work area behind the counter and the open kitchen gleamed with stainless steel. Tables out on the floor were surrounded by chromed-legged chairs. The tables and counter top were covered with gray, wavy-line-patterned Formica. The sides of the tables and stools were banded by chrome-plated metal. The booth seats, chairs and counter stools were covered with a deep-red, shiny, vinyl plastic.

At one end of the counter was a server station, separated from the row of stools by a curved, chrome-plated metal tube that was braced out from the counter. At the back of the station next to the kitchen was a chrome-plated order wheel with small clips, mounted on a spindle. Wait staff simply tucked an order under a clip, then spun the small wheel half-way around where a white-uniformed short-order-cook plucked it off.

To top off the authentic 50s motif, in one corner of the room was a colorfully-lit, period jukebox with a rounded top. The mechanism seen through the small curved window appeared to be extracting music from a spinning, shiny-black, thinly-grooved 45 rpm record. Customers pushed buttons on the jukebox, or on the chromed jukebox selectors at the booths, to select music for free. The old music did not overwhelm the restaurant, but played softly in the background so people could converse and the older ones could reminisce. From the walls hung framed black and white images of that bygone, innocent era: Chuck Berry, Elvis Presley, Fats Domino, Bill Haley and the Everly Brothers.

A waitress walked over. She was dressed to fit the *d*écor and the time in American history it represented. She wore a single-piece pink uniform dress, down to the knee, with a white collar and white cuffs, low white socks and low-quarter white shoes. Her hair was done-up, or rather piled-up, in 50s fashion, with a pencil slid through it. She wore a pink plastic tag with an engraved name: Sara. She set two glasses of water down on the table and got right to the point. Sara pulled an order pad from her pocket and the pencil from her hair, "What'll it be, folks?"

For both of them, all this brought back a flood of memories of quite similar restaurants back in Salina and Enid. From the menus at the table they gave Sara their orders: eggs over easy, hash browns, whole-wheat toast and tea for Jen; pancakes, sausages, muffin and black coffee for Chris. The menu also featured hamburgers, fries and milk shakes, but they always wanted breakfasts, regardless of the hour that started their flying day. Sara jotted-down the order.

"Comin' right up." She walked to the server station, clipped the order on the wheel and spun it around, "Order in."

Sara returned with cups filled with hot coffee and hot water with a tea bag. Chris said, "Quite a place. I've read about these old restaurants. Some were found on the long highway out of Chicago to California." Those restaurants and US Route 66 predated their childhoods by decades.

"Yeah, Route 66. For some, this is a trip down memory lane. For the young ones, they'll have to pull up Route 66 and 50s restaurants on their cell phones to even have a clue."

"Jen, you may remember dancing to these tunes."

"Hey, now. Careful. I'm only a few years older than you. How many, I'm not saying."

"You don't have to. I can guess by the stripes on your sleeves. Say, I know it's policy and just common sense for us to not eat the same food during a flight. I suppose it's OK to eat at the same place before a flight as long as the orders are different."

Jen thought for a moment, "I remember something about some bad pudding on an international flight out of Boston back in the early 80s. All the crew members got sick, pilots included, over the Atlantic and the flight had to return. I avoid the gas-generating stuff. That can do a number on you, and others, when the cabin altitude reaches 8,000 feet."

As always, each of their preflight meals would intentionally be different, should one meal or the other be somehow tainted, rendering only one of the crew incapable of flying the aircraft safely. The requirement for two healthy and alert pilots in the cockpit was always a good thing. It had been more than a good thing when Chris had to rapidly coordinate with the control tower at San Francisco as Jen skillfully avoided the light plane on final.

Jen and Chris had reviewed the final FAA report and they discussed it over their breakfasts. The light plane had been flown by a student pilot in his late 70s on his first solo cross-country flight out of San Jose. The report confirmed, by test, that he was also hard of hearing. He had always wanted to fly, and to fly over the Golden Gate Bridge. He had not changed his radio from the control tower frequency at San Jose. Radio or not, how he could have missed the huge layout of the San Francisco airport, bounded by the Pacific Ocean on one side, and the bay on the other, and shown on an aeronautical chart, was a mystery to Jen and Chris, and to others in authority. Chris suggested, "The CFI rating of the student's instructor pilot should be lifted."

Jen and Chris finished, stood up, left a hefty

tip for Sara and went to pay their bill at the cash register at the end of the counter opposite the server station. They both took the opportunity to carefully examine the kitchen from where they stood. It was open for all to see. The kitchen fairly sparkled with cleanliness. The well-scrubbed cooks had uniforms and hair-covering caps that were white as snow. This gave confidence to customers. The food was prepared in plain sight and not behind swinging doors in a hidden greasy area. Other restaurants, even some very fine ones, did not offer such visual openness.

They walked out to the lyrics of "Great Balls of Fire," Chris chuckling again, hoping that this 50s song would not describe a future landing. Jen and Chris were impressed with Route 66. They would be back, if not together, then by themselves for future Aster Air flights out of PDX. A comfortable routine had been started. And noted.

†

Aster Airlines Captain Jen Grissom and First Officer Chris McDonald settled down into professional airline pilot routines: logging instrument approaches and holding patterns, intercepting and tracking courses using electronic navigation systems, all to maintain currency;

logging simulator time to stay sharp, practicing emergency procedures; staying current on any and all changes in the aircraft they flew; reviewing FAA and Aster Airline's policies and procedures; staying fit and healthy; maintaining medical certification.

Beneath that required umbrella of commercial aviation was the daily grind, although Jen and Chris viewed the magic of flight as anything but a grind. But there was daily routine: checking aircrew scheduling; arriving at the right airport at the right time before flight; checking weather and filing flight plans; eating separate meals before flight; checking out and firing up assigned aircraft; safely flying routes; going into crew rest; unwinding and drinking modestly, strictly adhering to minimum hours between bottles and throttles; getting a good night's rest; starting over again for their next day's scheduled flight.

Jen and Chris often found themselves headed on the ground to PDX to fly the first of three legs: the flight to Salt Lake City. He came by MAX Line from his downtown condominium; she by her own car from her Mount Tabor home. For them, Route 66 became a "must stop" for breakfast. When they were teamed with a different pilot, they would eat in 50s ambiance alone, then join up and form a flight team in the Aster Air operations room about 90 minutes before scheduled takeoff.

When flying together, Route 66 was the last step of their comfortable, predictable routine before boarding the aircraft.

One early morning, as Jen dug into her eggs and hash browns and Chris was finishing his coffee, she just happened to notice a clean-shaven handsome, muscular young man with short blond hair and blue eyes, wearing jeans and a t-shirt, paging through magazines in the newsstand right across the concourse from the restaurant. He looked like he had been fished right out of a Norman Rockwell painting, as wholesome and American as apple pie. He wore large, horn-rimmed glasses that he kept adjusting on his nose, and kept glancing at Jen until she just stared back with a look that said, 'OK guy, just what are you looking at? I'm more than twice your age.'

He quickly looked back into his magazine, pretending to read. As Jen and Chris left for the gate, peripherally she saw that his gaze followed them. At the gate Jen looked back and noticed that the young man had redirected his attention to other flight crews that happened to be in Route 66, or were just walking by. Jen thought this was no big deal, just some nice young man, maybe interested in aviation as she had been in her youth over the cornfields of Kansas.

For another flight, Chris was in Route 66

eating and waiting. Jen was on leave visiting her aging parents who were still living in the family farmhouse near Salina, her cousin now running the farm. Chris chatted with the assigned captain that he had convinced to join him for breakfast. Chris pointed out the special features of the restaurant. He noticed the same young man, this time sitting on a stool at the counter by the busy server station, sipping morning coffee. He kept glancing over his shoulder in Chris's direction then quickly turning back. He removed his glasses and used a small spritzer bottle to spray them with cleaner, turning his glasses over, methodically, almost as if he were putting on a show. Chris thought that the young man worked at the airport as a cleaner or baggage handler, or in one of the many concourse shops. He did have a plastic-covered security tag on a cord around his neck.

A few weeks later, Jen and Chris were on the same Aster flight to Salt Lake City. "Peggy Sue" wafted around them in Route 66. Again they noticed the same young man, this time by a water fountain near the newsstand, drinking and furtively looking in their direction while bent over to take a drink. Chris mentioned, "Hey. See that guy over there, by the water fountain? He seems to be here a lot, always interested in us."

"Yeah, I've noticed him, too. He must work

here. See the tag? I wouldn't worry about it. We're on the safe side of security. He's been checked."

The young man did work at the airport, a recent hire to clean arriving aircraft after disgorging their passengers. He had been vetted by the airport's human resources department and interviewed by security staff. His all-American good looks had been a bit disarming. He passed muster and was given the special badge worn by airport employees. Without their realizing it, this airport employee had become part of Jen and Chris's preflight routine at Route 66.

Venom

The noble Saudi family had a long lineage and immense wealth through the biochemistry that lay beneath the sand: layers of once-living things trapped and heated under tons of sedimentary earth for millions of years – oil and gas. There would be nothing but the best for the eldest son. Clinging to long cultural tradition, Kashif had been groomed to be the second father, if and as needed, playing a vital role in the family, supporting and guiding younger siblings. The family home in Riyadh was palatial: intricately-patterned hand-woven rugs; sweeping marble stairways; rare crystals on hanging chandeliers; large-mirrored walls with frames gilded in real gold.

Kashif grew from a bright child into a very smart man. Islamic theocracy enveloped him, forming and cementing his views of the world, of life, its fundamental purpose and his role in it. Praying at the local mosque, intently listening to the *mullah's* sermons and responding faithfully to the five daily calls to prayer from its *minaret* were not enough for Kashif. As if he had been divinely called, he honestly thirsted for more. With his father's pride and blessing, he attended an exclusive *madrasa* in Riyadh, for the elite, to learn the full breadth of Arabic history and culture, master its beautiful flowing script, and understand the *Qur'an*, memorizing important sections, if not all of this revealed book of *Allah*. Fahim sermonized at the nearby mosque and taught at the special *madrasa* and gave Kashif private lessons in his home. *Islam* became Kashif's very soul.

Kashif's acceptance as a graduate student at the University of California, Irvine had been based, in part, on his excellent grades at King Saud University in Riyadh. There, he had studied English and had mastered the language. Professors at Riyadh's famous university thought Kashif bordered on genius considering his ability to quickly absorb, memorize, and thoroughly understand very complex subjects, especially organic chemistry.

The family had a number of homes in various corners of the globe, including a long yacht moored in Monaco. In Kashif's youth, they had spent time in their mansion on the cliffs of Corona del Mar, overlooking the Pacific Ocean, just a few miles from the university. This had been one of Kashif's favorite places. Some years before Kashif applied to UCI, the university had received a rather large endowment from Kashif's family. A biology and biochemistry research laboratory had been built in their name on the campus.

While they certainly knew of the problems, Kashif and his family were shielded from the political turbulence and the fierce fighting in Iraq, Afghanistan and Syria. They had read about it, but lived in their own wealthy world. Kashif was conflicted, trying to reconcile grisly earthly reality with his ethereal faith and comfortable life.

Before Kashif left for Irvine to start his classes, *mullah* Fahim visited the family home in Riyadh. Fahim was an animated, excitable man with deep-set dark eyes that flashed when he spoke of Muhammad and *Allah*. He made no secret that he leaned strongly towards the conservative, fundamental teachings and writings of Muhammad ibn Abd al-Wahhab. This latter-day *mullah* was fervent in his belief that only Wahhabism could reform the lost, wandering, secular, sinful world, even if that required the sword. This belief had been further strengthened when non-believing infidel Americans had first launched military strikes into Iraq and Kuwait from Saudi Arabia; physical blasphemy and desecration, in his eyes.

Three knocks; a servant opened the door. Fahim entered wearing his white turban and flowing gray robe of the finest cloth. His thick, black beard stood out in contrast, as if making a statement of his authority in the faith. Fahim placed his right hand over his heart when Kashif and his father walked into their ornately-decorated room. Fahim felt he was more than just a devoted *mullah*, but rather a member of this very wealthy, influential family. He spoke first, "Kashif, my dear Kashif. You must study very hard and not be seduced by godless, Western ways. I am not fit to fasten his sandals, but for you, I have humbly walked in the footsteps of Muhammad, peace be upon Him. I fasted and prayed on a desolate hill in the desert west of here. I asked *Allah* how to guide you."

Kashif felt the divine importance of the moment. He slowly reached out and reverently placed his hands on Fahim, one on each shoulder, and looked directly into his penetrating dark eyes. "How did *Allah* answer?"

"I heard nothing. I waited, prayed, fasted, but heard nothing but the desert wind. I thought perhaps the archangel Gabriel would speak to me for Him. But His ways are not our ways. He did speak, but in a different manner. In my sleep under His desert stars, I had a vision. You are to serve as a special soldier of *Allah*, for the return of the *caliphate*. You are to learn *Allah's* secrets of the chemistry of living, not for life, but for death."

Kashif's eyes widened. For the benefit of his father he forced an outward appearance of acceptance and bowed, but hid his doubts. Even Kashif's keen mind did not understand this apparent revelation. He had visions of finding cures for the world's diseases, maybe even to cure the dreaded cancer. Kashif did not wish to question Fahim's wisdom and vision publicly, and possibly embarrass both of them.

In a fit of disturbed sleep that night, Kashif, too, had a vision, an epiphany, a revelation: he would develop a special kind of death, as a weapon. What that was to be was not revealed as he slept. The next day, after the dawn prayer, Kashif decided he would just let *Allah's* path unroll before him, trusting that *Allah* would guide which direction he must take when he came upon a decision.

†

At UCI, Kashif studied very hard, lived in the family mansion and prayed at a beautiful *mosque* in Irvine. Its *mullah* was similar to Fahim, but one whose sermons were given in understandably muted tones after 9/11. American Muslims understood that their faith swam in the country's predominantly Christian sea. The mansion's garage held three cars. Kashif usually chose the BMW to drive to the university, or anywhere else he desired. His post-graduate student life was not lean.

When meeting someone, Kashif would only use his first name so as not to be outwardly connected to the modern laboratory with the family name that had been funded and built with the family wealth. But everyone knew. Inwardly he was proud whenever he passed the engraved plaque at its entrance, or parked in the space with a sign indicating that it was reserved for him. Adjacent spaces also had reserved signs, but with professors' names, not a student's. Kashif knew that all of this was on the path set before him by *Allah*. Who was he to question others' lives of poverty?

He sat attentively through the lectures for difficult courses, took copious notes, read volumes into the early morning and learned many of *Allah*'s secrets on the path to earning a Doctor of Philosophy in Biochemistry. Along the way, Kashif was drawn to the research of a particular professor on antidotes for venomous snakes, so-called antivenoms. The professor agreed to be his adviser for doing supportive research that would add to the professor's work aimed at saving lives.

Kashif was drawn to the topic because of Fahim's vision and his own dreamt epiphany. He would be dealing with life – and death.

In the laboratory, there were live species of the world's most venomous snakes, some with neurotoxin venom that could kill a man in tens of minutes if tailor-made antivenoms were not injected quickly. Among the snakes was the notorious Black Mamba found in Southeastern Africa, its name derived from the Zulu people's name for poisonous snake, *imamba*, and the color of its mouth. Also in the deadly menagerie were cobras and the colorful red, white and black-banded Sonoran Coral Snake, one *Micruroides euryxanthus*, found in the deserts of Southern Arizona and Northern Mexico, its venom second in lethality only to that of the Black Mamba.

Harboring such lethality required the approval of federal import-control agencies, government permits, university approval of escape-proof rooms, and the accounting of the snakes they held. Locked cages were in a room guarded by two sets of locked doors on either side of a small vestibule. Each cage had a red danger sign with cautionary language: Venomous Reptiles. The status and location of each snake was accounted for, reported and documented daily by laboratory staff, usually graduate students. When a snake died, that was accompanied by a witnessed death certificate, and the accounting changed accordingly.

Finding an irritated twelve-foot Black Mamba, its head lifted to the height of a student, capable of slithering down a university hallway faster than a terrified student could run, was to be avoided, even though the Black Mamba used that speed in the wild to avoid confrontation. Accidentally cornering a shy, reclusive, short and thin *Micruroides euryxanthus* could more than ruin a student's day, or an unwitting professor's.

But the risks were worth it. Their venoms were needed for studies to save human life in the wild. The efficacy of antivenoms was tested on laboratory rats and larger condemned animals, but not humans. Promising samples were sent to universities in South Africa who distributed them to aid stations in the habitats where antidotes to Black Mamba venom were necessarily being studied. Specific targets were the fields, forests and orchards found in Swaziland. Reaching in to pick fruit from the same limb upon which a startled Black Mamba was draped had ended the lives of many workers. Reports were compiled and sent back to UCI. Developed antivenoms for varieties of snakes also were sent to hospitals and clinics in North American regions that were inhabited by people. Anecdotal reports were sent back to UCI. A comprehensive database was maintained, carefully analyzed by Kashif and his thesis adviser, compared to laboratory results, and published in scientific journals.

Kashif dug deeply into the complex biochemical interactions between snake venom, antivenom, muscular tissues, neurological pathways and cellular receptors. He learned how to isolate specific toxins from the mix found in various venoms. In particular, the venom of the coral snake was intriguing. It interfered with how the brain communicated with muscles, affecting movement such as walking or speaking, and also caused blurred vision and a twitching tongue. But ultimately it paralyzed muscles and caused the cessation of cardiac and respiratory functions. Coral snake victims, in their last throes of life, felt like they were having a heart attack, which in fact they were. Kashif made careful note of another aspect of coral snake venom. From the time of its bite, a victim may not have any symptoms at all for many hours. Kashif, and others, questioned: Why the delay?

With his advisor's guidance, and the touch of the hand of *Allah*, his research narrowed down to the latest discoveries of the potent neuro-toxicities caused by three-finger toxin proteins, so-named because of the three molecular loops (fingers) that extend from the central core of the protein. It was the amino acids on these more-exposed loops that interacted with the muscles and their neurological connections of a hapless victim. As research scientists are wont to do with a discovery, this special class of proteins had been given generic scientific shorthand, 3FTx, the x denoting a specific toxin variant, and there were very many.

The complexities of 3FTx research were mind-numbing, but not for Kashif. With intense reading, research, conferences, and scientific collaboration, Kashif learned that 3FTx proteins were enriched, to various degrees, in the venoms of the King Cobra and the Green Mamba, but that the Sonoran Coral Snake had a 3FTx proportion of nearly one-hundred percent. Given his desert heritage, which of many paths to take was almost obvious, as supplemented by prayers at the *mosque*. He chose the venom of *Micruroides euryxanthus* as the center of his thesis.

More decisions and paths unrolled before him; 3FTx proteins had been synthesized in the laboratory. From there, it became possible to engineer protein mutations, creating altered DNA sequences that coded an engineered toxin protein. Each would have unique – and maybe desired – reactions when interacting with the nervous system of the human body.

✝

During his years at UCI, Kashif had flown back to Riyadh often, always in First Class, as his classes, his research schedule and his professors allowed. But considering the name on the laboratory, they were usually very accommodating. During these visits he would always stop by the *mosque* in Riyadh to pray and speak with Fahim who continued to give Kashif focused encouragement. During each visit, Kashif would explain his research in as much scientific detail as Fahim could understand. Fahim became excited when he learned that Kashif could possibly engineer and design a neurotoxin to achieve a desired effect. He encouraged, almost directed Kashif to follow this research path, but one narrowed down to a toxin that led to death predictable hours later. When Kashif told him of the delayed effects of natural coral snake venom, Fahim's eyes narrowed in thought.

Back at the UCI laboratory, Kashif's adviser was enthused about this narrow research, but for more altruistic reasons. Kashif fed a variety of synthetic 3FTx neurotoxins, laced in food, to laboratory rats and rabbits. He sometimes used larger animals, but was careful to not raise the hackles of people concerned about the ethics of using them for laboratory experiments. Some engineered 3FTx synthetic variants could withstand hostile enzymes found in digestive juices of the stomach and be absorbed into the bloodstream. An assigned graduate student was given the task of watching the poor animal, timing from when it had eaten to when its head and legs stopped twitching, followed by a non-beating heart.

How a particular synthetic neurotoxin reacted with the components found in the blood of a test animal was theorized, tested, and correlated with the observed time lags. The number of distinct components in the blood of an animal, or a human, was very large, making the combinations and permutations with synthetic 3FTx variants enormous. Kashif enlisted the help of the Department of Computer Science. Huge databases were used and complex models were run using supercomputers to help validate and explain laboratory results. Some synthetically-induced deaths were delayed by hours with little or no initial symptoms. At least they had not observed any symptoms until the end. Some rats and rabbits happily ate the poison-tainted food, moved contentedly around in their cages until muscle paralysis set in.

Kashif's thesis focused on this aspect of 3FTx synthetic neurotoxins which he successfully defended before a UCI board of senior research biochemists. With his adviser,

Kashif co-authored articles that were published in prestigious journals. With that, his adviser was placed on the secret short list to someday take over the department. With this research win-win, UCI conferred a PhD in Biochemistry, Molecular and Structural Biology on Kashif when he walked across the commencement stage in his distinctive graduation robe and proudly grasped his diploma. His father had come to witness the event and called Fahim back in Riyadh.

Fahim then made a very short call. The receiver was picked up at the other end, without answer. Fahim simply voiced, *"Khalaset."*

In the dimly-lit, windowless underground room, a steady hand checked off the first in a long list of actions.

Mentors

If anybody needed mentoring, it was Gene Fitzgerald. He grew up in a dysfunctional household in Hillsboro, Oregon. His father's alcoholism netted bruises for him and his depressed mother. His middle school vice principle called the police when Gene had showed up with a swollen black eye. His explanation that he had fallen on the sidewalk did not carry the day. A counselor accompanied by a police officer showed up at the Fitzgerald house. That eased things a bit. But Gene's frustrations started boiling over in high school. Fights in the cafeteria and vulgarities thrust at teachers did not sit too well with school administrators. His father's pistol showed up in Gene's locker during a school inspection. There was another visit to the Fitzgerald household followed by a school suspension.

Before finishing high school, Gene eventually lived with his divorced, psychologically-damaged mother. His father had moved to California, never to return for a visit or even call. Gene was pretty much on his own. His mother did not oversee his study habits in his bedroom, but wondered why he had seen fit to cover the window with aluminum foil. The darkened room was illuminated by dull purple lights and the glow of the computer screen that showed bloody, violent interactive video games.

Gene's grades were poor, but he did manage to graduate. He spent a lot of time at his desktop computer, his link to the outside world, his only world. A website with well-designed content drew him into a much different culture, far away. His online chats asked for more information; inquisitive texts flowed back into the darkened bedroom. As arranged, an olive-skinned man met Gene at a local McDonald's, treating him with burgers, fries, a milkshake and a very motivating discussion.

†

It was just another day in the life of professional airline pilots, except that Jen and Chris were in their favorite place at PDX: Route 66. They watched their Aster Air 737-700 being rinsed, sprayed from elevated positions by high-volume hoses with a special solution. It cleared snow and ice from the fuselage, control surfaces and most importantly the wings for a clean laminar flow on takeoff to generate the needed lift. Chris recalled his high school paper and how it had described that ice on wings was a bad thing for both lift and weight.

Almost on cue, a young man that had been watching them since Route 66 had opened, walked up to the eating counter and again sat down on a stool by the serving station. He glanced at Jen, even nodded as a sort of greeting.

Sara came over to take orders, "Hi guys. Nasty weather, isn't it? Problems with your Salt Lake run?"

Chris sighed and said, "Just a little delay to get the damn ice off. Weather in Salt Lake will be clear, cold and calm. We'll have the same, as always."

"Comin' right up."

Jen stopped her, "Sara. Do you know that guy over there?"

"Sort of. He came in and applied as a short order cook. Can you believe it? He had never cooked before; had no references. Our manager said he had to work more hours at another restaurant before he would even consider him working here, not even as a dishwasher. We have standards, you know."

Chris laughed, "Yep. Everybody has to log hours to get ahead."

Sara replied, "It's too bad. He's sure cute."

As Sara went off to give their order, Chris took it upon himself and waved the young man over to join them in the booth. It could comfortably hold four people. Jen and Chris slid over and made room. Chris welcomed him, "How are you doing this morning?"

"Great. I love airplanes and would like to fly them someday."

Jen reached out her hand, "I'm Jen Grissom, a captain for Aster Air. This is Chris McDonald, my first officer. What's your name?

"Gene. Gene Fitzgerald. I got work here cleaning airplanes. It's not much, but it's a start. I live in Hillsboro, near the airport there. Grew up watching planes come and go, sometimes right over my house, depending on the wind."

Chris asked, "Have you ever flown before?"

Gene smiled, answering with the best straight face he could muster, "Yes, a little. Before I graduated from high school, I paid for couple of lessons in a Piper Cherokee 140, but ran out of money. I'm trying to build up my bank account and learn more about flying, working at this airport."

As Gene spoke he took off his big horn-rimmed glasses, pulled out a small bottle of cleaner, spritzed them, wiped them clean with a table napkin, held them up to the light and examined them carefully. Jen inquired, "How's your vision? You have to pass a flight physical before you can solo or get your private license."

"I think it's OK. I've had to wear these darn things since my grade school teacher found out why I was having trouble learning."

Jen attempted to comfort the awkwardness, "I'm sure you'll be fine. I was just asking. Sorry."

"Please don't worry. I've had to suffer being called four-eyes. My eye doctor prescribed these large lenses because I have problems with my peripheral vision."

Gene changed the subject, "How did you learn to fly and get to be senior pilots for a big airline?

That's all it took. Jen began first and regaled the young men with stories of her first flight out of the Salina airport and flying a twin jet plane into PDX in dense fog. Chris kept interrupting with stories of his military training, of combat pilots at the officer's club bar, and a few harrowing stories about flying around Europe in their foggy winters and low level MC-130 flights at night over desert sands, "… dispensing death to bastards, damn ragheads."

Gene flinched. Jen topped it off by the story of their near miss at SFO.

She glanced at her watch, "Well. Got to be going. Flight schedules, you know. Looks like the snow and ice has been taken care of."

Gene slid out to let them pay their bills, "Ma'am … Sir … thank you very much. I'd like to learn more and get your advice when you're here getting ready to fly."

Chris patted Gene on the back, "We'd be happy to. I'll bring some of my early flight manuals to loan you. They're just taking up space, anyway. I'm sure Jen has some, too."

†

In the coming months, they spread their collective wings over Gene, even paying for his breakfast on occasion so his flying bank account could grow to sustain flight for future lessons. Gene had also now become part of their Route 66 routine. Jen and Chris enjoyed being flying mentors. They did not always sit with him. Sometimes Gene just said hello and sat at the counter for coffee, and leafed through Chris's flying manuals. Jen just shook her head as Gene spent some time spritzing and cleaning his glasses next to the server station.

During one breakfast all three of them were again sitting at the same booth. Jen pointed to a graph and tables in a training manual she had given him, about computing take-off role using aircraft weight, pressure altitude, air temperature and wind. An apparently unhappy supervisor in the concourse waved to Gene, getting his attention, motioning for him to come over quickly. An inbound flight had landed late and the aircraft needed to be cleaned right away. Gene got up and left, not wanting to put his job at risk.

In his hurry, Gene left his glasses on the table. When they were out of sight, Jen picked up the glasses and looked through them to see if Gene's vision could be a detriment to learning to fly. She did not put them on but looked through them at the newspaper on the table. Surprisingly, the lenses seemed to provide no change in how the newsprint appeared. She whispered, as if Gene were still at the table, "Chris. Look through these. There's no correction that I can tell. It's not even a no-line bifocal."

Chris put them on, then back on the table, "Yes, you're right. But, hell, I'm not an eye doctor. There must be something, but it isn't any of our business. A flight physical will sort that out."

Out of the corner of her eye, Jen saw Gene returning, in a hurry. When he came up to the table, she said, "I'm glad you came back. We were going to leave your glasses with Sara."

"Thank you very much. They're expensive. Wouldn't want to lose them. See you next time."

†

Months later Gene walked in to Route 66, over to Jen and Chris and stood by their booth. Jen had hoped that he had not been fired after seeing their unhappy supervisor. Finally, as Chris was finishing his coffee, "Well, where has this young aviator been? We've missed you."

"Oh, it's a long story. My grandmother had a stroke. She lives in Boise. I had to help our family and stay with her while things were worked out. We don't have much money and nursing homes are expensive. Our boss was good about that; gave me a long furlough. Anyway, I'm back. Oh, got to go, planes got to be cleaned."

He left and walked down the concourse. An older man had just purchased a newspaper, folded it under his arm, quickly left the newsstand and appeared to follow Gene, weaving through the sea of people. Jen noticed, but did not think anything of it. In the following months, Jen and Chris noticed the same man just hanging around the newsstand or strolling down the concourse. He was easy to identify sometimes wearing a black leather jacket and a British cap, chewing gum rapidly with a partially-open mouth.

Always observant, Jen sensed a correlation. When mentoring Gene in Route 66, she noticed the same gum-chewing man in the newsstand. She mentioned this to Chris. He answered, "Aw... he's probably just a frequent flyer with a business schedule that matches ours. Not to worry, Jen."

One morning, after sitting with Jen and Chris, Gene walked down the concourse to the gate where an arriving flight was slated to dock. The gum-chewing man, in a short raincoat, followed, at a distance. He watched as Gene pulled out a cell phone and sent a text message. Gene waited as arriving passengers walked out, then walked down the jet bridge to the waiting empty aircraft. The curious observer took out a small notebook from his raincoat, jotted down a few things and left the airport. The beginning and end of Gene's five-month disappearance had been carefully noted.

ar-Raqqah

Masoud avoided Iraqi and Kurdish forces, sometimes driving off road over barely improved trails. The destination was another ancient city on the bank of the Euphrates, upstream of Ramadi. Occupants tumbled out and entered through a guarded door. In darkness, status reports were given to two of the passengers, a one-armed man and a battle-scarred *mullah*. They disappeared quickly down a stairway, then through a maze of tunnels, then deeper. The *caliph* had summoned them.

Masoud and Dabir covered the van with a gray canvas tarp to match the surrounding concrete rubble. They took Akmal and Ramza down the same flight of stairs into the basement, leading with words and a flashlight. It revealed a hole in the concrete floor that led straight down to a tunnel entrance. They were directed to climb down through the cramped opening. Ramza hesitated; claustrophobia gripped him. With blunt encouragement, he descended. Akmal followed. They hunched over and were led through a labyrinth of inter-connected earthen tunnels. They climbed up into a familiar interior, a bomb-damaged *mosque*. There were others inside.

Military forces from Iraqi Kurdistan were part of a broad coalition backed by the United States in the fight to wrench control of ar-Raqqah from the Islamic State. Over 12 centuries earlier, it had been the capital of a *caliphate*, an extremely strong motivating fact used by *imams* and *mullahs* to draw people to the *jihad*. The might of air power had been brought to bear. Precision guided bombs were used for maximum effect and to lessen the odds of civilian casualties, to some degree. Target intelligence and knowledge of the disposition of the populace were less precise.

The self-declared Islamic State had been euphoric with their early successes. The dominoes had fallen in their direction: al-Fallujah, Mosul, Tikrit, Ramadi. A modern *caliphate* had appeared within reach. Now the dominoes had fallen the other way. Strategic cities had been re-taken. But the capital of the *caliphate* remained: ar-Raqqah.

The *caliph* and Hadi had to face reality. In addition to being outnumbered on the ground, they were vulnerable to the might of coalition air power. They fought fiercely in the streets, but conserved their materiel and human resources in the tunneled underground. Residents of ar-

Raqqah were encouraged to help, or conscripted into labor squads to dig and dig, to exhaustion. Those that resisted fell to the sword or a gunshot to the back of the head. Word quickly spread through old neighborhoods and discussed among multi-generational families; there was little choice. Virulent enforcement of *Shari'ah* law dictated their lives.

There was much discussion in the underground command center. Some argued that they should resist until the end, in the name of *Allah*. Others felt that if they could hold out long enough, exacting severe losses on the infidels, they could exceed the time-scale of American will: months and years compared to the decades and centuries of a *jihad*. Hadi stood and firmly stated that they should continue inflicting death and injury with snipers, mortar teams, mines, booby traps and suicide bombers. But rather than sacrifice all in Ramadi, he had proposed a plan to dissolve into ar-Raqqah, the surrounding desert and other cities, among them sprawling Aleppo and Baghdad. Hadi was very convincing that the *caliphate* of minds and souls is not so easily defeated and can be brought together at a future date to control land and its people under a theocratic *Shari'ah* government. Muhammad Talib spoke with passion supporting this position. With that, they held sway. The *caliph* nodded in agreement.

Death rained down from fighter aircraft and drones as a Kurdish special rifle team crept into a low bombed-out building on the southeastern edge of the city. Coalition forces would be advancing on the city from their rear, from a bank of the Euphrates. The three-member team went up a stairwell to a room on the third floor. The roof had been partially blown away as was the east wall. One of them was an American, an adviser who had supervised their selection and training as snipers. From a shuttered window their lines of fire were good. Islamic State forces had not detected them, but that would change when sniper rounds found their targets. The adviser was a tall husky man, a seasoned Marine, Gunnery Sergeant John Kelly. A Kurd sniper spread the shutters slightly apart and set up the forward legs of his rifle on the wide window ledge. Smithy was not fluent in their language, but could make do with what he had picked up on previous deployments. He had taken it upon himself to study Arabic on his own. The sniper team knew some English. Important things could be communicated accurately enough. Smithy was armed with a standard automatic rifle, a holstered Glock, a spotting scope and a hand-held short range radio. The sniper's rifle was one Smithy was very familiar with, having used it in combat and given instruction with it back in Quantico, Virginia.

Now it was down to business. It came soon enough. At the top of a high building, they spotted two men setting up a mortar, but their movement was too rapid to pick one off with a sniper round. With his scope, Smithy watched a group of six men, faces covered, lugging obviously-heavy canvas bags along the side of the wide street, the same street that would be used by Coalition forces when their operation kicked off. He patted the Kurd sniper and his spotter on their helmets and pointed firmly in that direction. They all watched as one of the enemy combatants took an explosive device out of his bag and set it up on the street. The Kurd sniper chambered a round and dialed in adjustments for the distance. The rifle kicked and the man in the street died instantly where he stood. Another round was chambered and released. Another fell as the others took cover, shouting and pointing in their direction. Smithy reported back by radio that they were engaging the enemy. The commander of the Coalition operation knew their position, as planned. Smithy looked at his watch. The planned incursion would begin in four minutes. But it didn't. Targets down the street were now out of sight.

An enemy sniper round struck one of the wooden shutters, ricocheted off a side wall, then out the open back of the room. It came from the rooftop where the mortar had been set up. Smithy caught the puff of muzzle smoke with his spotter scope. Another round struck the edge of the window. They had been located!

Soon a swarm of fighters charged down the street, firing wildly in their direction, zig-zagging across the street from behind building corners to doorways. The Kurd sniper took out two of them, but the onslaught continued. If the morning operation did not start soon, they would be overwhelmed. Smithy helped direct sniper fire, then returned fire with his own weapon. There was a brief lull. Silence.

Smithy turned around to the sound of footsteps on the stairs. Two attackers leapt into the room spraying it with automatic fire killing the Kurd sniper and wounding his spotter. Two quick bursts from Smithy brought them down, then silence, followed by excited voices from the stairwell. Sitting with his back against the wall by the window, Smithy radioed back, confirming their location, that they had been discovered and were under attack, needing immediate help. Another sniper round burst through a shutter with a shower of splinters. Smithy looked out the open back of the room, into the daylight, and saw a grenade lobbed up from the street and bounce across the floor. He flattened himself behind the body of the Kurd sniper. The blast was deafening, but the shrapnel had embedded in the Kurd's body, not Smithy. The spotter now lay dead. Stunned, Smithy's ears rang. He barely heard the shouts and the footsteps that ran across the floor in his direction. He knew that this was part of what he had signed up for. Thoughts of his father at the anvil, his mother, walnuts and Sister Mary Joseph crowded his mind.

They looked over at the huddled prisoners in the war-damaged *mosque*, their hands tied behind their backs, ankles tied together. Akmal and Ramza were each given a Kalishnikov with one clip of ammunition. A long scimitar lay on the table alongside a pile of orange jump suits. Their duties were explained: guard the prisoners, kill them when ordered. Their beheading executions would be video recorded for posting on websites and sent to news outlets to bring terror to their enemies and motivate those to come and join the *jihad* for the *caliphate*. It had been working. Iraqi soldiers in Mosul had fled rather than be captured and executed for their families to see. Fighters from across the Mideast, North Africa, Europe and even America had filtered in to fight and die for the cause. Some were motivated enough to strap explosives to their chests.

Prisoners were capital to be spent, but very

selectively. In the meantime, they were to be kept alive. Akmal and Ramza were ordered to take them, one at a time, outside for defecation and urination, feed them in the *mosque*, then retie their hands and feet. The *mosque* was chosen because some Coalition forces were hesitant to destroy a structural icon of Islam, especially if intelligence revealed that innocents were inside. Even if the Islamic State were to use a *mosque* for military purposes, its destruction may not sit too well with the populace.

Hours turned into days, days into weeks. They had charge of only a few prisoners. Akmal and Ramza had been well trained back at the camp. They were loathe to care for infidel prisoners, but they had their orders. Under extreme conditions, they would be ordered to leave the prisoners and join fighting in the streets to repel their enemies. They cared for the prisoners, but had not been given advice as to their comfort. Spitting and kicking were added to their shouts to move a prisoner around. They got some satisfaction from that. The number of prisoners grew. A recently-captured prisoner was dragged through the underground passageways and up into the *mosque*. He was bound tightly and tossed with contempt to the ground in front of Akmal and Ramza with orders to take special care of this one. He is of greater value, but is very strong and must be watched carefully. The prisoner struggled to roll over. He looked up with piercing blue eyes at Akmal. Contempt became a two-way street. He wore the uniform of a US Marine. It was Smithy.

The next day, the order came down to behead two prisoners. Lights and a video camera were set up, right in front of the other prisoners for them to see their eventual fate. A senior fighter came in and selected an older one. He was dragged in front of bright lights, forced to wear an orange jump suit, forced to kneel, head down. Smithy looked and made his own internal preparation, hoping his parents would not watch his execution. Akmal took the scimitar from the table and severed the unfortunate man's head with one swift blow. Ramza was ordered to do the same for the next selected one, but hesitated. Akmal whispered in Ramza's ear, whose eyes widened. Motivated, Ramza raised the sword and brought it down, but not hard enough. A senior fighter finished the job with a large knife. Lights and camera were removed. One prisoner cried aloud for *Allah* to rescue him. Smithy had been intentionally spared for greater propaganda value: the recorded execution of a US Marine.

In the coming weeks, the frequency of aerial bombings increased and the sound of automatic fire was heard more often, closer and closer to the *mosque*. Idle talk, rumors, were overheard by Akmal that preparations were underway for tactical relocation and to be prepared to execute the remaining prisoners. A man in near panic ran in, shouting orders to evacuate. There was not enough time to use the scimitar, so Akmal and Ramza prepared to use their Kalishnikovs and hose down the prisoners with bullets. With their fingers on triggers, another man ran in and shouted, "Stop!" He was immediately recognized, confirmed by his missing left forearm. Hadi commanded them to untie the prisoners' feet and take them outside. They took Smithy first. In the alleyway was a large Mercedes delivery van. Smithy was pushed in, then the others. Ramza jumped in. Akmal ran back into the mosque, returned with the scimitar, climbed in and closed the rear doors. The van accelerated quickly; Akmal and Ramza fell over. When they managed to stand, two familiar faces looked back at them from the front seats. Masoud was at the wheel. Hadi had vanished somewhere, but had given them strict orders. They took a special route and escaped the city to the north, then turned west. As they drove, Masoud and Dabir bragged that they had driven armored personnel carriers made in America in the final battles for the city.

Hadi was being driven to the same location by Gamil, a brave soldier who had fought alongside him in the final hours. Hadi trusted him. That would be very important in the coming months. Hadi was not sure why he gave to the order to save the prisoners, but had had a premonition that they may be more valuable alive than dead. His mind raced, framing a plan that had been in the back of his mind for some time. He had discussed this often with Muhammad Talib, how to bring *jihad* and terror to America in ways not thought of in Western minds. He had spoken to the *caliph* just before ar-Raqqah fell and had been given the authority to form a special group, the Army of God: *Jaysh al-Allah*, to carry out terror against Americans, on their soil.

Urban Cave

A Land Rover was driven down the alley and pulled up to the building's back entrance. Its lights were flashed in a specified sequence as a digital signal. Two men walked over to the all-terrain vehicle. Another remained in the shadows, his automatic weapon trained on it. Gamil rolled down the window and the men peered in. Nothing more was needed to gain entry, the one-armed man and the scar-faced *mullah* were immediately recognized. Hadi told the security guards that a large Mercedes van would be arriving soon. It did. Lights again were flashed. The van was carefully inspected and let in and the door rolled down. The first elements of *Jaysh al-Allah,* and its prisoners, had arrived.

Many factions with different political and religious beliefs lived in the large, ancient city of Aleppo. Hadi and Muhammad Talib had visited there and had met with supporters of the *caliphate* for recruits and cash, and to plan. Hadi had personally overseen the purchase of this safe house where they could meet clandestinely. It was an empty warehouse in an old industrial area that had been owned by a retired merchant that sold hardware, furniture and furnishings, including expensive Persian rugs. The ground-floor of the single-story building could be used for any number of things: a place to store supplies, weapons and explosives, a place to park cars and trucks. It had only small high windows for natural light. Hadi had forbidden turning on electric lights so the building always looked to be unused. What was inside could not be seen from outside, and very little on the outside of the building, except small frames of the sky, could be seen from within. The flat roof could be accessed by an interior spiral staircase to a small room with a door to the outside.

But it was the basement that had caught Hadi's attention. It had separate walled-off areas with electricity, plumbing, running water, an Internet connection, but no windows. A small room had a toilet. Three areas had rows of storage rooms with lockable doors. The merchant had used the largest room as an office, the other rooms for storing expensive items. The merchant's desk and chairs were left behind as part of the sale. A small cadre lived in the warehouse to oversee and maintain the place. The closets had cots, blankets and pillows for visitors that needed to lay low for a while. The *caliph* had even stayed there to make Internet recruitment videos. Food was stocked on shelves and in a refrigerator. Electric and water bills were paid on time. Comings and goings were done carefully in the alley so as not to arouse suspicion from neighboring industrial buildings. A low-profile satellite communications antenna was mounted on the middle of the roof, unseen from the street. Its coaxial cable was threaded down to the office. For the freshly-minted *Jaysh al-Allah*, the warehouse was the urban equivalent of an impregnable mountain cave complex in Afghanistan in the Tora Bora for *al-Qaeda*.

While Ramza and the welcoming guards watched the prisoners, especially Smithy, Akmal was shown the basement layout and instructed to set up a prison; the small rooms would be its cells. Masoud and Dabir were shown to a bunk room and told to wait for further instructions. In the basement, it was hard to hear the calls to prayer. One of the duties of the semi-permanent guards on the main floor was to come down and make such announcements, even though an accurate clock and calendar could have done the same thing. Prayer rugs were rolled up in the office. A yellow arrow had been painted on the floor. They all knew where it pointed.

In the following days, Hadi and Muhammed

Talib spent many hours in the office. Everyone else was strictly told that they could not enter without permission, nor could they linger outside of the office door. This level of secrecy was new, but nobody openly questioned it. Hadi sketched out a plan to bring terror to America, a complex plan, again beyond the thinking of those in US federal agencies responsible for the security of the nation. A different plan, equally complex, had succeeded in doing this, resulting in the terror of 9/11. They had often discussed how to bring more death to America. Various schemes had been discussed in al-Fallujah, Ramadi and ar-Raqqah. But there had not been time to plan and prepare. They were busy enough as the geographical *caliphate* was collapsing around them. Now they had the time, the place and the motivation. The *caliphate* of the mind had not lessened.

In the dark basement room, they decided that chemicals would be used as weapons of mass destruction. Saddam had done so against the Kurds. But the chemical for their plan was to be special, a biochemical nerve agent. If quietly slipped into a link of the food production chain, or into a reservoir, mass deaths and mass hysteria could result, especially when credit for the terror was publicly taken. A critical component of their plan was a lethal poison with special properties, including having minimal odor or taste. Hadi's premonition had been correct; the prisoners would be used to test the poison. But they did not have such a poison, nor did they have biochemists among them to develop it. It would have to be purchased or made somewhere, very quietly, and a secret test location determined, not at the warehouse.

Two of the building's trusted staff had been sent out to find where poisons could be purchased, or manufactured. The required properties were scribbled on a sheet of paper. Hadi's operatives returned with discouraging reports; the unique poison could not be found, nor did they find anyone who might be able to produce it. They had also driven to cities where such underground expertise might be found: Homs and Damascus.

Hadi asked his *mullah*, "Where can we find such knowledge?"

"Europe and America, in their research universities. We have believers in the *jihad* embedded there, including some professors. Others have already brought death by shootings, bombings and driving trucks into crowds. Some have given their lives for the cause."

"What about Riyadh? They have many universities. Some involved in the research for oil. They know of chemistry."

"Yes. That may be a good option. There is a *mullah* there, Fahim, a brother in the faith that believes as we do. I have heard from him. He knows of a genius with a private laboratory."

"Let us visit there ourselves. But the time must be right."

Wabar

A wooden arm with a fingered hand lay on the desk. The leather socket and binding straps hung over the edge. It had replaced what he had left behind on a backstreet of al-Fallujah. The prosthetic had been hand-carved by a loyal fighter in the *jihad*. Hadi did not always wear it, sometimes purposefully; the missing arm was his badge of honor. He leaned on his stump, fingertips of his remaining hand reverently turning the pages of his *Qur'an,* scanning for revelation. A large map of the Arabian Peninsula was rolled out next to him in the dark basement. A single light bulb hung from the ceiling. There were many remote desert places in the broad peninsula, far from Aleppo. Hadi needed only one but wanted the hand of *Allah* to guide him. To carry out this part of the plan, local chemical testing on prisoners in the warehouse carried too much risk. A very remote site would be needed.

At a village *madrasa* Hadi had studied the *Qur'an* in his youth. But the holy book still held some obscure writings lost to his memory. The scar-faced *mullah* stood by his side as he had in al-Fallujah after the sniper's bullet had cleaved his arm. He had no way of knowing that the US Marine, in a basement cell had squeezed the trigger, nor did Smithy know that he had shot the arm off of his captor.

In secret solitude, *mullah* Muhammad Talib was here to interpret the word of *Allah*, through the recitations of Muhammad the Prophet. He was much more educated in such holy matters. The next page was turned. A verse of *al-Haaqqa* reached out and drew Hadi in. He read aloud from this chapter of the *Qur'an*.

"And as for Aad, they were destroyed by a screaming violent wind."

Hadi looked up, "I recall reading about this. Who were these people?

Muhammad Talib leaned down and quickly pointed out an accompanying verse that described the deadly sins that brought their destruction.

"And that was Aad, who rejected the signs of their Lord and disobeyed His messengers and followed the order of every obstinate tyrant."

Muhammad Talib looked to the ceiling, took a deep breath, and answered as a patient teacher would do, "The ancient people of Aad were very wicked and lustful as was their ruler. They had turned away from the face of *Allah*, despite the admonishments of a prophet He had sent them. The hand of *Allah* swept them away."

"Where was their city?"

"In the vast desert shown on this map, in an ancient city once known as Iram, Ubar to the nomadic desert dwellers, the Bedouins." With authority, he placed his finger down hard on the map with a resounding *thump*, "Here!"

Hadi smiled, nodding his apparent approval. The location was indeed remote, surrounded by a vast ocean of sand: the Rub' al-Kahli. As if it were an epiphany, he declared a self-evident truth, "The infidels that now walk our land, that blaspheme the truth, are just like the people of Aad! They must be swept away from the *caliphate!*" He leaned back in his chair, "Tell me more of Ubar."

Muhammad Talib became excited and angry, "Blasphemers from America claimed to have found this lost city using cameras on their satellites they claimed could see through the sand."

"Where do they say Ubar was located?"

"Farther south than where my finger rests, in the mountains of Oman. But I do not believe their lies.

"They are infidels! Arab scholars of our

history and learned *imams* have contradicted them."

"What do you believe of Ubar?"

"I believe the Bedouins, their ancient oral histories, that it is located southeast of Riyadh in a remote part of the Rub' al-Kahli, in a place now called Wabar. Here, where I have shown you, *Allah's* wrath is written in the sand."

"What do you mean?"

"Craters. Large iron meteors from the heavens struck there long ago. Some have been uncovered. One as large as a camel is on display in Riyadh. I believe *Allah* rained down fire on the wicked people who had rejected Him, against the teachings of a prophet that He had sent to save them. The hellfire from *Allah* created a destructive wind, a flaming, withering *haboob* of *Allah*."

"When did this happen?"

"Before the time of the Prophet, peace be upon Him." Muhammad Talib became more agitated, pacing back and forth, waving his hands to the ceiling then slamming his clenched fist on the table. "Infidels, wicked infidels, claim that time of the fire from the sky was not long ago, long after Muhammad, peace be upon Him, recited the destruction of Aad."

"What do you believe about the time of this divine wind."

"I believe the Bedouins and their legends,

that *Allah* threw down His iron from the heavens before the time of the Prophet, peace be upon Him."

Hadi looked up at the low concrete ceiling and the dim light bulb for a long time, wrestling with his thoughts, tapping his fingers on the table. He sat forward abruptly announcing, "This must be the place to bring death to the infidels, like *Allah* had done with fire from the sky and its violent wind to wipe from the land those who had rejected Him. We will be the cleansing wind!"

"*Allah* be praised!" echoed in the room.

Planning requirements went from spiritual to practical, "Our location must be far from curious eyes. Heavy trucks must be able to get there and back out, driven by Masoud and Dabir. They will prepare trailers in al-Mukalla, to hold our prisoners and biochemistry."

Muhammad Talib elaborated and cautioned, "Wabar is indeed very remote. The sands there shift with the wind, covering and uncovering the craters. I believe the dunes are not high but they cannot be crossed by a heavy truck with large trailers; their wheels will sink deep into the sand. But there are uncovered areas between dunes, salt flats, *sabkhas*, which are hard and strong, covered with thin veils of sand. However, we must confirm this."

He pointed to a labeled spot on the map, Bir'

ash-Shalfa, "Here is a small settlement northwest of Wabar, an oasis also with tanks of gasoline for modern travel. This map shows a road to the place from the north and a road that leads east, passing north of Wabar." He hesitated, stroked his beard and added, "There may be geologists at Wabar. It is famous and researched. Herding Bedouins likely roam the area, orbiting the water found at Bir' ash-Shalfa, as they have always done. There could be unwanted curiosity from Bedouin tribes. They will know when strangers stay on their desert sand. They may need to be convinced."

"What do you suggest?"

"We must send a trusted scout. I suggest Gamil."

"Yes, I agree. He is not only a brave believer, he is intelligent. Call him in."

†

The old Land Rover approached, its four wide, deep-treaded tires gripping the sandy road. The cluster of large trees stood out like a beacon. Their roots had found water beneath the sand. Two pickup trucks were parked in the shade. Rusty tanks sat upon elevated concrete supports. White trailers were scattered around the periphery of the central well and its trees. Only a few people lived at Bir' ash-Shalfa. One walked over to greet the visitor. A short gray beard and mustache covered his lower face under a tightly-patterned red and white *keffiyeh* held on his head by a black cord headband. A long white garment shielded the rest of his body from the midday sun, but its weave let the wind drift through. He spoke cautiously to Gamil with a different Arabic dialect. In this very remote area, there was always suspicion that had to be erased with conversation and maybe riyals. Despite the stack of cans of gasoline in the rear of the Land Rover, among large bottles of water, Gamil thought it prudent to conserve what he carried and refill his tanks at this desert gas station. As gravity pulled gasoline through a rubber hose into his vehicle, a woman stepped from the shade. Her curious eyes peered through a narrow slit in her black *burka*. The old attendant waved her back, out of sight among the trees. As Gamil handed over the requested money for the fuel, he asked about any Bedouins in the area. The old man just pointed to the east as he asked Gamil's purpose. With a straight, unflinching face, he answered, "To visit the craters of Wabar."

The old man nodded and pointed to the southeast and said a small convoy of scientists, in vehicles like his, had recently passed through this oasis heading in that direction after purchasing gasoline. Gamil noticeably raised his eyebrows at this unwelcome news, but said nothing.

Gamil headed his Land Rover back to the main road, then turned left and continued east, the GPS application on the hand-held tablet computer on the seat leading the way; it was an iPad. Eventually, he saw tire tracks in the sand leading south. He turned off the road and followed them. The remaining distance shown on the iPad to the location of the crater field lessened as he drove. Traction varied considerably along the way to Wabar but Gamil was skilled. He accelerated to cross soft sand dunes to keep from sinking in and getting stuck, a death sentence if alone in the blistering unforgiving heat of the Rub' al-Khali. Eventually, he came upon three similar Land Rovers, newer ones. A long white canvas tent was strung between two of them. Men in khaki tan pants, shirts and hats were gathered around electronic equipment on the sand around a slightly elevated rocky ring: a sand-filled crater. Wires led into the tent. A similarly dressed woman stepped out and shouted some numbers to the men. Then they all looked over at the approaching vehicle. As Gamil stopped and stepped out they came over to greet him, thinking that he could be another scientist. Gamil noticed the logo of the University of Cambridge on the doors of the other Land Rovers.

The lead geologist, a research professor from the university extended her hand and welcomed

Gamil in the Queen's best English. Gamil withheld his hand and just nodded, pretending to not understand. More English words went unrecognized. With the false language barrier, an attractive blond woman with blue eyes stepped forward and spoke in very good Arabic; she had been to Saudi Arabia before. As conversation ensued, she translated for the rest of the research team. Gamil said he was on a religious pilgrimage to visit this holy site. They understood the legend that enveloped the craters, but did not believe it. The lead geologist waved her hand in the direction of the crater, inviting him to walk over to it. Gamil did, but stopped at the edge of the ring, out of respect. He believed that the hand of *Allah* had been here to cleanse the sand of wicked people. He frowned, now that ignorant infidels were spoiling the place with their mere presence. He stood silently for a minute as they watched, then turned abruptly and walked quickly back to his Land Rover, averting his gaze from the pretty British face that said farewell in his native tongue.

As Gamil drove back north he stopped on hard, stable land, out of sight over the next dune and wrote in his notebook that a large truck could not get to the Wabar craters and that even if it could, infidels could be there. As he continued back to the main road, the irony was not lost on him that he drove a rugged off-road vehicle designed and built in England.

On the main road Gamil continued his main task: find a remote area among the low dunes near the Wabar craters that could be reached by truck and trailers, but away from curiosity. This could be a difficult balance to achieve. He drove east and probed a number of off-road areas that looked promising. None satisfied the requirement that a large truck could be driven to them. He turned around and headed back towards the gas station oasis at Bir' ash-Shalfa. About ten miles from the settlement, he saw a few sandy *sabkhas* and drove a few miles over them to where sand dunes were high enough to prevent being seen by a passing motorist on the main road; one requirement for secrecy. He made notes about each of them as his iPad accurately recorded routes and locations. He wrote notes on a paper map as well. As he drove on a third hard-surfaced *sabkha* he came upon a Bedouin encampment. But Gamil had come prepared for such an encounter.

From one of the tents he had been seen by an alert, armed man. These were self-sufficient desert dwellers who lived great distances from any security assistance, whether by camel or by motor vehicle. They had their own defenses. A tall, stern man in desert garb walked out from a tent and stood as a guard. An automatic rifle hung on a shoulder strap, his hand on the trigger grip. His other hand held a deadly-serious long sword, a razor-sharp scimitar. Gamil stopped. An elder Bedouin stepped out and stood next to his guard and placed his hand over his heart, a welcoming gesture, then folded his arms as if ready to defend the camp. Gamil was motioned to enter the large, low square tent held up by tall poles and pulled taught by ropes tied to stakes set through the shallow sand. The tent cloth was hand made from the hair of animals they herded, a coarse brown-black fabric that could withstand sun and wind.

Outside stood a few camels. Farther out was a small herd of goats that were nibbling on scattered, scrubby shrubs. Young boys and women watched over them. These Bedouins were not wealthy in material possessions, but were rich in the pure spirit of Islamic belief. They had not replaced camels with Land Rovers or pickup trucks, nor would they have wished to do so even if they could. They were ensconced in nomadic tradition that stretched back centuries, very proud of their simple life.

Hot desert wind buffeted the tent as they spoke. Open, elevated sections of the tent let the wind through. The seasoned elder, the Bedouin leader, stared with squinted eyes set amid tanned, wrinkled skin, weathered by a full life in the desert. They conversed effectively despite their own dialects as they reclined on worn cushions set on threadbare rugs that covered the sand. Soon, upon the old one's command, a wife brewed strong coffee in a small copper pot over a small fire outside. She brought in a tray with a plate of dates and nuts and two small cups. In them, gritty coffee grounds were still settling. The unknown visitor was now a welcome guest, to be defended as a family member, if necessary. An old rifle hung by a leather strap from one of the center poles. With devious sincerity, Gamil explained that he was a research scientist looking for meteor fragments to the north of Wabar, in this general area. The tribal elder nodded with a glint in his eyes as Gamil spoke of Wabar, where *Allah* had vanquished a city of sinful non-believers. Cups of coffee were raised to this belief. Gamil asked to be excused to retrieve some things from the Land Rover. The young guard walked with him, watching carefully. Gamil went and returned, twice, once with plastic gallon jugs of pure distilled water, something not found in the well at the gas station to the west, then with a long object wrapped in a blanket. The guard tensed, thrust his sword into the sand and lowered his rifle in Gamil's direction.

The use by a visitor, a welcomed one, of remote, sand-covered land in the Rub' al-Khali was done according to ancient desert custom, not with a deed or lease, but with raised cups of coffee and an understanding handshake with a Bedouin tribal elder to share the area, sometimes accompanied with something of value to show sincerity. Who really owned the arid shifting sands and barren *sabkhas*? Gamil unwrapped a beautiful scimitar and held it forward as a gift, laying it flat on the palms of his two open hands. That satisfied the nervous guard. The elder reached out, accepted the gift, slowly turned the blade, admired the skilled craftsmanship that had made it and asked about the beautiful engravings on each side in Arabic script.

The elder was not an educated man, nor a literate one. He had never seen a *madrasa*, or any type of school house or classroom whatsoever. But he had learned much from other desert dwellers or from passing nomadic caravans. He had memorized some verses of the *Qur'an* and had even purchased a small copy from a passing merchant. He had often visited the oasis, trading meat, wool and cheese, asking for access to the well. There were some at Bir' ash-Shalfa who could read. He had asked for their teaching and for them to read from the *Qur'an*. This elder was wise beyond his years. He asked Gamil to listen as he described the harsh conditions of the arid desert, as if Gamil surely did not understand. He said that by necessity, Bedouins were more practical than fastidious in the ritualistic practices of *Islam* than their urban brethren. City dwellers had more distractions and temptations, and certainly more food and water. When it came time to fast, his nomadic commune hardly noticed the difference. Fasting was a way of life. Life out in the open was simple and free, but merciless and hard. The elder emphasized that his relationships were simple: his family, his people, his animals; that he was unencumbered for the more important relationship with *Allah*.

With that, Gamil explained that the words on the sword were from the opening *surah* of the *Qur'an,* and read them from the scimitar, "In the name of *Allah*" on one side, "The Most Gracious, the Most Merciful" on the other. They faced each other in silence; seasoned suspicion remained in the old man's eyes. He asked directly why a poor nomadic shepherd such as he deserved such a wonderful gift. Gamil spoke slowly for emphasis, "No other scientists in the entire world know of our research this far north of Wabar. They must not know of our work and steal the credit for any discoveries of the ancient wrath of *Allah.* Such distinction must go to our university. We must park trailers and trucks and set up a secret research camp. Nobody must know or ask."

The wise elder knew what he must do. The curiosity of his people would be held at bay;

any questions from any other visitors would go unanswered. He nodded his agreement; Gamil reached out and clasped his hands, thanking him for his understanding. The moment of this verbal contract was interrupted by a more-immediate need. The old man stood and shouted a command and some in the camp came out of their tents. Older men and women knelt on small plain rugs or swatches of tent cloth and prepared to kneel and bow down in the same direction as the elder did. How he knew it was time was uncertain. There was no *mosque*, *minaret*, *mullah* or *muezzin* anywhere near this small encampment on the vast desert. But he had a clock purchased years ago at Bir' ash-Shalfa, and he watched a small stake in the sand and the shadow it cast. From this, he knew it was about that time of late afternoon for the *Asr*.

In the early years, his desert ancestors had judged the time to pray by the elevation of the sun relative to the horizon, the length of cast shadows compared to an object's height, the sun's highest point in its arc across the sky, an estimnated time after sunset and when the sky was judged to be completely dark. The times of the dawn, noon and sunset prayers could be estimated reasonably well, but the times of the afternoon and night prayer had more error in their estimates when compared to the dictates of the strict administrators of Islam. But in their hearts, they had known that it was vastly more important to strengthen a pillar of the faith with prayer while kneeling towards Mecca, even if the time was not met accurately.

The elder estimated this direction. Gamil asked him to wait just a few seconds as he ran to the Land Rover and returned with his prayer rug. He rolled it out next to the elder and followed him in action and prayer, as did the others. In this role, the tribal elder became the *imam*, the leader of Islamic prayer for the members of his nomadic tribe. The bond with the driver had now been sealed by much more than the engraved scimitar.

Gamil and the tribal elder exchanged light kisses on both cheeks in parting. He got back into the Land Rover and set his rolled-up prayer rug on the seat beside him. He drove out of sight, stopped and made written note of the main tent, its size, that they were held against the wind by ropes tied to stakes set through the sand, and that the tent cloth was not white, to better reflect the sun, but dark brown and black, made of coarse threads spun from the hair of goats and camels, woven by the women. He pulled a communications handset from the glove box. He stepped out to get a better link with satellites, keyed in a number and a

word, *Khalasset*, checked them carefully, pressed
the transmit key, then drove to the roadway and
turned west, past the oasis, then north to the wide
paved road leading to Riyadh, and points farther
north to Aleppo.

The sun was setting in the west. Completely
out of sight, with nobody to impress, he
determined the accurate direction to the Great
Mosque of Mecca from his iPad, rolled out his
prayer rug on the sand in the middle of nowhere,
used some of his water for ritual purification,
knelt and bowed down, touching his forehead
to the rug and recited the *Maghrib*. He had done
this before in much harsher conditions, not at
the purported research university, but during the
battle for ar-Raqqah.

†

In the dark basement, Hadi and Muhammad
Talib questioned Gamil in private, discussed
the details of his data and his verbal report. He
handed over his paper map with marks and notes.
Of the six possible sites, Gamil suggested one; he
defended his recommendation. The path leading
to it was wide and hard, with only thin layers of
sand that change frequently with the winds. The
dunes were high enough to hide the site from
the road. A heavy truck and trailers with a wide

footprint of tires could make it in, and the tractor back out; the depth of the sand would not be higher than the axles, if the site was used in the next few months. If there was a delay, deeper sand could be a problem. If there was a soft sand risk, they could let air out of the tires to halve the pressure. He mentioned that there were more remote sites in the desert without the risk of a big truck getting stuck, but had not thought enough about the hand of *Allah* in the history of Wabar before he spoke. Muhammad Talib dressed him down in front of Hadi who did not look happy. Gamil took this uncomfortable opportunity to emphasize that the suggested site was as close to the Wabar craters as possible, and that even if a truck could make it to Wabar, there would be no way of predicting if scientists would be there, or not. Hadi looked up, slapped the desk and pointed to the map. The site was chosen. Gamil was ordered to absolute secrecy, lest the sword cut his life short.

The plan was coming together. Gamil left; Masoud and Dabir were invited in. They were given a hand-drawn copy of Gamil's map, hard cash and ordered to return to al-Mukalla, purchase a semi-truck tractor, two tandem trailers, and to build-out their interiors as Hadi demanded and sketched. The precise latitude and longitude were written on the rear of the map. They were good trusted soldiers, told to not disclose the map or anything about it, to trust it with their lives, and that only they were to do the trailer modifications. They were given a satellite communications handset, told how to report when the task was completed, when the trailers were in place, and that time was of the essence.

Trailers

The phone rang breaking the deep bedroom silence in a modest home. Yasser rolled over groggily and picked up the receiver. He was on call and there had been unexpected problems at the al-Wadiah border crossing before. He expected to hear the voice of the chief guard telling him to come in for special duty. But what Yasser had heard was a soft, muffled voice recite the names of his wife and two young children, and their ages, perfectly, then weave physical threat with financial promise. Yasser had not slept well since then. Three days later he put on his uniform and had a rushed breakfast: dates, nuts and spiced tea. Today was the day. Yasser said goodbye to his wife, patted the heads of his son and daughter and drove to his assigned border checkpoint as the day-shift supervisor. The *Hajj* was still a month off so he would not have to contend with pilgrims and try to sort out the dangerous ones. This day he would have to contend with lines of cars and trucks coming from Yemen, one in particular.

By mid-afternoon the pleasant morning had

turned hot, brutally hot and desert dry. Withering wind blew through the desolate checkpoint, sucking moisture out of everything and everyone, including Yasser. Sun-glassed fellow guards stood in the shade of the elevated span that straddled the highway, checking documents handed out through vehicle windows by cautious drivers. With powerful binoculars, Yasser could see it through the shimmering heat. The massive vehicle, literally a train on rubber wheels, approached at some speed from the south over the long black ribbon on the sand. It had to slow rapidly to join the end of a long line of cars and trucks that slowly crept forward as guards did their duty, one vehicle at a time. Machine gun like *dat-dat-dat* sounds belched from its exhaust stacks as it slowed using engine compression to assist the wheel brakes.

The region still suffered armed conflict for control, fueled by family and tribal histories, religious and political division, and modern thoughts of black liquid beneath the desert. Blood had been soaked in the sands around al-Wadiah and continued to be shed to the west across a still-disputed border. Lines on old paper maps had been drawn, with some British influence, using a ruler that did not bend to ancient realities.

Suspicions remained high. Weapons were checked as the truck neared. They prepared to protect modern Saudi Arabia: its land, its people, its oil. Yasser recognized the number on the Yemeni license plate that he had committed to memory during the phone call. The truck's tractor was a powerful beast with a large snout for its huge diesel engine, a sleeping area behind the cab and tall, twin, chromed vertical exhaust stacks. It pulled two long trailers in tandem.

Yasser stepped south towards the northern edge of Yemeni territory, in the direction of the truck, and raised his hand. For emphasis, a machine gun hung on a strap from his shoulder. He pointed and waved the truck to a side area in the sun before reaching the shade of the overarching span so that following vehicles would not be blocked during the inspection. The tractor and its trailers ground to a final halt with a loud collective squeal punctuated by the whoosh of air from its pressured brakes. The white trailers were huge, each over fifty feet long. The logo of a research university in al-Mukalla was affixed to the side doors of the tractor and the trailer doors. Installed on the front of each trailer was a small electric-powered air conditioner. They were not running, but the one for the cab was, powered by the *clack-clack-clack* of the idling diesel engine. Yasser noted the small slits, narrow vents that had been installed at the tops of the sides of the trailers. To the unsuspecting, it all looked like a mobile research facility, or the cargo for one. The guards had seen and checked many tractor-trailer rigs in pursuit of cross-border commerce and trade. This one was different. The tractor had three rear axles with pairs of wide tires on each end, 12 tires in all, providing traction and bearing for a heavy load. The front of the first trailer was connected over the tractor's rear wheels. The rear wheels of this trailer had a similar set of 12 tires. The second trailer had 24 tires; 3 axles with 12 tires in front on a road dolly, 3 axles and 12 tires mounted on the back end.

Masoud and Dabir climbed down from the towering cab. Yasser walked over and looked stern for the cameras that recorded everything. He had a growing family to feed and a wife that liked nice things, and probably would like to live a little longer. Documents were handed over by Masoud; they loosely listed the trailers' loads. Yasser carefully examined them as he glanced down again at the Yemeni license plate. He had to be sure. The destination shown on the transport papers was the zoo in Riyadh. Masoud pulled out a short step ladder from the cab and set it at the rear of the last trailer. Dabir stepped up, unlocked and unlatched the doors and swung them wide open. Guards stood nearby with automatic rifles, rounds chambered, muzzles lowered. Yasser climbed up and into stifling heat to inspect

Masoud's and Dabir's handiwork as had been
dictated by a one-armed man in Aleppo.

In the rear of the trailer, Yasser noted a
portable, diesel engine electric generator and
an extension ladder by a high stack of folded
dark canvas. The interior had been modified; a
long workbench was fastened on one side with
electrical receptacles along its length. Beneath
the workbench were rows of cardboard boxes
with partially-folded lids that barely hid canned
goods and packages of dates and nuts. Next to
them were large plastic buckets, inserted one into
the other in vertical stacks. In the forward area
of the cavernous interior were stacks of folded
chairs and folded canvas cots. Alongside them
was a man-portable aluminum ramp used to more
easily load and unload the big trailer if an elevated
loading dock were not available. At the far end
were two large, cylindrical stainless steel tanks
fastened firmly to the floor. One was mounted on
a low platform, a spigot at the bottom. The other
had a narrow pipe extending from its bottom
through the forward wall of the trailer, connected
to an outside spigot. There were no labels as to
what the tanks held, but they could be sampled,
if requested. Yasser placed his hand on each tank,
but did not ask.

Yasser paced slowly up and down the length
of the trailer, writing notes on his clipboard,

looking as official as possible. Masoud and Dabir stood outside peering in, feeling the tension of weapons pointed at them. Apparently satisfied, Yasser returned, climbed down the short ladder and waved his approval. Outwardly calm, Dabir nodded and then shut, latched and locked the big doors.

The inspection routine and the short ladder were moved to the back of the forward trailer. The rear doors were opened and Yasser stepped up and in. Again, the air inside was very hot. He walked down the full length of the trailer. A ramp was strapped to the trailer wall with two long telescoping poles. On the other side, he was flanked by six, tall rectangular cages that almost took up the entire length of the trailer. They were completely covered, sides and top, by chain link fencing. Galvanized pipes were threaded through the edge loops of the fencing. The outward side of each cage was also a hinged door with a clasp for a padlock. The long trailer looked to Yasser like a mobile dog kennel. The bottom corners of the cages were bolted to the floor with metal straps bent over the bottom pipes. Yasser hesitated, thinking, 'What kind of a dog could grasp a round pipe and lift a cage? What kind could lift an un-padlocked clasp and swing open a door?' He shrugged. The convincing nighttime phone call helped him conclude that the cages were for transporting zoo primates bent on escape.

The last cage at the forward end was padlocked. Inside were two long wooden boxes and two cardboard ones. Yasser hefted the padlock with his fingertips as he stared at the boxes, then let it swing back against the cage pipe with a metallic *clack*. He had the authority to require their inspection, for weapons or bomb-making materials that could be used for an attack, maybe the final act of a strict follower of *Allah*. Such men had made it through the checkpoint before with explosive consequences for unsuspecting citizens.

Gun barrels, guided by suspicious eyes, pointed at Masoud as he climbed into the trailer and walked towards Yasser. He stepped close to Yasser and spoke quietly in the hot shadows. Back turned, Masoud hid the transaction. A sealed envelope was quickly handed over. Yasser snatched and hid it under his uniform shirt, down and alongside his ample belly; he ate more than dates and nuts.

Finally satisfied, the trailer doors were closed and locked. As he walked toward the guard house and shade Yasser again looked at the sets of large, wide double wheels. Signed papers of approved passage were returned. Yasser motioned the other guards to stand back and waved the truck through. Masoud gave a small nod before heading out on the long drive to Riyadh. As the truck passed, Yasser placed his right hand over his heart, then down and patted the slight bulge under his shirt.

†

The drive through the blistering summer desert heat would be much farther than Riyadh. But Masoud and Dabir sat in an air conditioned cab with room for one to sleep while the other drove, a small living space with a septic holding tank to provide non-stop travel endurance. Before reaching the capital city, and its zoo, they curved to the east through al-Karj, then due east to Haradh to top off their diesel fuel tanks. This was their first time there. They laughed a little that this was a good place to refuel. Over the wide desert landscape were spread many large structures and much equipment to suck oil from the ground and refine it. Underground lairs also gave up enormous volumes of gas to be processed and shipped well beyond the borders of Saudi Arabia. All of this returned great wealth to the country. Masoud and Dabir also knew that the birth of fossil fuel extraction in the country began with infidels walking the land decades earlier with the creation of Arabian-American Oil Company. They had angrily discussed such things at the dockside coffee shop in al-Mukalla.

Refueled, they headed south into the very heart of the Rub' al-Khali, the vast arid Empty Quarter of Southern Saudi Arabia, one of the largest, most barren deserts on the planet. They had made a great loop since crossing the border at al-Wadiah. A more direct route to their directed destination would have been difficult, if not impossible. The well-maintained part of the road ended. Dabir entered a latitude-longitude pair into the navigation application on an iPad. They drove south of Bir' ash-Shalfa and followed the road east toward the dot on the iPad map. As they drove, they gazed over a seemingly endless sea of sand dunes. The monster truck seemed out of place, but they had their orders. Finally, they turned off the road onto a load-bearing alkali flat, bare in places, covered with a thin layer of sand in others. This wide *sabkha*, one of many, spoke to moister times when monsoon rains had nourished the area many thousands of years earlier. But the climate had changed. Now bone dry, wind-blown sand moved and collected on the flat *sabkhas*. Some heaped into dunes. This one had been chosen as the path to their destination.

The truck rolled to a stop on a wide area of shallow sand at the edge of a dune. Dabir checked their coordinate position on the iPad. They set to work in the blistering afternoon heat in the hot desert wind. The second trailer was unhitched, its front end still resting on the interconnecting road dolly. The hitch pin was removed; air-brake hoses and electric lines were disconnected. The tractor and remaining trailer were pulled forward. Dabir paced perpendicular from the front of the parked trailer, measuring the distance by foot, and stood at a space. Masoud drove around and lined up the remaining trailer parallel to the disconnected one, offset to the side. Dabir motioned him slowly forward with hand signals for adjustment left and right then clenched a raised fist to stop. Stabilizing jacks with wide flat bottoms were lowered to the shallow sand. They hand-cranked them down to take the load off of the trailer and the decoupling procedure repeated. This ballet had been practiced, and timed, in a remote area of southern Yemen. They had performed it to perfection. There was more to do before the next unseen satellite passed over. But its timing was known to those in the warehouse basement and it mandated their schedule.

Ramps were slid out from each trailer and set in place, slanting down to the sand from the rear doors. They brought out four large sections of dark brown canvas, each with brass grommets along the edges, a long coil of rope, a sharp knife, long stakes and a heavy hammer that had been hidden within the folds. The canvas had been dyed to match the cloth made

by Bedouins for their tents. They pounded stakes
in at an outward angle through the sand into the
alkali crust beneath and threaded loops of rope
through their eyelets, like large desert needles.
The canvas sections were knitted together with
rope threaded through adjacent grommets. With
some difficultly, using the tall ladder, they tugged
on connected ropes and pulled the large canvas
sheet over one trailer, then the other, and pulled
it taught in all four directions through the eyelets
of the ground stakes that surrounded the two
trailers in a circumscribing rectangle. It looked
like a squat pyramid with the top lopped off. The
grommeted seam parallel to the trailers down
the center line between them was not threaded
together at one end. The ropes to the stakes could
be removed, allowing a smaller vehicle to enter
under the tarp and park unseen. The area between
the trailers was shaded, as were the outer areas
under the sloped canvas, leaving ample space to
use the ramps and keep things out of the sun and
out of the prying eyes from high above.

Yet, those in the basement in Aleppo were
nervous. There were those much farther away
that viewed images from high-flying drones or
from even higher American satellites in low-earth
orbit. Unnatural shadows with straight, angular
edges could be noticed, but so could Bedouin

encampments; their tents had similar straight edges. The schedule of drones was known only to the few that controlled them, but there was little reason to surveil this remote area. But satellite orbits had been predicted by Hadi and had governed the arrival of the trailers and the departure of their tractor.

The stretched canvas and the heavy padlocks on the trailer doors were checked and re-checked. Everything was in order. But Masoud and Dabir had not been let in on the purpose of this very remote encampment. They had some suspicions, but did not know and had not asked. Under penalty of the sword, they had been instructed to never discuss the camp with anyone, not even each other. Masoud looked at his wristwatch and circled two vertically-pointed fingers at Dabir. Only a few minutes were left on the countdown; it was time to go.

As the mass of tires had rolled across the sand-covered *sabkha*, Masoud climbed back into the sleeper and turned on a hand-held satellite communications handset. As he had been trained in the secret basement, he keyed in a number and a very short message, then sent it skyward with the press of a button: *Khalaset*.

They returned on the same long, circuitous route past Bir' ash-Shalfa to Haradh, fueled up again, then proceeded back to the al-Wadiah border.

On the Saudi side, Yasser was on duty as the tractor passed with the university logo on its doors. He was inside the small, air-conditioned guard house behind tinted glass. He saw Masoud and Dabir and smiled, but they did not see him. He was happy since his wife was happy, who was now wearing some new gold jewelry.

On the Yemeni side of the border, even with no trailers, the tractor still prompted caution, if not suspicion. Yemeni border guards dug through the cab interior and inspected the underside with a mirror on the end of a long rod. Terrorist bombs had been brought through the checkpoint before, fastened underneath trucks to be later parked next to a doomed *mosque* or market square. With nothing to hide, except the intentions of those in Aleppo, the tractor was waived through.

Miles later, the satellite phone was used again. This time the next incremental digit was keyed in followed by the same text, a single word. With the press of a button, it rode the back of a radio signal and arrived at its destination almost instantly: *Khalaset*.

Rub' al-Khali

The big Boeing 737-700 of Aster Airlines was lined up on final, on glideslope, perfectly. The runway at Salt Lake City rose up to meet their descent. Eyes darted side to side driven by the *déjá vu* of San Francisco. With tray tables up and seat belts fastened, passengers looked out at the mountain peaks of the Wasatch Range, the Great Salt Lake and the large white *sabkha* to the west: the Bonneville Salt Flats. Nina was strapped into the fold-down seat just outside the locked door to the flight deck, subliminally rehearsing her smile and goodbye routine. Jen's hands lay lightly on the control yoke, eyes now focused straight ahead, precisely judging diminishing height. At just the right moment she added very-slight back pressure. Nina felt nothing as wheels met concrete. Only *chirps* from rubber tires announced their arrival.

Chris confirmed, "Nice one, captain."

✝

A half-day later, Akmal's hands lay lightly on the black steering wheel. The sun had baked it searing hot, too hot to hold firmly on the desert road. Akmal's eyes focused on the sandy road ahead. Ramza looked around at the standing waves of empty sand that stretched to the horizon in every direction. The tan dunes were interrupted by salt-encrusted flats and barren rocky hills that stubbornly would not be moved. Small ripples crawled slowly on the backs of the dunes, pushed and formed by the wind that had moved and sculpted the Rub' al-Khali for uncountable years. Ramza looked over at Akmal in the driver's seat, both now soldiers in the fight for the *caliphate*. They held Syrian passports and the necessary visas to cross into Jordan and Saudi Arabia, forged in the Aleppo warehouse.

Akmal and Ramza had been grilled and instructed in the basement room. They had good battlefield recommendations and had been specially selected. They had guarded captured prisoners, putting some to the beheading sword without hesitation when directed. Not born to it, they had been molded by foreign invasion and conflict...and *mullahs*. They had come a very long way since innocently playing by the waters of the Tigris or kicking a soccer ball in al-Zawraa park.

With firm orders, they had left Aleppo driving a white, rusted, dented, four-wheel drive Toyota pickup without the luxury of air conditioning. It, too, had been in ar-Raqqah, a small, mechanized part of insurgent mobile infantry, capable of traversing soft sand with the soldiers of *Allah*, firing a machine gun mounted in the bed of the truck. The pedestal for the gun had been removed when the truck had been transferred to the warehouse garage in Aleppo.

Along with instructions, a satellite communication handset and an iPad, they were given a ring of labeled keys, a box of padlocks, and a specific time-frame within which they must arrive. The instructions were repeated to make sure they had sunk in, plus they were advised that *Allah* would be watching, with due regard for their afterlives.

The desert destination had been carefully selected. Even though well-hidden in their urban cave among the populace of Aleppo, suspicions, questions and surveillance hovered around them. A new, very special operation in their warehouse, with unusual comings and goings, could possibly stand out and be discovered. A desolate site was needed in a different country far away, where curious Americans paid little heed from the air. Satellites in space, however, were a different, unavoidable matter. A very remote place had been found in the central part of the Rub' al-Khali, near an area described in the holy *Qur'an*.

Akmal and Ramza had preferred to drive at night when temperatures over arid desert land plummeted to comfortable, even chilly levels. With windows rolled down, soft dry late-evening air swirled around them. Through the night, they had taken turns dozing off, stopping periodically to relieve themselves on the desert sand like their nomadic ancestors had done. They had passed near Damascus and border check points for entry into Jordan and Saudi Arabia. The rear bed of the truck held cardboard boxes of food, metal cans filled with gasoline and rows of plastic jugs filled with the more important water, just in case the truck gave up the ghost in the middle of nowhere, and the Rub' al-Khali had plenty of nowhere.

They had told border guards that they were construction laborers headed for work in the Empty Quarter, that the pay was higher when working there in the searing heat of summer. The guards had searched through the boxes for weapons and contraband. Akmal had casually pulled out his small copy of the *Qur'an* from the glove box and laid it on the seat. When the cab was searched, the guards had seen it, stood back, placed their right hands over their hearts and waved them through; best not to interfere with a believer and tempt the judgment of *Allah*.

After crossing the Saudi border, they had driven into Riyadh a half-day later. Both had been unaware that the reason for their directed trip lived not far away in that large city. The less known individually the better; each a pawn on the Aleppo chess board was just following orders, but watched collectively. They had been ordered to arrive on a specific date within specific times, driving during the hottest hours of the day. They had made a short stop at a *souk* in Riyadh. They were very familiar with such markets since they were boys. They still enjoyed the haggling. After topping off the gas tank at a station near the *souk*, Akmal had taken the wheel.

Wind through the open windows felt like a hot hair dryer blowing on their faces. The temperature in the open desert had reached a high of 135 degrees. They had a schedule, but planned for survival. From the back, a plastic gallon jug of water was set between them. They took swallows from the jug almost continuously as the hot, dry air evaporated sweat from their skin instantly, providing some measure of natural body cooling. They knew that they had to stay hydrated, lest they pass out and succumb to the unforgiving desert.

With the aid of the iPad's GPS application, they turned off onto a barren *sabkha* and soon found the expected canvas-covered trailers cooking in the sun in the middle of the planned nowhere. It was indeed desolate, but they had their orders and they were good soldiers. It was first things first and time was running out. Eyes in space would soon pass over them and their truck. Toggling back and forth between images for the same area, a computer operator could detect differences to be investigated by intelligence analysts. A straight-edged shadow at sunrise or sunset could trigger attention. But, there were many other areas in the Middle East to take up photo analysts' time. Yet, covert security was paramount to those in Aleppo. Ramza lifted the edge of the canvas over the Toyota as Akmal drove in between the trailers.

Akmal stepped out in the shade of the canvas cover undulating in the desert wind. He fumbled through the ring of keys and found the one for the padlock on the doors of the trailer with the workbench, the doors with an identifying small black dot. He walked up the already-placed ramp, unlocked and swung the heavy, hot doors open and stepped inside. Ramza followed. The trailer felt like the very hot oven it was. Then it was hard work in the stiffening heat. They pulled and slid the diesel generator down the ramp. While not large, the generator was heavy and awkward to move. They tugged, lugged and slid it to the edge of the canvas cover farthest from the air conditioner intakes, and turned it so that its exhaust pipe pointed outwards under the edge of the tarp, lest lethal carbon monoxide make its way into either trailer. They plugged two electric cables into the generator and the other ends into receptacles on the sides of both trailers.

Using an empty jug, fuel was transferred from the outside spigot of the inside diesel fuel tank to the generator. The other tank held water. Akmal pulled on the handled-cord a few times. The generator fired up; it had been repeatedly tested in Yemen. Akmal yelled a command. From inside, Ramza threw a switch. The air conditioner came to life. Soon, cool air started to fill the trailer. He flipped another wall switch by the rear doors and rows of florescent ceiling lights came on, as did lights over the workbench. He leaned out and looked around the back corner of the trailer at Akmal who was standing next to the gently-purring generator, "He has sent us blessed air, and given us light. *Allah* be praised!"

Akmal walked up the ramp to the other trailer, ring of keys in hand. With rear doors swung wide open, he stepped inside and quickly walked past the cages to the front in the oven-like heat. There he threw a switch and the air conditioner began dispensing cool air. Another switch, ceiling lights came on. He saw the boxes in the last cage. He unlocked and removed the padlock, moved the restraining clasp and pulled open the cage door as he called out for his brother. They moved the boxes out and set them by their truck; automatic rifles and ammunition were inside.

Akmal and Ramza walked back into the cage trailer. They stood there for a moment, in thought, and gazed down the row of cages. They nodded slowly.

Akmal tended to his work. He went back into the work bench trailer and used the iPad and the satellite phone to check each workbench receptacle. They all worked, confirming that workmen, somewhere, knew what they were doing, but not for what. He left them plugged in to recharge their batteries. They had been firmly instructed to communicate only by the satellite phone, and absolutely not by iPad. That was to only be used passively for GPS navigation. Akmal looked at his brother, his arms raised, bathing in the cool air flowing down from the forward vent, as if standing in a shower. Akmal lectured, "Brother. We do not need cool air. We are not women. We are strong soldiers of *Allah*. Everything works. To save fuel, until we know more, I will stop the generator and leave the doors open."

Akmal ran out, quickly returned and set his copy of the *Qur'an* on the workbench. He had not been instructed to do that, but his faith compelled him. Now they had to wait for the special delivery that was slated to arrive in two days.

As instructed, the cage trailer had to be cool, not for them, but for others. But now, their assigned work done, they had to report.

Akmal walked back into the workbench trailer and stepped out with a fully-charged satellite phone. Akmal sent a single number and word to the location in Aleppo. The weak signal spread upward from the small antenna and was relayed among the cluster of communication satellites, then downward to a warehouse rooftop.

A handset beeped and awakened a man who had been asleep in the afternoon heat, in the shadows on the roof, waiting. He quickly pushed a button and read text. Excitedly, the young, bearded man ran down the steps of the abandoned warehouse to the basement. He slowly slapped the heavy door of the room, five times; twice ... pause ... thrice. The door was carefully unlocked and slightly opened as a careful eye peered out. The excited man was let in. He held up the satellite phone and announced, "*Khalaset.*" Hadi made a check mark on a big ledger spread out before him and said aloud, "*Khalaset.*" Muhammad Talib just nodded. Hadi gave the order.

†

Smithy and his fellow condemned prisoners were bound firmly, hands and feet, and gagged, but not blindfolded. The drivers of the Mercedes van in the warehouse, and an assigned guard, worried more about attention-getting shouts than what their prisoners could see. Nothing could be seen through the high small windows from where the van was parked, and nothing could be seen from within the rear of the big windowless vehicle. They were herded past Hadi and Muhammad Talib and the hateful eyes of others, then upstairs into the waiting van; they were tied to the internal bracing of the interior, just to make sure.

Hadi's admonition to proceed with haste drove them to leave while it was still daylight. It was late afternoon as the young guard for the trip started to shut the rear doors of the van. The afternoon call to prayer, the *Asr*, penetrated the walls of the warehouse. Feeling that his career, or very life, may be at stake, he hurriedly pushed the doors shut and retrieved his prayer rug from the front of the van, then knelt down in prayer with the others.

All was in order as the big entry doors were opened to let the van out. The driver turned down the street and pressed the accelerator down hard. The rear doors had not completely latched; they swung open. Smithy looked out at a daylight street scene. In the distance, he saw a very tall tower bristling with telecommunications dishes and antennae. The sun was directly behind the top of the tower. Smithy's quick mind recorded everything as the driver stomped down on the brakes; the van screeched to a stop and the doors slammed shut with a loud *bang*. Smithy heard some swear words directed at the guard, just a boy really, who humbly got out and checked again to make sure the doors were shut, latched and locked. The van then moved on, destination: the Rub' al-Khali.

Orders

With his PhD diploma proudly in hand, Doctor Kashif returned with his father to Riyadh. A surprise gift had awaited him: a private laboratory paid for by his father, built near the *mosque*. There, he would continue his research as an extension of King Saud University. Kashif prayed at the *mosque* and *mullah* Fahim would visit the laboratory frequently, fire flashing in his dark eyes. Occasionally, visiting true believers would accompany him. They, too, had fire in their eyes, and in their hearts. Some visitors were special, having been directly involved in the noble, violent struggle for a modern *caliphate*, a latter-day succession following the death of the Prophet. The struggle in Syria had not been going well; ar-Raqqah had fallen. A different plan arose in the vengeful darkness of a hidden place. Kashif would be drawn into it as a critical component.

The laboratory was fitted with the best equipment that their money could buy. The family had very deep pockets, as deep as the oil beneath the desert. Hired laboratory assistants cared for rats and rabbits in rows of cages in one room, and more carefully cared for desert coral snakes living in sturdy glass cages in a locked room. Another room contained a plethora of small snakes and lizards, but not for testing. Kashif's coral snakes were fussy eaters and these were their natural diet. The coral snakes were expensive, made even more so to ensure that import and export controls were conveniently overlooked. That was no problem. Kashif's family had enough money which wound up in the hands of government inspectors and snake hunters in the Sonoran Desert of the Southwest United States. He was unsure just how his research would be used to attack the Great Satan, but thought it divine justice that snakes from their land would somehow be part of it.

In his private office Kashif had a large mahogany desk with brass inlays of Arabic script from the *Qur'an* around its edges. On the wall were his framed Masters and PhD diplomas. Research continued apace, detailed notes were written in bound ledgers and duplicated in computer files. On the book shelves behind his desk were research periodicals with articles on rather unique subjects: *Micruroides euryxanthus* and 3FTx.

When not interrupted by the daily call to prayer from the nearby *minaret*, he tediously synthesized and modified a large array of 3FTx neurotoxins for testing. With genius and patience, he prepared droplets of water that contained selected DNA fragments, nucleotide building blocks, salts, buffers, and the critical DNA-replicating enzyme. With special, precise equipment, the carefully-mixed droplet solution was cyclically heated and cooled for measured hours in a specific order to enable the exponential production of a long piece of DNA by way of the polymerase chain reaction. These products were then mixed with a few bacterial cells that were subsequently retrieved by a small probe and placed in a petri dish. In another calibrated laboratory device, the dish and its contents were warmed gently overnight to a specific temperature to build a bacterial colony that was later incubated in a broth to promote a mass production of the target toxin protein. The cells were bathed in ultrasound to collect, purify, and concentrate the toxin protein in sufficient quantity for testing. Hired laboratory assistants helped with the very tedious process, but only Kashif understood what was taking place.

Kashif kept *mullah* Fahim informed of his progress. Initially, the synthetic toxins were applied by tiny drops on finely-chopped vegetables. Rats and rabbits enjoyed their meals, but later fell over, legs kicking sideways, heads twitching, until death by a non-beating heart or asphyxiation from non-moving lungs relieved their suffering. From eating until the first twitch, he tested and timed, over and over.

Through Fahim, he learned that certain, unspecified people wanted a couple hours of delay, not minutes. Very specifically, he learned that the eaten toxin must not take effect before two hours, but not to exceed three hours. Kashif thought that to be a strange, unexplained request, but just another node in the path set before him by *Allah*. Who was he to question?

With the two-to-three hour delay window met on rats, rabbits and larger goats, and confirmed by repeated testing with 3FT**3b-23**, he ran next door and into the room where Fahim studied and prayed. When he understood the gravity of what Kashif told him, he stood, looked to the geometrically-patterned ceiling with up-stretched hands, "*Allah* be praised."

Kashif cautioned him. It would have to be tested on humans, to be sure, as their blood, muscle tissues and nervous systems were not the same as rats, rabbits and goats.

As he mentally labored at his desk, reviewing more data and test results, there was a knock on his door. He arose and opened it and there stood Fahim, with two visitors. Kashif noticed that one of them wore a wooden forearm. The other wore a black turban and had a deep scar on his face.

As Fahim had strongly been advised days earlier, there were no introductions, no names, just hands placed over hearts. Soon they found themselves sitting around Kashif's large desk. At the visitors' quiet request, Kashif dismissed the laboratory assistants for the day. The discussion would be life-changing, if not for Kashif, certainly for others. Hadi spoke, deadly serious, "With respect, you must move your laboratory and testing. We have made preparations."

"Where?"

"In the Rub' al-Khali. It is far from anything, except a wandering Bedouin tribe, but they have been convinced to avoid the place. There you will find water and electricity, prisoners in cages and two of our warriors to control and care for them. In the great desert, you will find a place to work and rest, to set up your laboratory equipment and to make the final tests."

"When?"

"In two weeks. Please arrive there at three o'clock; not before two o'clock, not after four. And, please, make sure to park your vehicle under the stretched canvas that awaits you." After giving these orders, he reached into his canvas carry bag with his remaining hand, pulled out a satellite phone and gave it to Kashif along with a few pages of written instructions with the precise latitude and longitude of his destination, and a small folded paper map. He pointed to the room with the snake cages as if he were very familiar with them, which he now was, and continued, "Bring the snakes and their food, if you must. You will perform tests on infidels we have captured in Syria; one is an American."

Kashif hid his enthusiastic reaction to the prospect of human testing and carefully disagreed, "I will not need the snakes. We have milked their venom and I have used it to make a whole new class of synthetic neurotoxin in sufficient amount for testing and further refinement. But I will need my precise laboratory equipment in case I have to make further modifications during testing, and to make the final solution in quantity. How much do you need?"

"I do not understand your technical knowledge. But remember carefully, the burden of *Allah*'s wish is upon you."

As if on cue, a small cardboard box was slid across the desk. Kashif opened the lid. Inside were sixteen small glass bottles with laboratory-grade ground glass stoppers, each bottle wrapped in foam rubber. He pulled one out and examined it. There was a French word printed on the bottle, in flowing script.

Hadi directed, "Fill these bottles, carefully seal them and give them to those you will meet in the desert. When you have succeeded, return here for further instructions from Fahim. The word on the bottles is the name of an expensive French perfume, to confuse any border guards, if necessary." Kashif had seen that word before.

Hadi continued, "There has been a change, please listen wisely." He pulled out a small, clear plastic bottle with a finger plunger on a screw-on top to spray out the water it held. "You must spray the poison on the food to be eaten from this position." He pulled Muhammad Talib's hand to the desk and pushed it down, palm up, held the spritzer bottle vertically about twelve inches up and twelve inches away from the dry hand, then pushed the plunger down four times, ejecting a fine water mist out horizontally that settled slowly down onto the *mullah's* palm. "Push the sprayer down four times, from this position, four times, not three, not five...four times. Do you understand?"

Kashif nodded and merely accepted these instructions, without question. He knew it was the will of *Allah* unfolding before him, even the unnecessary precision for application of the toxic liquid. *Allah* had sent this general from His army – with orders. Hadi stood and placed his only hand on Kashif's shoulder, "You are now a warrior in *Jaysh al-Allah*."

☨

The next days were busy. Kashif purchased a new Mercedes van, top of the line. Of course, it came with an air conditioner. Beyond his own comfort, he did not want to subject his equipment, and the developed toxins, to the extreme temperatures found in the desert, especially in the Rub' al-Khali in the summer months. He had found that the engineered toxins were stable through a normal range of temperatures up to a limit, and he did not want that limit exceeded *en route* through the desert. The engineering and production of synthetic 3FTx was temperature-sensitive; he trusted the one-armed man, and *Allah*, that the facilities in the desert would meet his needs. The sun's hammer on the anvil of the Rub' al-Khali was well known, worse than in Riyadh, and it was mid-summer. Kashif was thankful for the air conditioning in the van. He had known comfort all his life, and he thought that he deserved high rank in the Army of *Allah* and the perquisites that came with it.

The evening of the day of departure arrived softly. Kashif loaded the last of his laboratory equipment and a supply of synthetic 3FT3b-23, DNA samples and bacteria. The truck's engine idled outside of the gated brick wall; the air conditioner hummed. He locked the van's rear doors and looked towards the northwest through a gap in the city's buildings. There, the blue sky overhead started turning black, some stars showing, and transitioned downward through narrow bands of pale blue, orange and deep red at the horizon in the evening twilight. The beautiful desert evening scene commanded, as it had done since the time of the Prophet, the call to prayer. It spread over him from the *minaret*, over his father and Fahim who had come to see him off. Together, the *Maghrib* was recited as they knelt down on their prayer rugs towards Mecca, a well-known direction from Kashif's laboratory. They did not need a compass to determine the *qibla*, the direction of the holy *Kaaba* in the Great Mosque of Mecca.

Kashif embraced his father and Fahim, clasped their hands firmly then stepped into the van. Without stopping, driving at a safe speed, he estimated he could reach his destination in about 14 hours. With all things considered, with some comfort stops along the way, it could possibly take one or two hours longer. He started in the cooling evening, but drove to the special site to arrive in the hottest part of the day, adjusting his speed and time to arrive within the required frame of time, as ordered.

He was guided by the iPad beside him on the seat, destination coordinates set in. A folded paper road map lay beside the iPad, just in case. If all else failed, in an emergency the satellite handset was to be used to contact those who waited. As the Mercedes disappeared down the street, Fahim stood feet astride, arms akimbo, watching, then raised his hands and looked skyward, "*Allah*, be praised." Then he called Aleppo with a number and said, "*Khalaset*."

Preparation

In the remotest of areas of the Rub' al-Khali the sun was lowering in the sky as the stretched canvas slowly fluttered up and down. From boxes in the bed of the truck, Razma fished out slabs of flat bread and a box of fresh dates they had purchased in the Riyadh *souk*, and two plastic bottles of quite warm water.

Akmal retrieved two blankets from another box. From under the canvas, they walked out and over to a soft, wind-drifted sand dune and spread them out. They could have slept in air-conditioned comfort in one of the trailers, but Akmal feared that their diesel fuel could become scarce, not knowing the duration of their stay. With the generator off, it was quiet, desert quiet. They had often camped together as children on the banks of the Tigris under clear, star-clustered nights. The open desert had had a spiritual feeling for them, as it did now. Plus they felt that they were tough, not having had the luxury of air conditioning when American bombs had fallen in ar-Raqqah. Akmal continued his command, by virtue of his age over his younger brother, and directed, "We will eat and sleep here, under the stars. Get the shovel and a paper roll."

Razma pulled them out from behind the seat in the cab of the truck where they lay next to the long, razor-sharp scimitar, an ar-Raqqah battlefield award, wrapped in a black flag. Without any remorse, its sharp edge had been used to sever heads from bodies. Ramza announced, "I will be first." He walked some distance to the other side of a smaller dune, out of sight, dug a small pit, relieved himself and filled it in with sand. He returned to the open-air camp site, "Here. Your turn."

When Akmal came back, they feasted much like their nomadic ancestors had done and watched the sun drop below the horizon. Akmal and Ramza looked at each other knowing their obligation, by the time of day and the position of the sun. There was no call from a *minaret* in the middle of nowhere to remind them.

They ritualistically prepared. Akmal looked around and thought for a moment. He turned on his iPad and touched a geographic application that yielded a map to determine the bearing from one point to another. GPS satellite signals automatically had been used to determine where they were and how to get there. He touched a name on the displayed map, rotated the iPad to the indicated true north and pointed his hand almost due west in the direction of Mecca. They stood shoulder-to-shoulder, placed their upward-cupped, outstretched hands together, bowed their heads and recited the *Maghrib*, one of the five daily prayers that they had learned in their youth. Being alone, they did not feel the need to kneel. They had also done this in ar-Raqqah, a tactical prayer when bombs were falling. They assumed that *Allah* understood such temporary exemptions. During those air attacks they deeply loathed the infidels in the sky who were interrupting the sacred daily ritual of praying to *Allah,* confirming *Allah's* infinite importance.

They finished the prayer. Akmal looked at his battlefield brother, "Ramza. Someday we will make the *Hajj*, together. Until then, we face Mecca, together."

As the clear sky darkened to twilight, the brightest stars and planets came out. They lay back on their blankets and looked up as the familiar display of *Allah's* distant creation came into view; more stars could be seen. Ramza said, "Our ancestors lived like this, simple, pure, their minds open to *Allah*, as they wandered and looked at those very same stars. I think being alone in the open desert clears the mind, like it has done for *Allah's* prophets when they wandered in the desert." He looked over at the Toyota and laughed.

"That truck is a poor excuse for a camel if we had to cross over a steep, soft dune. But now, when we have roads, it is faster. We are spoiled."

Akmal's voice turned serious, "Muhammad, peace be upon Him, looked at those same stars when he looked out of the mountain cave near Mecca." Sleep weighed heavily on their eyelids and lifted them away to dream, as they thought of Muhammad in the cave of Hira.

In the early morning, the sands had cooled, and so did the air that touched the grains. The cool air densely slid down the face of the dune next to them. Both had rolled over in their sleep and had pulled their blankets over themselves, keeping their heat in and the relative desert chill out. They needed their rest. The day would be bright and very hot, and they had to be ready for an arrival. The sun brushed their cheeks and awakened them. After morning prayers, they used the shovel and finished the flatbread.

Akmal unfolded the papers he had carried from Aleppo and read the instructions again. He fired up the generator and shut the cage trailer doors with its air conditioner on. He turned off the air conditioner and lights in the workbench trailer and left the doors open.

In each cage they placed a sleeping cot, a plastic bucket with a roll of toilet paper, plastic bottles filled with water from the trailer tank.

From the boxed stores under the workbench they placed packages of dates and nuts on each cot. Akmal hung an open padlock on each cage door after checking that he had the keys that would unlock each.

Ramza spoke the obvious truth, "Prisoners are coming and we must watch over them, like we did in ar-Raqqah. But why bring prisoners all the way out here? Better to have finished them off in Aleppo. They must be important, maybe as hostages for ransom. They will be cool and have some comfort as they await the will of *Allah*."

As they waited, Akmal periodically went in to check the temperature and adjusted the thermostat. It had to be just right.

They stood, almost at attention under the canvas in the fierce afternoon heat. Akmal and Ramza watched a trail of dust kicked up by the big Mercedes van coming down the long, meandering flat *sabka* from the main road. It stopped right in front of them, but Akmal motioned for the driver to park the van under the canvas. With a pole, Ramza lifted the canvas high enough for the van to pass under. There was room next to their Toyota.

The drivers and a guard stepped out. They carried rifles and stern, unhappy looks. Hands were placed briefly over hearts; they knew each other from their time in the Aleppo warehouse. The rear of the van was next to the doors of the cage trailer. Ramza stepped up the ramp and opened the big doors; cool air spilled out. In the van were six men, bound and gagged, squirming in discomfort and fear – except one. They started dragging each one out, letting them tumble to the ground.

This had been done a number times after passing border check points with bribed guards after the van had left Aleppo, one prisoner at a time on remote side roads. While one stood guard with an automatic weapon, prisoners had been untied and gags removed one at a time, given some bread and water, let urinate, defecate and clean themselves, then bound and gagged and shoved back in. It was not a comfortable trip for those that had been captured in ar-Raqqah and held in the basement in Aleppo.

Akmal and Ramza knew these men, captured in the course of battle. One was an American, a Marine, a military adviser to their enemies, an infidel son of a whore of the Great Satan. With that, Akmal and Ramza removed ropes from legs, then lifted and shoved each up and into the cool trailer and into separate cages where gags were removed and wrists untied. Smithy was first. The drivers cautioned, "Watch that one. He is big and strong and tried to escape on the way here." A bruise on the side of Smithy's face bore witness to his attempt.

Smithy was taken to the far end of the trailer, shoved in the cage, hands untied at the end of a gun barrel, and the door padlocked shut. Smithy sat down on the cot in his cage. Akmal spat on him. Each of the remaining prisoners were locked into their desert dog-cage accommodations. Akmal then walked up and down past each cage, scimitar in hand, along with Ramza who held a loaded automatic rifle. They had done this many times before, in ar-Raqqah and in Aleppo, to show that they had the upper hand. Smithy understood Akmal's taunts and the chatter among the other prisoners, but he continued to hide this linguistic talent from his captors. The strength of Smithy's mind was comparable to his physical strength. Akmal and Ramza left the prisoners, closing the big doors behind them.

Before leaving, the drivers again firmly instructed them, "Feed and care for them. Do not harm them. They must be healthy. It was very difficult to sneak them across the borders. Much money was required to make eyes look the other way."

On their cots in their trailer cages, the apparently-doomed men slowly unfolded themselves, rubbing the pain from their joints. A couple of them started to speak as all dug into dates and nuts, gulping down water from plastic bottles. Smithy remained silent as he ate and drank, leaned against the wire mesh of his cage, and listened. He then folded his arms across his chest revealing sculpted steel biceps. Smithy's eyes did not hold the same fear as the others'.

Akmal and Ramza watched the van disappear down the *sabkha* as the sun was setting. Evening prayers followed. They did not know anything about the next one to arrive, except that they thought that he must be very important. Akmal surmised that he would stay in the workbench trailer, that it was there for his purpose, whatever that was, maybe a special torture. Even if they were to be invited inside, they planned to sleep outside under the stars, as they had already done.

Akmal walked up the low dune with a satellite phone. He looked out over the desert and the encampment below, all now bathed in the soft colors of twilight. He rubbed his forearms. The evening air was unusually damp. He pressed the transmit button on his satellite phone. A keyed-in number and one-word message was relayed at near the speed of light. It matched that sent by the driver of the van as it was leaving: "*Khalaset.*"

Divine Wind

Ian topped off his morning black tea with a spot of cream. A career investigator, he had been assigned to the Portland field office of the Bureau. It had been a very wecoming change from the heavy snows of Buffalo, New York. Ian Hadley had fallen in love with with the city, its tall green trees, its much-gentler climate and its welcoming people, despite the gray, rainy winter months. It reminded him of his time in London.

Ian had rented a small home in the city's near east side close to an authentic British pub he had stumbled upon. With family roots that stretched back to the British Isles, he had visited relatives there...and their pubs. In Portland, Ian had found a similar warm place with excellent craft beers and ales. He had become a regular. As with public houses back in the UK, this pub within walking distance became his home away from home.

A clap of thunder brought him back to a rare early-morning reality. He put on his sporty leather jacket and jaunty tweed cap, walked into the gargage and put the top up on his British racing green MG convertible. As he backed out, the early morning sun illuminated billowing white clouds towering over their dark undersides. Moist air in the Pacific Northwest was certainly nothing unusual, but the lower layers of air that now covered the valley had streamed in overnight from the south. Temperature decreased with altitude at a rate that made the air vertically unstable. A mid-level pressure trough was moving over it from the west, converting the instability into thunderstorms.

On the main road to his office, close to the aiport, he skillfully shifted through the gears and brought the MG up to speed. The exhaust sounds from the finely-tuned engine were again a wonderful way to start the day. A sudden deluge of rain, mixed with with small pellets of soft hail, turned the roadway wet and slick; he slowed. At a stop light, he reached into the glove box and pulled out a packet of chewing gum. The mint flavor fairly exploded in his mouth. This habit had replaced cigarettes. Ian chewed rapidly as he drove on. He stopped at the main gate, then pushed the button on his transmitter fob. Heavy vertical bars of iron rolled sidewise, letting him enter, then closed behind him. Ian drove to his reserved parking space near the entrance to the FBI four-story brick building.

In his office, he took off his cap and jacket

and sat to review his secure overnight message traffic. After a short meeting with two others, and his boss, he put on a nondescript raincoat, then asked for a lift to the airport a mere mile away. It was another day for the special surveillance team that he led. It was his turn in the concourse.

The plain unmarked sedan he rode in rocked suddenly as a stong gust of wind from the collapsing storms swept against and around it. Ian looked up as an arriving big airliner on final approach tipped side to side, resulting in a rough landing. Ian was glad to be in the sedan rather than that plane.

In a special line at the passenger security checkpoint, he opened the lapel of his raincoat, revealing a special badge. He was let through into the same concourse as the day before, and some days before that. He stopped for more tea at a Starbucks, then went to his usual newsstand and leisurely looked through magazines and paperback books. And looked at other things.

†

A shallow layer of vapor, evaporated from the very warm waters of the Arabian Gulf, had crept in quietly to cover the middle of the Rub' al-Khali. It was a distinctly-felt, moist, unseen blanket. Such moist intrusions had almost disappeared over the thousands of years of inexorable change, change having been the only constant of the globe. The vast Empty Quarter, waves upon waves of sand, absorbed the intense rays that burned down from the sun. Dunes in the afternoon could singe bare feet. They heated the moist air that touched them and thrust giant columns upward that condensed as the heated air expanded and cooled. Kashif saw them as he drove east, past Bir' ash-Shalfa, billowing brilliant white in the blinding sunlight. He knew that these were somewhat rare for the Rub' al-Khali in summer. Kashif thought that they were a prophetic welcome, producing a divine wind, sweeping the path set before him by *Allah*.

Equally uncountable raindrops, birthed in towers of white mist fell through the collapsing centers of the thundering storms. They would never reach the sand below. As martyrs, the drops willingly evaporated, cooling and dragging down denser shafts of air to spread out across the desert in a fierce wind that lifted sand grains into a speeding brown wall that swallowed everything in its path.

A thousand needles of flying grains stung the faces of Akmal and Ramza as they crouched under the wildly-flapping canvas cover. Akmal walked out to get a better look down the *sabkha* and was buffeted by the gritty violence that swirled and gusted around the canvas cover. He shielded his squinting eyes. He returned to check that the air conditioners were on for both trailers and that the prisoners were well, if not fearful.

Akmal had received a satellite phone transmission, just a set of numbers, confirming date and time of arrival. He felt that *Allah* must be divinely testing them with the sandstorm. The whole reason for their secretive assignment would be arriving in a raging *haboob*.

As the time approached, they stood in the lee of the encampment. There was some protection from the blinding sand, but they could not see the alkaline flat that led to the highway, but they knew which way to look. Ramza pointed and shouted, "Lights!"

Akmal did not hear anything above the roaring wind, but saw Ramza's extended arm. He cupped both hands over Ramza's ear and shouted, "What did you say?"

Ramza pulled his brother's head and ear over to his lips and shouted back, "There. See. Two lights. Over there!"

"Yes! Now I see them." He switched on a flashlight and waved it side-to-side to help guide the driver.

The Mercedes van stopped just a few yards

from them with the sound of tires skidding on the shallow sand. Sophisticated Kashif stepped out and shielded his eyes. Akmal grasped Kashif's hand and pointed back to the cab of the van, motioning to sit in there, where they could converse. Kashif did. Akmal went around to the other side, slid in and shut the door. Despite the whistling sound of the wind and of the grit peppering the van, the interior was relatively quiet. Akmal just stared at the elegant man next to him. He exuded a natural air of wealth, education and Arabic refinement, and extended his hand. "My name is Kashif, from Riyadh."

Akmal placed his right hand over his heart, nodded in greeting, then grasped Kashif's hand, "My name is Akmal. That is my younger brother, Ramza. Please drive forward under the cover."

Kashif got back into the driver's seat, put the van in gear and pulled it slowly forward. With a pole, Ramza lifted a section of canvas and guided him next to the pickup truck. Under the cover, Kashif got right to the point, "Show me the infidels."

Akmal climbed the ramp, unlatched the door, turned around and extended his hand to Kashif, to help. A gust of wind swept in as they entered. Ramza followed and pulled the door closed. Kashif stopped by the last cage and stared, "Who is this?"

"He is an American soldier."

Smithy did not look back, but stared up at the ceiling in silent contempt. Kashif walked back down the row of cages looking at the huddled fear crouching on cots in each. They all looked to be healthy, at least physically. Kashif smiled his approval. He inquired, "Have they been fed and given water?"

"Yes, this afternoon, before the flying sands came. We feed them three times a day. When *Allah* stops the wind, we will take them to empty their buckets. There's a trench close by, on the other side."

"Fine, just fine. Now, show me where I will do the work of *Allah*."

They made their way out and up into the other trailer. Ramza had pulled the doors shut. Kashif walked down the length of the workbench, letting the fingertips of his right hand drag along its smooth surface. He smiled and nodded, noting the electric power receptacles. He stopped by the folding cots and the large stainless steel tanks.

Akmal broke the moment. "Kashif, Sir, this tank holds fresh water; this one holds diesel fuel for the generator outside, both enough for a long time to do your work. We are your servants and soldiers in the battle, Sir."

Kashif relaxed a little and replied, "You need only call me Kashif. Will you sleep in here? You are welcome to do so."

"Thank you, but we prefer to sleep outside, under the desert stars. But we will use the cots. The sands of *Allah* become hard in the night."

"As you wish. Now help me, very carefully, move my equipment and chemicals in here."

Under the flapping canvas, Akmal and Ramza were introduced to a much different world. They had never seen a laboratory in their short lives. Kashif carefully supervised their help moving the contents of the van. Some items he insisted on moving himself: the vials of 3FT3b-23. He supervised the positioning of the equipment on the workbench. When all was done, Akmal showed Kashif the location of the septic trench and a small shovel near their cots outside. Back inside, Kashif inspected the boxes of food; then he gently commanded, "Thank you, Akmal. Thank you, Ramza. Now I must do some work, and rest. Tomorrow we begin."

Kashif spent the evening re-calibrating equipment to his precise standards. The voltage of the generated power was correctly filtered and sufficiently smooth. He carefully checked all of his equipment to make sure it had not been damaged by bumps in the road from Riyadh. All was in order.

Before Kashif's arrival, Akmal and Ramza

had taken turns, pacing up and down by the padlocked cages with scimitar or rifle, again for show of intent. This had provided daytime cooling, despite their thinking that they were tough soldiers in the Army of *Allah*. The space under the canvas cover was not always comfortable, only a place to stand outside in the shade. The generator noise was not loud but it was persistent. Located near the far end of the cage trailer, it spewed carbon monoxide into the desert air. If Akmal or Ramza slept near there, they might not wake up after a calm, windless night. They had chosen the cover of the desert stars, away from the generator exhaust.

They had prepared paper plates of food, then slid each under cage doors. Akmal used these opportunities to spit on Smithy. Akmal and Ramza had taken prisoners from their cages, one at a time, to empty their buckets into the ditch. Prisoners had to use their hands to cover their dumped defecation with sand. They were not given a shovel, as it could be wielded in a fit of desperation, requiring the sword or the gun, resulting in an unapproved loss. They handled Smithy differently. They tightly bound his ankles together for the trips to and from the pit. He had to hop like a kangaroo. Each prisoner was returned and locked in their cage, after which Akmal and Ramza filled and tossed in plastic bottles of water.

They had just finished feeding the prisoners. Kashif had slept well on his cot in air-conditioned comfort. When Kashif stepped out to the rising sun, Akmal pointed towards Mecca. Akmal and Ramza joined Kashif, knelt, and recited the *Fajr* together, further cementing them in their common objective.

Kashif invited Akmal and Ramza to come into his trailer for his careful advice. "I am ready to start my tests. Continue to prepare meals as you have done since they arrived. I will apply a special substance to one of the plates and will make a small mark on it. Give each of them their plates for the midday meal and watch carefully when the selected man begins to eat it."

Akmal and Ramza looked at each other, but Ramza asked the question, "What if we touch the food or the paper plate?"

"It will not harm you, unless you have an open cut. I will wear rubber gloves, but you must just be careful with bare hands. Gloved hands will raise suspicions."

Akmal asked, "The American. May I leave him for last, for the special final justice of *Allah*?"

"As you wish. Here are two stop watches, one for each of you. Practice with them; starting, stopping, timing. Leave them in your pockets, out of sight; press the start button when the first poisoned bite is taken."

Ramza interrupted, "What then?"

"Let them all finish their meals, then remove the plates as you have always done. After that, return and bring the selected man here. By now they must suspect that they will be meeting their end, but they must not know that their meal is what brings death."

Akmal quickly analyzed the circumstances, "When one of them is taken, the others will assume that he has gone to meet his fate by the sword. Yes?"

"Yes, that's the way it must appear. Have your scimitar at your side for all to see when you bring the prisoner here to my laboratory."

On a laboratory table, Akmal noted a box of small glass bottles with glass stoppers. "Do these contain the poison?"

"No. They are empty now, but they will be filled when we leave here with them. Here, you may look at one."

Akmal held it and turned it around. It had a small label affixed, the same as did the others in the box. The lettering was small, so he held it closer. On it he read a name in French. Akmal did not know what that name meant, but Kashif and his family certainly did. This exclusive perfume cost over 10,000 riyals an ounce. His father had often purchased it for his wives; the first was for Kashif's mother. Kashif saw that Akmal was perplexed and explained, "Our final liquid will be transported in these bottles. In case officials find and ask about them, we can tell them that they contain very expensive perfume for the wives of important people."

Akmal trusted the wisdom of this obviously educated, wealthy man and did not ask further. Such things, expensive things, were beyond his understanding and appreciation, things not found in areas of urban combat, or in their father's market stall in Baghdad. But he knew about men whose wives could number more than one. He and Ramza had privately discussed such things in their youth. They had only one mother, their father only one wife. But like other young boys in Baghdad, they had dreamed.

They dug into the stored food that had been trucked in from Yemen and prepared meals on six paper plates on the laboratory workbench, as they had done each day. Now, it was midday. They had just finished the daily sanitation ritual, taking the prisoners one at time, under armed guard, rifle and scimitar, to the sand pit. They definitely were not chefs, by any stretch of the imagination. They had visceral hate for the infidel prisoners, especially the American. Ramza had even hoped that they had pork to force on the Iraqi soldiers. But the food they handled was *halal*, permitted under Islamic law. Dates, nuts and canned meats, lamb and chicken, had been the daily fare for the prisoners whose days were numbered.

Akmal moved one plate to the end of the bench, as directed. Kashif sat down before it, spritzer bottle in hand. He held it away and up from the plate at the required estimated distance, then pumped the clear toxin out in four small bursts of sprayed mist. In the workbench lighting, they could see the mist settle slowly down onto the exposed food. He pulled out a pen and put a small mark on the edge of the plate, then handed it back to Akmal. "Remember, start the watch at the first bite."

The prisoners had become accustomed to the feeding times: morning, midday, evening. Despite their fearful unknown futures, they had actually looked forward to their feeds. They were hungry. This provided some pleasure and respite in the confines of the long trailer. The plates were slid under cage doors, each with a plastic fork. They took to them, some ravenously; Smithy ate calmly. With some precision, stop watches hidden in pockets were started when the man in the first cage took his first bite. Then all were let finish while they watched. Ramza picked up a large plastic bag at the far end of the trailer and walked past each cage. Each prisoner slide out his fork and plate and they was tossed in the bag by Ramza. Being the younger, he had been assigned garbage duty. The prisoners had to remain healthy for the testing. Clutter and filth was to be avoided.

Ramza stood guard with an automatic weapon. Akmal unlocked and entered the first cage in the trailer and roughly dragged the prisoner out, then down the ramp. Akmal wore the scimitar in its scabbard across his waist. Ramza followed them up the ramp into Kashif's trailer, shutting the big trailer doors behind him. The test subject was tied to a chair, legs bound together, but hands left free. His eyes were wide with fear. He expected torture. He looked at the laboratory equipment on the bench. He thought electric shocks would follow. He had seen such things in ar-Raqqah, wires from a wall socket clamped to testicles, followed by screams; military information had flowed out. Tall, elegant Kashif walked around him, then sat down and waited with his notebook in hand. This only heightened the prisoner's fear, expecting some new high-technology pain. Kashif put a finger across his lips, "Please. Do not speak. Do you understand?" The prisoner nodded.

Akmal and Ramza sat down on chairs to watch, stopwatches in hand. Eyes glanced at other eyes as tension rose in the trailer. The prisoner's eyes flicked nervously side to side; he let out, "Please. What are you doing? What do you want?"

Kashif gave the poor man a gentle slap on his

face. With finger again to his lips, he reminded with a more-stern voice, "No speaking. Do you understand?" Minutes dragged on. An hour passed. Then more minutes. Kashif watched the digital numbers increase incrementally on the electronic watches. He made some notes. At one hour and forty six minutes into the test, the man started gasping for air, clutching his chest. He tried to speak, but only slurred gibberish came out. Kashif watched closely and held his hand up to prevent Akmal or Ramza from stopping their watches; not yet. The man writhed and struggled, still clutching his chest. Then, his head fell forward, his body motionless. Kashif dropped his hand. Watches were stopped. He wrote the times and their average in his notebook – 1:48:32. He shook his head – too fast.

Akmal's and Ramza's eyes were wide with wonder. The fine mist they saw settle on the plate was strange, holding its power unnoticed, then a later painful death. A few more minutes passed. With stethoscope, Kashif listened for the telltale heartbeat. Finally, he put it down, "Dispose of him. Now he faces the wrath of *Allah*."

Akmal and Ramza dragged the corpse out of the trailer, then towards a larger dune where the sand was deeper. Ramza carried the shovel. Despite being an infidel, they followed *Shari'ah* law and buried him before sunset. But with contempt, and for the labor involved, there would be no bathing and shrouding of the body, no coffin, nor a final prayer. They dug and labored in the late-afternoon heat, rolled the body in, then covered it, leaving no marker for the grave. They reported back to Kashif, who informed them, "The next test will be in two days. I must make adjustments. Care for them."

After the condemned man had been dragged from the trailer, there was considerable chatter in the cage trailer that increased when he had not returned. They had seen similar things while they had been held captive back in ar-Raqqah, even beheadings. Some in the cages thought that this must be what awaited them. Smithy just listened, but thought that torture to get information was the game, torture to the death if necessary. But he was puzzled. That didn't fully square. Military operations had certainly changed, as did their plans and the disposition of forces. What information did these Kurdish soldiers, or he, have to offer that was so important?

It was midday, two days later. The sun was intense, temperatures rose. Kashif had carefully modified the toxin. He labeled it 3FT3b-23-1. The cage at the front of the trailer was now empty. The occupant of the second cage had been given the poisoned plate, stop watches had been started.

He now sat in the chair in the laboratory trailer, watched closely. Frozen with fear, he had not tried to speak, for which Kashif was thankful. Conversation had its own risks. It could break through the walls of hatred, opening the mind and heart to human compassion. That could interfere with the tests. Kashif wanted to treat them as test subjects, as if they were rabbits and rats back in his laboratory in Riyadh.

Minutes turned to hours. Kashif paced up and down the trailer, upset. It had been over four hours, well past the required time window, and the man had not succumbed and even appeared to be alert. What had he done wrong with the second batch? He sat down at the workbench, pouring over notes and data. He read digital data from his instruments. Were measurements inaccurate? Had calibrations drifted? Was the sensitivity to small changes too great? He had not seen such sensitivity when testing on rabbits and rats, even larger goats. Finally, he threw up his hands. "Dispose of him."

Akmal and Ramza looked at each other. Why? Kashif could read their puzzlement and questions on their faces. "His blood and tissue are tainted. I do not know how long it would take for his body to cleanse itself completely of the toxin. Testing on him again would only reveal the effect of two different toxins in combination. Dispose of him!"

They untied him from the chair, tied his hands and gagged him. He struggled when he realized that they were taking him away from the trailer he had come from, in the direction of a hill of sand. He knew his end was coming and started making his peace with *Allah*. He wished they would remove his gag so he could ask his executioners to bury him according to *Shari'ah*. He was a believer, but their enemy in the fight for a *caliphate*. Ramza forced him to kneel, then held his back down to steady him for Akmal. The prisoner started to shake as he closed his eyes tight. He had seen Akmal withdraw the scimitar, the sun-glinting off of its polished blade. Akmal raised the sword up and brought it down swiftly. The head fell to the ground, rolled to a stop, eyes open, looking up. Sand soaked up the blood. Ramza thought he saw the eyelids blink. Both could not help but wonder what the man, the man whose consciousness resided in his brain, had felt and thought when disconnected from his body. Did he feel the impact on the sand? Such questions had been asked for centuries by other executioners with the blade. They buried both parts of him. The winds had remained calm since the first burial.

Over the next days, two more tests were

conducted, but only after Kashif had completely checked every last bit of laboratory equipment. This time he was pleased as he reviewed his notes: 2:21:21 and 2:36:52, plus two more bodies for the desert. Beside the times, he wrote 3FT3b-23-2 and underlined it. He knew he needed more tests, many more, to achieve results with any statistical significance. But test subjects were hard to come by, especially if they had to be transported to this remote, clandestine location. Not an ideal test environment, but the only one given him with great difficulty. He thought that it must be the path set before him by *Allah* to accept a small sample for test confirmation. He instructed that he would make another test tomorrow, then another for confirmation.

The test on the fifth prisoner was successful: 2:25:33. When this last prisoner was taken from the trailer, Akmal looked at Smithy. He slid the edge of his hand across his throat in a gesture of intent. Smithy was now the only one in the trailer.

One final test subject remained: Smithy. Akmal scowled. He had wanted to taunt and behead the American alive on the hot desert sands, with him hopefully pleading for his life, but this was not to be. Another burial was expected, and Akmal intended to desecrate the body.

The next day, white thunderclouds had

risen to the north. The severe down-rush winds now reached the trailers, carrying sand. They could hear the *haboob* outside and remembered Kashif's arrival during one. Akmal prepared the plate of food misted by Kashif with 3FT3b-23-2. There was no need to mark the plate. Akmal and Ramza walked over to the cage trailer as gusts of wind and sand blew in under edges of the stretched canvas. The paper plate was covered with a cloth to protect the food and prevent it from being blown off. Akmal held his scimitar with a rifle slung over his shoulder. Ramza held his rifle at the ready. He opened the trailer door.

Deliverance

From his cage, Smithy had watched closely since has arrival. His fellow inmates, Kurdish soldiers that he had advised and fought with, had been taken out one by one, not to return. He did not know exactly why they did not return, but suspected the sword or a long knife had been used. He had been forced to watch heads cut from bodies in ar-Raqqah and had heard screams of pain that were literally cut short. He felt certain that they were at final peace, buried somewhere under the sands of the desert outside.

Since Smithy had been thrown into a trailer cage he had reflected on his role, helping the Kurds fight like Marines to eradicate terrorist evil from Iraq and Syria. He knew that these were America's enemies, but a thought nagged him: America may have brought this on themselves, to some degree, by their very presence in the Middle East, attracted there by the immense reserves of oil under the sand. He never did quite agree with statements that what the terrorists did not like was America's freedom. Smithy had discussed this with Marine buddies in the barracks, in forward operating areas, on the battlefield, or with his Kurdish counterparts. He acknowledged the possibility that what was not liked were not just Americans and their freedoms, but Americans and their freedoms on their ancient land.

Smithy studied the large hexagonal nuts on the ends of vertical bolts that held metal straps to the floor, straps folded over the galvanized pipes at the corners of the wire cages. From the first day in the trailer, he set about planning his deliverance from certain death. The end of each folded strap was fastened to the floor by a large tightly-wrenched nut on a carriage bolt that extended through a hole drilled through the wooden trailer floor, then through the strap. The unseen rounded head of the bolt had an adjacent square section before the threads began. When the bolts had been hammered through from below, the square sections embedded in the wood, preventing them from being turned when their nuts were wrenched on from inside the trailer.

Masoud and Dabir were good truck drivers and could use tools, but they had never built anything before. Hammers, wrenches, drills, nuts and bolts; those were the things of others. They had been forbidden to have anyone else involved. It was only they who were to fasten the purchased dog kennel cages to the trailer floor. Masoud had ordered the cages from an American company. They arrived in a shipping container offloaded on the docks of al-Mukalla. The cages had been ordered by dimensions and the strength of the chain link metal that covered them. Masoud had ordered the strongest mesh, the chain link with the largest gauge wires so that nobody could escape. Also, as ordered, the cage edge wires were looped around the pipe frames so nobody could separate fencing from pipe by brute force. The carriage bolts purchased from the hardware merchant in al-Makalla had ends with cross holes for nuts that looked like little castle turrets, with spaces for cotter pins, cross pins to be bent over to prevent the nut from being turned by vibration, or by somebody that didn't have pliers to unbend and remove the pins. In a back alley of the Yemeni port city, the cages had been set a foot apart in a line along one side, metal straps bent around pipes at the bottom, and holes drilled through each strap and completely through the trailer floor. Dabir had crawled under the trailer and hammered the bolts through the holes until the base of the rounded heads were flush with the underside. In the trailer, Masoud had threaded on the nuts, twisted them down by hand and fastened them tight to the floor with a socket wrench. They had not purchased cotter pins. Masoud and Dabir had thought that nobody could loosen the bolt without a wrench, plus they were on the outside of the cages, on the other side of the strong chain link, unreachable. They did not think further, but proceeded until all six cages were firmly wrenched to the floor. If they had, the bolts would have been set the other way around, rounded ends in the trailer, tightened nuts underneath. But they were truck drivers.

As the number of prisoners decreased, one by one, when Akmal and Ramza were not around, Smithy gripped the vertical corner pipes of his cage and jerked up with all his considerable might, again and again. The bolts and straps did not give way. But he noticed that the nuts had been lifted from their straps, ever so slightly, unnoticeable. His beefy hands could almost fit through the 2 1/2-inch wide chain link. After a couple of martial-arts punches from his pile-driver arm, the openings above two straps at one end of the cage spread apart to where he could push his hand through and bring it back out. Before his young guards returned, he carefully pushed the wires back to where it appeared that nothing had been done to them. When alone, he tested the nuts with his vice grip between thumb and forefinger. They were not Maryland Black Walnuts, but they felt about the same. Smithy did not try to crush them, but turn them, counter-clockwise. They had indeed been wrenched down tightly, but not tight enough to withstand Smithy. The nuts on two straps gave way, loosened. He did not remove them. In Arabic, he had announced to the remaining expectant prisoner who had been watching, that the nuts were fastened too tight. The prisoner's brief optimism turned back to the reality of his expected death.

The next day Smithy heard the moan of the wind, louder and louder. Now was the time to act. He had suffered through *haboobs* in dangerous battlefield operations and had heard one after he had arrived in the trailer. Now, if he could break free, the *haboob* could mask his escape across the desert, preventing accurate gunfire.

He thrust his hand through the mesh in two locations, removed both nuts and lifted the end of the cage. The straps unfolded easily. He continued lifting the cage, hinged over on the remaining straps, until the top of the cage leaned against the far end of the trailer. Smithy clambered out underneath, through the gap and lowered the cage back into place. He walked to the trailer doors looking for a way to unlatch the doors from inside. He heard Ramza doing just that from the other side. Smithy pressed himself back up against one of the two doors that was never opened. A gust of wind and sand blasted into the trailer as Ramza entered, followed by Akmal. As they walked to the far end, Ramza looked with shock at the empty cage and raised his rifle, ready to fire. Farther back, Akmal did not see Smithy in time, quietly creeping up from behind with bare feet. A hard right cross to his temple felled Akmal, unconscious. Smithy leapt over his body just as Ramza turned around. Too late. A bicep and forearm, as if driven by hydraulic blood, wrapped around his neck, as Smithy's large, beefy hand on his other arm vice-gripped his forehead. The cliff in the Hindu Kush came back in a mental flash. Smithy gave a simple, quick snap, with considerable strength. The last thing Ramza heard was the cracking and separating of his vertebrae as the spinal cord at the brain stem was severed. The light in Ramza's eyes and the thoughts in his brain disappeared.

Smithy held the shuddering, twitching body, then nothing. He released his headlock and Ramza slumped to the floor, still technically alive; death would follow. He lifted up the cage and reached in, grabbed a plastic bottle of water, then picked up Ramza's rifle. He stepped back over Akmal and dashed out the door, down the ramp, out under the canvas edge into the raging *haboob*. He was unsure of how many people were here, or where they were and how they were armed, and decided to flee rather than fight without full situational awareness. He made a quick, reasoned decision: leave the rifle and its weight behind.

Direction was elusive in the blinding sand. He had gotten a brief glimpse of the dune when he was pulled from the van that had transported them from captivity in Aleppo. Smithy had been taught to observe and remember everything. He took quick stock of the trailer and the trucks parked next to it under the flapping canvas cover, then headed at a full run away from them in an arbitrary direction out into the unknown desert. He was still in reasonable physical condition despite his reduced diet and lack of exercise since his capture in ar-Raqqah. He found himself laboring, breathing harder as he ran up the face of the unseen dune while the soft sand slid away beneath each step. He kept running, then found it easier. He loped down the other unseen side, tripped and tumbled to the bottom. He lay there, catching his breath, then stood and ran in what he felt was the same direction. The sand blinded his reckoning, but it also filled in the trail of foot divots he left behind, leaving no trace, becoming ripples among countless others on the dunes of the Rub' al-Khali.

Akmal came to and struggled to his feet. He touched the raised welt on the side of his head and looked quickly around at the empty cages, then down. To his horror, and there had been more than enough horror to go around, he saw

Ramza on the floor. He knelt down and shook the still warm but apparently lifeless body of his brother. He shouted, "Ramza! Ramza! Ramza!" Ramza's eyes blinked once. Then the light went out forever.

More horror followed. Akmal saw that the cage that had held the American was empty. He knew that this was not good and that Kashif must be told immediately. But not before he tried to find the escaped American. With his rifle held in the ready-to-fire position, finger in the trigger guard, he ran around the covered trailers in slightly expanding circles, hoping to find tracks to follow and bring the American down in a ripple of bullets. But the flying sand had done what it had always done and erased all traces of human presence: footsteps and graves. The storm could easily have put Akmal in a blinded direction, lost. He had the sense to not search farther out and found his way back to the barely-seen canvas tent.

Kashif was not pleased, not pleased at all. He immediately knew that there was a risk that the American could make his way to somebody, somewhere, maybe the distant highway where he might wave down a curious driver to hear his tale.

"We must leave – now! Do you know the place of command of our one-armed leader? I do not."

"Yes. I have been there, and with him in the fight for the *caliphate*. I was to return with whatever you provide me."

Kashif quickly pulled a small sealed laboratory bottle from the small electric refrigerator, wrapped it in foam rubber and nested it in an insulated cooler, added ice, then sealed the cooler with an insulating lid. It contained 3FT3b-23-2. He had intended to make a batch of the special toxin and seal it in the faux perfume bottles for Akmal to deliver. But time was running out quickly with the US Marine on the loose. Kashif now decided to make the batch in his Riyadh laboratory and Akmal could take it from there. Kashif changed the plan without approval. "This is more valuable than gold. We must keep it in the cooler. You will return to Riyadh with me. Leave the truck behind. It has no air conditioning and the toxin could be put at risk if you are delayed. I will message them of our new plan."

Akmal threw some food and jugs of water into the back of the van, carefully wrapped his scimitar in the black flag and slid it behind the rear seat. Kashif moved all the laboratory equipment into the van and made one final check of the trailers and turned off the generator. Akmal made sure his iPad and satellite handset were moved to the glove box. He ran back into the laboratory trailer and got his *Qur'an*. The automatic rifles were tossed in the back as well. Kashif felt uneasy about that, but reasoned that there were no borders to cross back to Riyadh.

"There is little time. We must go … now!"

"But … Ramza … my brother …"

Kashif hesitated then answered the unasked question. "Quickly now, we will ensure that Ramza faces Mecca in the eternal sands." They carried Ramza to a nearby area. They labored in the wind and blinding sand as they dug a shallow grave at an approximate right angle to the direction of Mecca. There was no time to ritualistically wash the body, nor sheets for a white shroud. Those in Aleppo had not planned for this, nor had he. They rolled Ramza's body gently into the grave. It came to rest on its right side, facing Mecca. Kashif ran back and brought out some white laboratory towels and placed them around Ramza's head and face. Kashif felt that under the circumstances, *Allah* would approve. Kashif shoveled in sand, but Akmal used his bare hands to cover Ramza's body. Kashif recited graveside verses from the *Qur'an*, exactly, from memory.

Considering all that had happened, Kashif nervously keyed in a message on his satellite phone and pushed the transmit button. There was no encryption. The message caused excitement in the basement room in Aleppo about the unusually-long message, and that it had been transmitted in the clear. They read the text with some concern, "American escaped. Killed Ramza. Akmal and I bringing chemical to Riyadh." Kashif slapped his forehead, cursing at himself for violating communications secrecy and forgetting the most important telecommunication of all. Kashif nervously keyed in an important number, *Khalaset* and pushed the transmit button.

Kashif drove in poor visibility towards the main highway, leaving all behind. He relaxed as they neared Riyadh, knowing that even if suspicion somehow pointed in his direction, he and his family had connections, and money enough to avert an investigative gaze.

A man in the basement room far away, unaware of the *haboob*, carefully examined the orbital tables for American spy satellites and announced, "He will be leaving during an overhead pass from the north. Should we message him to wait?"

Hadi calmed the small room, "Do not! It is in the hands of *Allah*. We will soon have what we need. Akmal is a brave, valiant warrior. The doctor knows not of our total plan; he has nothing to tell of it, nor does Akmal."

✝

Smithy labored running in the soft sand, but continued on, panting, sweating. He stopped to drink the last of the water from the bottle and tossed it away. He ran farther, over another dune. Then, right in front of him, desert tents appeared in the subsiding *haboob*. He stumbled against the opening to one of them. A man in the tent called out to others in the nomadic encampment. They dragged Smithy inside, out of the wind, giving him water and asking questions in Arabic. Smithy motioned for them to slow down so he could understand. One among them was the Bedouin tribal elder and spoke with calm authority, "Who are you? Where are you from?"

In broken Arabic, Smithy said that he was a US Marine and described the death camp from which he had fled. The elder nodded as he spoke; his face turned very grim. Pointing to the scimitar hanging on a pole, he explained that he had been given a gift, asked to not interfere or ask questions about the trailers not far away on the other side of the dunes, and that he feared that *Allah* would now punish him. Apparently, the elder had a more temperate view of the *Qur'an*. He had just wanted to live peacefully in the desert, as his ancestors had done, and not be lectured by radical clerics who lived off the labor of others.

Thinking more clearly, Smithy asked how far away the main road was, and how long it would take to reach it. The elder smiled and pulled him outside to where camels were tethered, lying down, their third eyelids closed against the flying sand. The elder shouted orders and others ran over and put saddles on two of them. He motioned for Smithy to get on, and hold on. With ungainly ease, the camel lurched up, as did the other with the mounted elder. Then it was across the desert sands at a fast gait, the elder holding the reins of Smithy's camel, leading it. Nothing in Marine boot camp had prepared him for this creature, but he held on firmly, his ride punctuated with twinges of nausea.

After some time they came upon the road. A car passed, its passengers staring at the pair of camels and their riders. Smithy waved at them as he jumped to the ground, but the car disappeared into the distance. They waited for a half-hour before a big Toyota Land Cruiser approached. It had a rack of blue lights mounted on top. Smithy stood out in the road, waving his arms. Saudi police stopped and got out, pistols drawn.

The police and an angry Bedouin elder would eventually find and examine the trailers. The empty cages, the septic pit were one thing, but unmarked graves quite another. With a keen-nosed dog and a little digging, dead bodies would speak to the Saudi police.

The Bedouin elder held the scimitar that he

had been given to seal his lips. He slid the curved
shiny engraved blade through a trailer door
locking latch. The big door was already open, a
policeman was inside. The old Bedouin looked
skyward. With a slow steady pull, he attempted
to bend the blade. Being brittle, only decorative,
not worthy of battle, it snapped into two pieces.
At the edge of the death camp he flung them out
across the sand, fell to his knees and begged *Allah*
for forgiveness.

Delivery

Kashif pulled up to the high wall around his private laboratory. He pushed a button. The big iron doors swung open. Kashif drove in and they closed behind him. The laboratory had living accommodations for assistants and himself should deep laborious research require overnight stays. Kashif instructed Akmal to stay in the laboratory until the chemical work was finished, to carfully increase the quantity of the deadly 3FT$_{3b-23-2}$ timed toxin.

Kashif went next door and pounded on the back door of the mosque. Fahim answered with wide eyes, "Kashif, my dear Kashif, what of your work? Success? "

"I have created a poison that satisfies what your visitor requires."

"*Allah* be praised!"

"Come with me. You must meet a young warrior, Akmal. He and his brother helped me in the desert. Very unfortunately, the last prisoner broke free somehow and attacked both of them, killing Akmal's brother, then escaped. He was a devil American. We had to leave quickly."

"Do you have the poison?"

"Yes, but I did not have time to make a larger amount, to fill the bottles given me. I will do that now in my laboratory, but it will take three days. Akmal will make the delivery."

Fahim looked worried, "Do they know of the murder, the escape?"

"Yes, if they received my transmission, and only that Akmal and I were coming back to Riyadh with the poison."

"You transmitted the words Riyadh and poison!?"

Kashif had been insulated from such stress, where his own life could be at risk, "Yes. I panicked. *Allah* forgive me."

Mullah Fahim almost lectured, "You must be very careful, as must I."

"Yes, yes. I must tell my father that I have returned, but not what I have done."

Fahim met Akmal; they spoke of the will of *Allah*. While he fervently believed in the *jihad* for the *caliphate*, he had never been in actual combat nor had seen a killing or a beheading in person. Fahim asked many questions.

Kashif carefully incubated 3FT**3b-23-2** broths, purified and concentrated the toxin protein, and carefully filled the small faux perfume bottles and sealed them. He purchased a new BMW for Akmal to deliver the poison. Despite the air conditioner in this luxury vehicle, the small vials were placed in an insulated cooler, each wrapped in white foam rubber.

A scene was eerily repeated outside of the laboratory's walled gate. The sun had set and the *Maghrib* was recited, this time by Kashif, Fahim and Akmal, who then drove off into the warm evening air. *Khalaset* would not be communicated to Aleppo, but a very careful phone call was made. But questions remained in their minds. They walked back into the laboratory. Kashif pointed to a newspaper on his desk and broke the silence. "I see that there will be a global economic summit in Istanbul this year. World leaders will attend, including the President of the United States."

"What of it?"

"Maybe my special poison will lace the food served at a banquet. That could explain the need for a specific time delay. Enough time for a kitchen helper or waiter to escape, a limited time to ensure scenes of world leaders collapsing at their tables, not in their rooms."

Fahim tensed and retorted, "It is not for us to wonder of such things. Only our one-armed leader knows, and it must remain that way."

"Yes, you are correct." Yet, Kashif's keen

mind could not help but wander through the possibilities.

Akmal drove north and soon passed near King Khalid International Airport. He looked over with a twinge of envy as a big British Airways Airbus A380 was lifting off. The impressive machine of the air had been designed by European engineers. But he felt that superior minds had used the West's technology against them to bring about 9/11. He patted the cooler on the passenger seat and hoped that Hadi would use its contents to somehow bring death and terror to the West.

Aboard that British Airways flight to London was a big strong man seated in First Class. An FBI escort sat next to him. Smithy unbuckled his seat belt, tipped his seat back, thumbed through the ads in a magazine then looked down as the lights of Riyadh spread out below him. The flight attendant set down a glass of the finest white wine. He was much more comfortable than he had been a few weeks earlier. Saudi police had rescued him in the Rub' al-Kahli and delivered him to the US Embassy in Riyadh. Embassy staff bought him new clothes and First Class tickets to America. Encrypted messages were sent to the State Department; hard copies were hand-carried to a very secretive location. Smithy, too, had something to deliver.

†

Akmal inched along in the burning sun behind a line of cars waiting to cross the border. He had been thinking carefully of how to handle border crossings and not put the precious vials at risk. The steel gates at the crossing were rolled back and forth, letting cars and trucks through, one at a time. Finally, Akmal was at the gate. Two no-nonsense armed Jordanian Army soldiers held up their hands for him to stop, as if the gate were not enough. As he stopped, Akmal placed his copy of the *Qur'an* on the center console where it could be easily seen. Through the open window Akmal calmly explained that he had been hired to make a special delivery to an important government official in Amman as he pointed to the cooler on the seat beside him. The guard requested to see its contents; it was big enough to hold a bomb. With a gun barrel pointed at his ear, Akmal moved the cooler carefully to his lap and pulled off the lid. He described that this was special very expensive perfume for the wives of his wealthy client.

The guard raised his eyes, secretly wishing he could afford to have more than one. He asked to see one of the bottles. Akmal lifted one carefully out and handed it over. The curious guard held it

up against the sunlit sky. He saw nothing but clear
liquid inside and a French word on the outside.
He held the top to his nose, but smelled nothing.
He asked, "What kind of perfume is this?"

Akmal replied, "It is the best money can buy,
from France. It is sealed tight, or the air may
touch it too early and ruin its fragrance."

"Please open it."

Akmal blanched then composed himself,
"As you wish, but if the perfume is damaged
our client, a government official, will be very
unhappy, as will be his wives. I'm sure he will
want you to repay him."

The guard thought for a moment, saw the
label, and thought that his career might be at
risk if the supposed client knew the head of the
Royal Jordanian Army. But he did not like being
threatened by the mere boy in front of him. He
handed the vial back, "I said, please open it!"

Akmal took a deep breath, twisted and gently
removed the stopper and handed the bottle to
the guard. He raised it to his nose. There was a
very slight hint of something, like a mild vanilla,
hardly anything, and nothing like any perfume
he had ever smelled. He expected the smell of
flowers or something sweet and fragrant. He
sniffed the opened bottle again. His curiosity got
the better of him. He put his fingertip against the
opening of the small bottle and tipped it briefly

over and back. He put his nose to his fingertip, still nothing. As if taste would help, he touched his finger to his tongue. Nothing. He handed the bottle back and noticed the *Qur'an* on the seat. He waved Akmal through. Akmal inserted the stopper, placed the bottle back with the others in the cooler, noted its position, and drove on.

Akmal knew that in about two and a half hours, an ambulance would be called to the check point. He would have to tell about the incident when he reached Aleppo, that the contents of a specific vial may have changed, having been touched and tasted by the Jordanian guard.

On the way to the Syrian border, he mentally rehearsed the next charade, hoping he would not have to put another vial at risk. If asked, he would hand the same, tainted bottle to the guard. This time his story worked, without having to do so. The guards flinched, knowing repercussions in Syria from an important husband and his wives could be much more than serious.

As he drove past Damascus, Akmal pulled the satellite phone from the glove box and sent numbers to Aleppo, his estimated time of arrival.

After winding through the narrow back streets, he pulled to a stop, flashed his headlights, and was let in. The guard recognized Akmal and led him into the secret basement room after slapping the door with the coded rhythm for the day. Akmal proudly held the cooler and set it on the table before Hadi, as if it were an offering to the gods. There were a number of people in the small room. One of them looked like he definitely did not belong there, or in this part of the world. He was young with fair skin, blue eyes, blond hair, wearing a t-shirt and western style jeans. Akmal suspiciously asked, "Who is this one? A captured American infidel? Let me put him to the sword."

Hadi spoke, "Do not worry. This is our converted brother. He has been in the field and has proved himself. *Allah* guided the words we put on the website; he found them. His name is Gene. He is a believer and will help us bring death to America."

Akmal wondered aloud, "How?"

"We have a way, beyond their limited circle of thinking, as when *al-Qaeda* touched an un-thinkable corner of their brains to bring down the towers. This American will help us. He joined the fighting north of ar-Raqqah after you and Ramza had left for the Rub' al-Kahli. *Allah*'s blessing be upon you … and Ramza. He died a hero in the fight and is now in the presence of *Allah*."

Akmal snarled, "The American prisoner was a cunning snake and bit when we had a careless moment. Ramza sleeps in the sand. I believe the American has died of thirst and heat in the desert."

He then opened the cooler, pointed to the tiny bottles and asked, "Are these part of *Allah*'s plan?"

Hadi did not answer the larger question, but merely said, "Gene is now our brother in the struggle. He will accompany these bottled weapons back to America, to the city of his birth, a wet, green place. He has well-forged provenance with signatures for the rare, priceless perfumes, and purchase certifications in case airport security requests inspection of his hand luggage. *Allah* will ensure that the aircraft flies and arrives safely."

Gene reached into his jeans pocket and pulled out a pair of large glasses and slowly set them on the vials in the cooler, then just stared at Akmal.

Hadi commanded, "Enough!"

Soon, Gene would be entrusted as a courier of timed synthetic death, flying back to Portland to keep his job cleaning airplanes at PDX.

†

Against all hope, the American infidel was not dead on the sands of the Rub' al-Khali. As Hadi spoke, Smithy was winging his way from London on a special government aircraft back to America to be debriefed by senior officers of the Central Intelligence Agency and the Federal Bureau of Investigation. His words were melded with reports from an agent operating in Portland: the observations of a young man working at PDX. Data mining of intercepted communications by enormously-powerful computers at the National Security Agency had pointed attention towards Gene from Hillsboro, Oregon, and an abandoned building in Aleppo. A single over-used word had stood out, *Khalaset*.

Mist

Jen peered sleepily through sheer window curtains. The black-out shade was rolled up; she had forgotten. The cell phone she had slid under her pillow awakened her with muffled lyrics sung in the minor-key harmony of the Everly Brothers, "Wake up, little Susie, wake up." She reached under the pillow, groped around, shut off the alarm and rolled out of bed.

Under clear skies, calm saturated air from the Pacific Ocean had collapsed softly on the city overnight: dense fog. She could hardly see the house across the street or the tall trees that towered above it on Mount Tabor. Jen thought her first officer should get a head start to get a handle on planning for the weather that might delay their takeoff for Salt Lake. But that could wait until she showered.

After drying off, she walked out of the bathroom with a big towel wrapped around her, holding a corner over her head, briskly drying her short hair. She started to reach for her cell phone to speak directly to a weather forecaster for PDX, or get the latest forecast from the Flight Service Station. Jen changed her mind, 'Hell, Chris should do this. I'm the captain for the flight.' She reached down, "OK, fly boy. Up and at 'em. Fog's got us by the ass."

While Jen dressed and put on her Aster uniform, Chris swung his legs out of bed and sat up, rubbing his eyes. Rather than use his cell phone app for automated information from the FSS for PDX, he called and spoke directly to a flight specialist about the fog. He learned that it was forecast to thin with visibility above takeoff minimums by their estimated takeoff time. While he had the specialist on the line, he asked about route and landing weather at SLC. He stood and stretched with a big yawn, "Fog's forecast to lift by our ETD, but there could be a backlog of planes waiting, and that could delay us. Oh, by the way, there were some thunderstorms near the Oregon-Idaho border yesterday, on our standard route. They're forecast in that area again."

"Great, weather puke. Now step away from the window before you get arrested."

Nina and her crew went to Starbucks for coffee and sweet rolls, their routine. Route 66 didn't take reservations, but Jen and Chris found the expected folded card with a hand-written

"RESERVED" on the table in their favorite booth by the window that overlooked the ramp. As they sat down at the Formica table, "Blue Suede Shoes" was on. Chris looked down; his shoes were black and not suede, but he thought, 'What the hell, they're close.' Sara came over, picked up the card and greeted them, "Mornin' Jen, Chris … on the Salt Lake run today? Looks a little misty out there."

Chris replied, "Sure are. Fog's forecast to lift in time. We'll have the usual."

Sara jotted down the order and slipped the pencil back in her hair with, "Comin' right up." As she had done many times, she walked to the counter, clipped the order to the wheel and spun it around, saying, "Order in." The short order cook reached up and plucked it off with a well-tattooed forearm that spoke to an interesting life of cooking. He knew exactly how they wanted their breakfasts prepared; Sara shared their tips with him. He had already started to prepare their breakfasts when he had seen Jen and Chris walk in. Service would be quick.

Sara smiled and gave a quick flirting wink at a young man sitting at the counter by the serving station, on the other side of the chrome metal tube, "Hi Gene, ya doin' OK?"

Gene just nodded and nervously pushed his glasses up to the bridge of his nose, "I'm fine.

Just studying these flight manuals I got from Chris and Jen over there."

Sara replied, "They're great folks. They'll help you get started. Say, we missed you. You were gone for a few months. Glad you're back."

"Yeah, me, too. I had to take care of a family matter," replied Gene.

It was a busy morning. Sara went to another table, then a second with six people. Before she returned with their orders, two hot plates with breakfasts were slid out from the kitchen, "Order's up."

Gene glanced at Sara, then slipped his hand into his jacket pocket and withdrew a small bottle with a spritzer top. He removed his glasses and rested his right hand on the chrome tube as he casually held them. He methodically pushed the plunger down, slowly, four definite times; the fine mist barely missing his glasses as he turned them over. A few of the tiny droplets settled down on the chrome tube, but most went onto the breakfast plates a few inches beyond. He returned the bottle to his pocket and used a napkin to wipe his glasses sparkling clean, holding them up to the light; rubbing, looking, rubbing, looking, as he had frequently done to the idle curiosity of others, and to the interest of the tattooed cook behind the counter in the open kitchen.

Sara clipped the next orders to the wheel,

spun it around with, "Two orders in."

She picked up both plates and went to Jen and Chris's booth while "Peggy Sue" played and set their breakfasts down, "Here you go. Just the way you guys like 'em. Eggs not too runny, real butter, sausage links crispy."

Jen smiled, "Thanks. They look great, enough tasty calories to get us to Salt Lake. We shouldn't need any in-flight snacks for refueling." They dug in with their usual early morning, preflight gusto. Out the window they could see their aircraft and people buzzing around, some tossing luggage onto the conveyor belt for the luggage hold. They could not see much beyond that as the fog held the airport firmly like a steel hand in a velvet glove.

Gene watched them, then took special note of the time on his wristwatch, jotted it on a napkin he put in his pocket. He paid for his coffee, stepped down from the stool with the flight manuals in hand, waved at Jen and Chris, walked over to the newsstand and picked up two carry-on cases held by the clerk under the counter, then left down the concourse.

Gene walked to a gate, not to clean an aircraft, but with a boarding pass in his pocket. The gum-chewing FBI agent followed, stopped and watched as he boarded a Boeing 787-8 international flight to Frankfurt. With the hint of a sneer, Gene flipped the flight manuals into a waste can by the gate. He entered a short text message that could not be seen by the agent, a number, a date, a time, and *Khalaset*.

Sated and satisfied, Jen and Chris left a good tip, paid their bill, gave a thumbs-up to the cook and waved to Sara on the way out, "See ya next time."

With a pencil in her hair, Sara replied, "Have a good flight."

In the Aster operations room Jen filed an IFR flight plan with Seattle Center. Chris updated observed and forecast weather for PDX and SLC and for the planned route for Aster Flight 2123, and any published notices to airmen. There was a weak trough in the mid-atmosphere that had not moved much since the day before. Thunderstorms were again forecast along their route over Eastern Oregon and Western Idaho. With a National Weather Service super-computer-model of at-altitude forecast winds, Jen calculated required fuel load and route timing. The eastbound climb up to 31,000 feet would be over the Columbia River Gorge, then southeast over the Umatilla National Forest, Baker City and Boise, Idaho, then letdown towards the Great Salt Lake. They had done this many times. It had become almost old hat, but this time the magic of flight was shrouded in fog at the start.

Nina was near the gate with her three flight attendants. With the Aster gate agent, she reviewed the number of expected passengers, number of children that would ride on laps, passengers with special needs and in-flight services. Nina assigned work positions and duties and reviewed how to handle medical and other emergencies. This required drill, too, had become old hat.

Nina and her crew boarded first to perform safety checks at emergency evacuation doors, confirm safety equipment, check door pressure gages, and locate the two automated external defibrillators, one in each cabin. Nina was strict on AEDs; she had saved a man's life with one at 32,000 feet. She and her crew had just gone through their required annual training on emergency evacuation, First Aid, CPR and AEDs. They were ready for this routine flight.

The aircraft would again be a Boeing 737-700, the same one they had flown in from SFO the night before. Chris had made a maintenance write-up. With her "good hands" Jen had very smoothly set the big bird down on the runway. They noticed a slight shudder that seemed to come from the main landing gear. With the write-up on their minds, Jen and Chris walked out onto the ramp and around the aircraft while it was being refueled. With a flashlight, they looked over the landing gear and up into their wheel wells and talked to the aircraft technician. He had just completed his inspection and had just reviewed the repair report that cleared the write-up. Jen looked up at the black tail with Orion the hunter and patted him on the back. "Thanks."

Before the Door

In their travelers' trance, passengers funneled down the concourse to the starting point. Security processing had become robotic and accepted as a just another part of modern life since 9/11. Identification was examined and boarding passes marked before they moved on to the security checkpoint. Shoes were removed and placed in gray plastic tubs along with hand-carried baggage, coats and jackets, laptop computers and anything made of metal. A special imaging device made things on the conveyor belt appear transparent to inspectors' weary eyes as people walked through a metal detector, just in case. On the other side at the end of the metal rollers, passengers put themselves back together. One was pulled aside after the red light on the metal detector turned on. A metal-detecting wand was waved closely to all parts of him. He had a metal hip implant that netted him an intrusive frisk.

Back at the starting point, an older couple hugged a younger man. They wore plain clothes, but looked to others as possibly being from the Mideast by their skin tone and facial features. When they spoke in Arabic, they removed all doubt. Passengers averted their eyes, pretending not to notice, lest they be considered fearful, or worse, profiling racists.

At the gate, the young man, just a teenager, sat with others waiting for the call to board the flight to Salt Lake City. He wore jeans, t-shirt and a jacket, carried a small satchel, and noticed others glancing at him. He was handsome: wide eyes, dark arched eyebrows, dense eyelashes and olive-brown skin. Two young girls kept giving him appreciative once-overs, then giggled to each other. He had become used to this back in Hillsboro, in his neighborhood, in grade school, in high school. But overall, he and his parents had been welcomed and befriended by many. He had stood out as a top student. At his graduation, his parents were extremely proud when he gave a motivating speech from the podium on the stage as the class valedictorian. His Iraqi heritage and his parent's immigration from Bagdad had been its central theme.

A young woman sitting next to him, thumbing through a magazine, felt the mild tension in the waiting area and asked, "Where are you going in Salt Lake?"

"The University of Utah. I've been offered a

scholarship there in computer science."

"Congratulations. I'm Carol. What's your name?"

"Mustafa, my friends call me Musty. I've received offers from other universities. I've narrowed it down to Oregon State University and the University of Utah. My parents paid for this flight so I can visit their computer science department and speak to their professors, like I did at Oregon State."

Carol was surprised when she heard his name. Musty's English was absolutely perfect, with just a hint of an accent tinged by hearing his parents' conversations. Her next question did not surprise him. He had heard these oblique probes into his heritage before, "Are your parents from Oregon?"

"No. They are from Baghdad."

A few others within earshot squirmed, pretending not to hear.

Carol wanted to probe further, but finished with, "Oh … well … good luck to you, Musty."

"Thanks."

Everyone glanced up as the flight crew for their flight to Salt Lake walked past them and down the jet bridge towing black leather cases on small wheels; a man and a woman in sharp Aster Air uniforms. Both wore black slacks; she a long-sleeved gold-colored shirt with a black band around the neck, he wore a blue shirt of the same design. Jen had three dark gold stripes on her sleeves; Chris had two. Waiting passengers knew the woman was the captain for the flight.

Preparing for periods of boredom, Chris had briefly stopped at a concourse news stand and picked up an interesting magazine. The cover grabbed his attention: "Ancient Mesopotamia." Jen and Chris walked aboard Aster Flight 2123. Nina welcomed them, "Hi folks. Breakfast good? Eat your hearts out. We had Lattes, Chocolate Croissants and Blueberry Scones at Starbucks. How's it looking on the first leg?"

Chris turned around as Jen went into the flight deck. "Fog's forecast to lift before takeoff time. There might be a thunder bumper or two near Boise."

With her 'been there, done that' smile, she just replied, "Got it."

As Chris entered the flight deck, Nina stuck her head in, "Hope you filtered out the grumpy passengers."

Chris retorted, "Above my pay grade, Nina, above my pay grade."

Jen keyed-in flight planning information into the FMS as Chris methodically went through system checks. Everything was routine, going smoothly; just another day moving people around the western part of the country, except this one was shrouded in take-off fog and *en route* thunderstorms.

Nina and her people determined that everything was ready. The gate crew let her know that the boarding announcement had been made. Nina put on her plastic welcome-aboard smile, but she sincerely did want to welcome passengers into her world of flight. The first to arrive at the door was an elderly man in a wheelchair being pushed by a gate attendant. A flight attendant assisted him into his seat, followed by a mother with two small children, one a babe in arms. After a brief delay, the rest of the passengers arrived and turned right to find their seats. As they passed the open door to the flight deck, some looked in at the complex array of computer displays, switches, knobs, and the two pilots going about their profession. This was comforting and normally the last opportunity to see inside the front end of the big aircraft.

Musty stopped to give the cockpit a longer look, with obvious interest. Nina had to ask him to please move on as others were stacking up behind him. It was hard not to notice his Mideast looks, but Nina just shrugged off her reflexive thoughts. He was just another passenger, and the cockpit door would be sealed up tight before taking off.

Through their headsets they heard Nina's report, "One hundred and thirty souls on board, one wheelchair, one lap, crew of four. We're buttoned up back here and set to go."

After tug push-out, engine start and taxi instructions, they finally were pointed down the runway that disappeared into the thinning fog. They could see the runway lights and centerline for a sufficient distance that nearly matched the reported visibility and were cleared for takeoff. Chris pushed the throttles steadily forward as the engines spun up to maximum power. As they accelerated down the runway, Chris glanced over at a row of gray, twin-tailed F-15s of the Oregon Air National Guard, hauntingly veiled by thin fog. Some were at the ready under open-sided shelters, deadly air-to-air guided missiles bristling under wings and fuselage. Chris knew their pilots were on hard alert to protect the nation. If things had been different high over the cornfields around Enid, he wistfully thought that he could have been a fighter pilot.

Jen noticed them too, and Chris's brief distraction. Their lethality was both comforting and frightening. With very powerful twin jet engines, the F-15 Eagles could takeoff, climb and overtake a passenger airliner quickly. For a terrorist-controlled aircraft, an absolutely cold-sober decision would have to be made; sacrifice the lives of all aboard to save many more lives in the tall buildings of an American city. The solid door behind them was also comforting. They knew that nobody could get past that door to force an F-15 decision.

Past the Door

The big Boeing 787-8 lumbered down the runway, rotated, lifted off and began its climb. Gene looked out the window, down at the concourse buildings with aircraft nosed into their gates. He could see the big black tail of Aster Flight 2123. As PDX and Aster's docked Boeing 737-700 drifted back from his view, he smiled and did a celebratory fist pump. Now for the long fight to Frankfurt. But others also had an interest in Aster Flight 2123.

✝

In the dark basement room of the abandoned warehouse, people gathered around Hadi and *mullah* Muhammad Talib. The iPad on the table beeped. He reached down and touched the screen to open the window and read the text. He read the hoped-for number, followed by the date and time, and *Khalaset*. On a large sheet of white paper, Muhammad Talib wrote the sent date and time with a black felt-tipped marker; below that he wrote their time-zone conversion, two more numbers after adding "2" and "3" to the computed local time. Biochemical gears had been set in motion. Hadi pointed at Muhammad Talib and nodded for him to send another message, to Riyadh.

Kashif and Fahim sat around the beautiful mahogany desk. The iPad lay there, waiting. Then came the audible notice that a message had arrived. Kashif touched the face of the iPad. He noted the date and times shown, quickly set a laboratory stopwatch in motion, displayed digits changing each second on the large display. It would beep at the two times also entered, an hour apart. Kashif leaned back and closed his eyes as he envisioned $3FT_{3b\text{-}23\text{-}2}$ coursing in the blood of people, somewhere, maybe in Istanbul, wrapping itself into and around the complexities of their cells and nervous systems. Without realizing exactly for what, Fahim looked to the ceiling, "*Allah* be praised!"

†

Aster Flight 2123 lifted off, Jen bade the tower farewell and switched radio frequency to Terminal Radar Approach Control for their departure vector east towards the Columbia River Gorge. As they left the PDX control area, Jen again switched frequencies, "Seattle Center. Aster two one two three leaving four thousand feet, climbing to flight level three one zero. Over."

"Aster two one two three, radar contact. Cleared. Report three one zero. Over."

"Seattle Center. Aster two one two three. Report three one zero. Over."

Above the shallow fog layer below, lit white by the risen sun, majestic Mount Hood slid by. Beautiful, as this part of their flights always were, but the white mantle around the snow-covered peak made this flight almost magical. Passengers by the windows on the right side of the aircraft also felt this magic, the dormant volcano affecting the thoughts of each differently.

Jen engaged the autopilot which accurately leveled them off at 31,000 feet on their approved route. She reported to Seattle Center; a few minutes later the aircraft automatically banked and changed direction to the southeast driven by route data that she had entered into the FMS. With cheerful smiles, Nina and her crew pushed the drink and food carts down the narrow aisles, avoiding overhanging elbows, giving friendly service to all, even the grumpy ones. It was all part of the job. They were over the Umatilla National Forest, headed towards Boise, Idaho.

They were still under the control of Seattle Center but nearing the zone controlled by Salt Lake City Center.

The sky above was a clear crystal blue but below was a sea of lumpy white clouds over farmland and forests. Directly ahead of them some of the clouds had congested together with their billowing cauliflower tops much higher than the rest. Jen glanced down. On the radar display, directly ahead was a green area with a yellow area within, to show categories of the strength of reflected microwave energy. "Hey, weather puke, looks like your buds guessed it right."

"Sure does. We might be able to clear the tops."

The slowly boiling clouds, brilliant white in the sun, appeared to rise to their altitude. The yellow area on the radar display now had a red center indicating stronger reflection from a central core of heavier precipitation, some frozen. Flying into or just near such convection could easily subject Aster Flight 2123 to severe turbulence, lighting and hail. This was to be avoided. Jen keyed her radio, "Seattle Center, Aster two one two three request course change to zero niner zero to avoid thunderstorms. Over."

"Seattle Center. Aster two one two three. Cleared zero niner zero. Over."

Chris's fingers danced across the FMS

keyboard on his side of the console. The aircraft banked left, turned, then rolled wings level on a heading of 087 degrees giving them a ground track of 090 degrees. Jen planned to avoid the thunderstorms to their north then turn south towards SLC.

Minutes droned on. Chris reached into his black leather valise and fished out the magazine he had purchased in the concourse and thumbed to the feature article. Skimming the introductory paragraph, he read how archeologists had discovered fragments and artifacts near an ancient city. Carbon-dating had confirmed that the environs of Baghdad was the earliest known clustering of human beings for mutual benefit, the origin of cities, and civilization, on the banks of the Tigris River.

Chris keyed the flight-deck intercom, "Hey Jen, you ought to read this. Interesting stuff. Jen … are you alright? Jen?"

Jen was rubbing her face and eyes, as if she was trying to wake up. Chris noticed, "Jen, how are you feeling?"

"Heartburn, or something; you handle the transfer to Salt Lake Center." She uncapped her bottled water and took a long swallow.

"Got it." Chris keyed the microphone, "Seattle Center. Aster two one two three leaving your control zone. Over."

"Aster two one two three. Contact Salt Lake City Center on one two one point five. Good day."

"Salt Lake Center. Aster two one two three to Salt Lake City. Entering your control zone. Over,"

"Aster two one two three. Salt Lake Center. Welcome. Monitor one two one point five. Over."

Back on intercom, Chris asked, "Feeling better, Jen?"

"No. Can't … catch my breath! Can't focus. Chest tight … pain … I think I'm … I'm having a heart attack! You have … control. Alert … Salt … Lake …"

"Salt Lake – hell! We'll set 'er down now in Boise. They've got two long runways and we've burned off enough fuel. Hang in there, Jen."

"Salt Lake Center. Mayday! Mayday! Aster two one two three declaring medical emergency. Request immediate clearance for descent into Boise. Over."

"Aster two one two three. Salt Lake Center. Cleared into Boise. Say emergency. Over."

"Captain Jen Grissom having heart attack. Have ambulance and EMTs ready. Meet on taxiway."

"Aster two one two three. Salt Lake Center. Roger. Alerting Boise. Over."

Chris set the transponder code to 7700, alerting all air traffic control facilities in the area that Aster Flight 2123 had an emergency situation. Controllers at Salt Lake Center redirected aircraft to clear the air space for an emergency descent. Boise tower was contacted by Salt Lake Center. Before Chris could disengage the autopilot, pull back the throttles and change direction, he doubled over from sudden sharp pains in his chest. His arms felt like lead, unable to reach for anything, except push the intercom button for the cabin. Nina was near the flight deck door, pulling trash from the food and drink cart. She heard the soft bell tones and saw the flashing light by the galley and picked up, "OK guys. What is it? Need some coffee?"

She could hear the strain. His speech was slurred and broken, "Nina … we're having … a problem …come in … now!" Chris struggled to reach a toggle switch on the pedestal and barely managed to move it to the unlock position. Nina saw the green light come on and heard the metallic *clack*. She did not need to use the secret procedure to open the door without approval from the other side. Nina opened the door to find a horrible, frightful scene. Jen was lying to one side in her seat, holding her chest, panting, unable to speak, but trying. She just looked up at Nina with wide eyes, filled with real fear. Chris was speaking, barely audible. Nina leaned down and heard, "Get me out … this chair … use headphones … find pilot." Nina turned around, jumped through the doorway to her forward work station. She threw a switch and a short series of soft tones were heard in the cabin. Her crew immediately understood, as they had reviewed back at PDX.

Those in the first rows saw the open door and the activity as three attendants almost ran down the aisle. Nina pulled them into the flight deck and took charge, "Help me get them out of their seats and lay them flat outside the door, where there's more room. Bring the defibrillators, now!"

As they struggled to move the still-breathing, limp bodies, Nina pleaded over the cabin speakers, "If there is a doctor or nurse on board, please come forward, now!"

As Jen and Chris were dragged out into the relatively open space, a woman came forward and leaned over them, "I'm a registered emergency room nurse. Move out of the way."

The nurse knelt down, took pulses and lifted eyelids, then started CPR forcefully on Jen with a steady rhythm, paced to the hit tune, "Staying Alive." She motioned to a large man in a forward seat to come forward and pointed to Chris, "Put your hands together, like this, heels down and push up and down hard on his chest in time with me. And don't stop." She shouted, "Get those AEDs here!"

She commanded the man performing CPR

to tear away Chris's clothing down to bare skin. She did the same with Jen. Just then, an attendant arrived with two AEDs, opened them and turned them on. Their speakers started giving voice commands. Before passing out, Jen and Chris had sweated heavily. Nina knelt down with a towel and wiped their chests.

Aster Airline training started to pay off. Two flight attendants attached the electric pads and pressed the analyze buttons. Both devices automatically announced that an electric shock was going to be delivered. An attendant yelled, "Stand clear!"

Bodies flinched. The nurse immediately started CPR again and commanded the volunteer to do the same for Chris. They continued while listening for directions from the AEDs. About two minutes later, they moved aside as two flight attendants again pressed the analyze buttons. Again, an attendant yelled, "Stand clear!" Then Jen and Chris flinched again, and CPR was continued. The third time the analyze buttons were pressed there was no command to press the shock buttons. The nurse placed her ear on Jen's chest, then on Chris's. There were faint heartbeats. She stopped CPR, waited a few minutes, then pressed the analyze buttons and followed voice commands. The nurse said that with help they could keep this up for a long time, hopefully until after the plane landed.

Nina froze, wondering, Who would do that?

Musty

Interest in the cabin turned to concern salted with fear as people craned their necks and gawked at the unfolding drama. That turned to panic when they heard Nina's measured voice, "Anybody with flying experience, please come forward." Nobody came. She had hoped for an Aster pilot to be on board, dead-heading to Salt Lake City; but she would have known that at the gate. She repeated the announcement, any pilot would do. The cabin chatter was mixed with passengers' screams and sobs.

Nina mentally shrugged her shoulders, stepped over the resuscitation operations that crowded the area by the main entry door, then into the flight deck and sat down in Chris's seat. A teenager ran from the back and stepped around the pile of people. Passengers were tense. They had noted the boy of Mideastern heritage at the gate. Some had eyed him as they had waited there or had heard him speaking Arabic at the start of the security line. More screams were heard as he passed them running towards the front of the aircraft. Musty's sprint down the aisle triggered a wave of cell phones, brought out from purses and pockets after he passed, numbers of friends and loved ones were entered. With high tech nerds managing Aster Airlines, a very good Wi-Fi system had been installed on all of their aircraft. Panicked calls went through. "Honey, this is Linda … I'm on the Portland to Salt Lake flight. Something's happened to our flight crew. An Arab terrorist just ran to the front of the plane!"

"Linda! What! Linda!?"

"I love you, Sam. I love you. Please tell the children I love them."

"Linda! Linda!" The phone went dead. Sam immediately dialed 911.

Musty stuck his head in the cockpit, "I'm not a pilot, but I've flown simulators on my computer for big commercial passenger planes, just like this one."

She looked at the young, handsome Mideastern face on a tall, skinny kid and said with exasperation, "Jesus! Oh, what the hell. Sit there, put these on."

Nina donned Chris's headset, he donned Jen's. As they sat there looking straight out at the clear, blue sky over a sea of billowing clouds, the plane flew along nicely, smooth and level, still on autopilot and heading east at 31,000 feet. Nina and her olive-skinned computer pilot didn't have a clue as to where they were except somewhere over Idaho, or in which direction they were headed.

He studied the computer displays and said, "We're on a ground track of zero nine zero, heading zero eight seven. We're at a pressure altitude of thirty-one thousand feet. True altitude thirty-two thousand and five hundred feet. We're on the two one five radial of airways beacon two nine at twenty six miles."

Nina stared at him thinking, 'Who the hell *is* this kid?!'

Mustafa looked at the question written on her face, "Oh … I'm Musty."

"I'm Nina."

"Aster two one two three. Salt Lake Center. Cleared for emergency descent BOI. Over."

Nina and Musty just looked across at each other, uncertain of their next steps or of much of anything.

The inbound call came again, "Aster two one two three. Salt Lake Center. Do you copy? Over."

Musty quickly found the microphone button, "This is Musty on the Aster flight to Salt Lake City."

Nina keyed her button and interrupted, "Both our pilots are unconscious up here, being given CPR. There are no pilots on board. Repeat, there are no pilots on board."

"Aster two one two three. Salt Lake Center. Say flight experience. Over."

Nina keyed in, "I've been a flight attendant for twenty years, three years with Aster. I've never flown the damn things. I'm not too sure about the young man sitting next to me in the captain's seat."

He keyed in, "This is Mustafa. I've never flown before. This is my first flight, but I have flown many types of commercial aircraft in video simulators on my home computer, including this Boeing seven three seven, seven hundred. I know the instrument panel, the keypad, knobs, lights, and the levers of this plane. Oh … over."

"Mustafa on Aster two one two three. Salt Lake Center. Are you flying the plane or are you on autopilot. Over."

He looked at the panel carefully, "Yes, we're on autopilot. We're not flying the plane and have not touched anything. We're heading due east. Call me Musty. Over."

"Musty, Salt Lake Center. Experienced Boeing seven three seven pilot coming. We'll get you down. Stay calm. Don't touch anything until we tell you. Over."

"We won't … Over."

Salt Lake Center was anything but calm. The on-call pilot with a fat log book in Boeing aircraft was being raced to the Center in a Salt Lake

City police car, lights flashing, siren wailing.
Aster flight 2123 had not squawked 7500 on its
transponder to indicate a high-jacking, but the
Center director was suspicious. In a deep, serious
voice, he radioed up, "Verify not squawking
seven five zero zero."

Musty and Nina just looked at each other.
What? The words came over their headphones
again, "Verify not squawking seven five zero
zero."

Nina keyed the microphone, "What the hell
is squawking?"

The director feared that the described
situation on the flight deck could be a ruse. Then
a call came in on his unlisted number – from the
Pioneer Precinct of the Salt Lake City Police
Department, "Greg. Charlie here. We've received
a number of 911 calls that something is wrong
aboard an inbound flight. Passengers have called
family members that the plane has been taken
over by a mideast terrorist!!"

That pushed the director over the edge. A hot-
line communication was immediately made and
other red lights flashed, this time accompanied by
a blaring, pulsing horn in the F-15 alert shack at
PDX. Crew chiefs ran to their Eagles to prepare
the alert birds and to assist their pilots. In flight
suits, with g-suits tightly over their legs, they
sprinted across the ramp, up the just-placed

ladders under the just-opened canopies, into single-seat cockpits of the very same fighters that Jen and Chris had seen on takeoff. The crew chiefs helped the fighter pilots strap in and don their helmets, and pull out the ground safety pins with dangling red tags. The two fighter pilots closed their canopies.

Taxiing commercial aircraft were held in place by ground control and the vertical climb corridor was cleared by the control tower, redirecting anything flying over the PDX control zone. Inbound aircraft would be stacked up, waiting for clearance.

Two interceptors lined up in ground formation and accelerated together with full afterburner to lift off in a few seconds, rotated to a near-vertical climb, did a quarter-loop from vertical and rolled wings level. Throttles were set for supersonic cruise and they were vectored by military ground controllers toward the location of Aster flight 2123 as determined from Air Traffic Control radar. Using their powerful radar, this pair of Eagles could detect distant prey like their feathered counterparts. Soon they acquired their target, slowed and approached Aster Flight 2123 that was in a descending turn.

By this time, the seasoned Boeing 737 pilot at Salt Lake Center, his eyes fixed on a radar display, hands on the microphone, had maneuvered Aster

Flight 2123 towards Boise, indirectly, through the hands and eyes of Musty whom he had instructed to not disengage the autopilot or autothrust. As directed by the pilot in Salt Lake Center, Musty turned knobs, pressed buttons, and entered relayed data on the Flight Management Computer's keypad, and engaged various systems. When not doing that, Musty was coached about where to find the landing gear lever, the flap lever, and the two thrust levers, each with smaller attached levers to activate thrust reversal. Musty felt completely comfortable with the instructions as he was very familiar with everything; they matched the simulator app on his computer in his bedroom back home in Hillsboro. He had never actually touched physical levers but certainly knew where they were.

As Musty controlled the plane by radioed instructions, he was distracted to his left. There he saw a single F-15 Eagle flying alongside, sliding in closer to get a better look. What Musty or Nina did not see was the second F-15 in trail behind, one of its air-to-air missiles locked on, with a sensitive gloved finger resting lightly on the launch button. The F-15 pilots had already changed to Salt Lake Center frequency.

The forward pilot chimed in, "Hi there. I'm Major Anderson from the Oregon Air National Guard. I'll be with you all the way to touchdown.

Just listen carefully to me and to the pilot down below. He's flown Boeing seven three sevens all his life, including the model you're in. He'll bring you in on a long straight-in approach. Should be a piece of cake."

Musty did not understand the part about cake, but keyed his microphone. "I'm listening."

"Good. Where are you from?"

"Hillsboro ... Hillsboro, Oregon ... near Portland."

"How'd the Blazers do last year?"

"Terrible, second to last place. They lost their center from a torn Achilles tendon."

Major Anderson smiled, as did the pilot in trail. It was the right answer to a quickly made-up obscure question. He unlocked the missile should his finger get too itchy.

As Musty watched the plane fly itself lower, a couple more passengers in back took turns keeping Jen and Chris alive, helping the nurse to the keep blood flowing despite hearts and lungs under the control of 3FT3b-23-2. On the way down, the pilot at Salt Lake Center instructed Musty how to lower the landing gear, set the flaps and how to reset smaller levers to reverse thrust. With autobrake engaged, he would not have to worry about using toe pressure on the rudder pedals; that would take touch and feel, something impossible to learn on a desktop computer using a mouse. Autobrake with manually set reverse thrust would slow the plane to a complete stop on the runway on the same alignment governed by the ILS. Musty had done these things before with keyboard entries, mouse clicks and dragging the cursor across images of controls and switches on his computer screen. He had used his desktop computer interface to steer simulated aircraft on the taxiway to the gate, but he had never actually touched a rudder pedal with his feet, simulated or otherwise.

At 3,000 feet above the ground, they were 10 miles out and lined up nicely, having intersected the ILS glide slope for the left of two runways: Runway 28L. Another commercial pilot, experienced in the 737, was now in the Boise control tower, taking over after closely coordinating with Salt Lake Center. Musty and the two F-15 pilots changed to the Boise tower frequency. Runway 28L appeared straight ahead of them. Linear strobe lights sequenced repeatedly towards the runway, almost hypnotically, as if pulling them in. Flashing lights, yellow, blue and red, could be seen alongside and at the far end of the runway: fire trucks and ambulances, filled with emergency responders.

Nina glanced right at the dome of the majestic building of the Idaho State Capital building. Off to the left the afternoon sky was dark. Musty was distracted by a thick lightning bolt to the ground, then another. The darkened sky, with embedded thunderstorms, gray shafts of rain extending to the ground, was some distance away and not on their flight path.

This was a different magic of flight. Musty and Nina watched with awe as the big complex machine descended all by itself towards the runway. Musty reported airspeeds, changed flap settings and moved the landing gear lever down when directed. He reported when three green lights appeared; the gear was now down and locked. Major Anderson radioed his visual confirmation from the outside that the landing gear for the main and nose wheels looked to be locked in place. The F-15 pilot in trail slid under from behind and also made his visual confirmation before pulling away. Major Anderson stayed in formation, but moved farther away to the left.

Nina's crew had everyone assume crash positions in their seats, leaning forward with their hands holding their ankles, except for those administering CPR to Jen and Chris, and using the AEDs. Two more passengers had come forward. They all relieved each other all the way down. Keeping hearts pumping and blood flowing was hard work. They weighed the risk of surviving a crash landing against the risk to Jen and Chris if they stopped CPR. Kneeling over them, they kept at it.

Musty's control tower mentor told him to gently rest his right hand on the thrust reverse control levers, and be ready to pull them back, but only after the wheels touched and remained on the runway. As they neared the ground, an unemotional computerized voice announced radar-altimeter altitudes above the runway: 500, 400, 300, 200, 100. When they reached 50 feet and crossed the runway threshold, Nina's commanding voice was heard over the cabin speakers, "Brace! Brace! Brace!" In their earphones Musty and Nina heard, "... 20, 10 ..." then tire *chirps* and a resounding *bump*; the automatic landing flare was not as smooth as Jen's would have been, but it was a thankfully safe contact with the runway. Nina's "Brace! Brace! Brace!" commands continued. Automatically, as the computer and mechanical engineers at Boeing had designed, when Aster 2123's wheels touched the runway, spoilers extended and auto-braking activated. Musty pulled the two small levers back into thrust reverse position.

Just as the main wheels touched, a down-rush from the thunderstorm had spread out over the ground and reached the airport. Wind direction swung around from the west, wind speed increased from 8 knots, almost straight down the runway, to 43 knots. It was a wind gust, a strong direct crosswind gust, well above the limits for autoland control or a manual landing, for that matter. This possibility had not been considered, even though Salt Lake Center knew about the thunderstorms west of Boise. The cross-wind against the large black tail weathervaned the aircraft to the left. Musty could have pressed down on the right rudder pedal, but he had not received radioed instructions to do so. A right foot pressed too far could have swung the aircraft across adjacent Runway 28R and into the terminal building, the crosswind becoming a tailwind. The big 737 ran off the runway to the left onto rain-soaked soft turf. There had been heavy thunderstorms the evening before. The nose wheel sunk down and folded back. The nose dropped and plowed a ditch in the ground. The main wheels sunk down, further lowering the engine cowls to skid across the grass-covered ground. The aircraft slowed rapidly, but not before skidding onto the concrete parking ramp of the Idaho Air National Guard. Showers of sparks flew from engine cowls grinding against dry concrete.

Parked A-10 Warthogs were lined up on the ramp. Two aircraft maintenance technicians were working on the last A-10 in the line, crouched under one wing. They looked up to see their fate: Aster Flight 2123. They dropped their tools and made an instinctive dash away from the ugly, but deadly, air-to-ground fighter and flung themselves face down on the ramp. The left engine struck the A-10, wing tanks ruptured spreading spark-ignited fuel, barely missing the Air Force sergeants. With hands clasped over heads they lay motionless until the intense heat singed their hair and exposed skin. Aster Flight 2123 spun half-way around to the left and ground to a stop. In severe pain, the sergeants sprang up and ran into the open hangar, shouting for help.

Nina saw the flames and keyed the microphone, "Release your seat belts and get out on the right side of the aircraft, the right side, right side!" Nina's well-trained crew quickly unbuckled, jumped up, and with passenger assistance opened the emergency exits on the right side of the aircraft and deployed the inflatable emergency slides.

In the fear and confusion, one passenger leaned into the emergency exit row on the left side and asked the man sitting next to the escape door to open it. He did, after fumbling with the levers and reading the instructions on the door. He wished he had paid more attention to the pre-takeoff flight-attendant briefing instead of reading a magazine. The left escape hatch was opened. The intense radiant heat pushed passengers back.

The attendants shouted and repeated to the panicked passengers, "Come this way, come this way. There is an exit over here." The commands were intended for a smoke-filled cabin when the emergency exits and the floor track lights leading to them would be difficult to see, but they kept shouting commands, leading and motivating. As passengers crowded near the exits, Nina's crew asked for willing passengers to go first and then to stand at the bottom of the chutes to direct following people to move quickly away from the aircraft. As the next passengers crammed forward, they responded to more commands, "Jump! Jump! Jump!" with flight attendants' hands slightly pushing on their backs. As the aircraft emptied, a remaining flight attendant held a mother's baby and jumped down the slide; holding her older child, the mother followed. Nina helped the old, disabled man from his seat and to the slide. She held him as they slid down.

Fire trucks drove up and foamed the fire on the left side of the aircraft. The heat was very intense. Panicked passengers ran away towards the runway. Nina continued to help the disabled man as best she could. Thick black smoke was carried by the gusting winds over the escaping people, both runways, and the main terminal on the other side. Overcautious responders foamed the rest of the aircraft. Even though some people looked like other-world, white foamy creatures, they didn't care – they were alive. With the aircraft's nose resting on the ramp, EMTs scrambled up the inflated slide and aboard through the now-opened forward right door not far off the ground. They went to work on Jen and Chris until they could quickly move them to ambulances to take them to the nearest emergency room. The ambulances were followed by a van from the local TV station that had been held outside of the security perimeter. In addition to news reporters, cameras flooded the terminal: cell phones and computer tablets. An emergency landing and a damaged aircraft, back-dropped by flames and smoke, unconscious pilots, and airmen with severe burns, was soon news well beyond Boise.

Heroes emerged in the following days: an emergency room nurse from Portland, a husky passenger from Iowa, a retired 737 pilot from Salt Lake City, bandaged Air Force sergeants, Nina, and a tall teenager from Hillsboro whose parents had immigrated from Baghdad. Their stories were told and re-told during televised interviews, followed by one with the hipster president of Aster Airlines. Nerds at computer screens across the country started downloading flight deck simulation applications for the Boeing 737. Google searches for this ubiquitous aircraft spiked, as well as hits on the Aster Airlines website. Interviews with Nina and Musty filled the airwaves. Politicians soon latched onto Musty, then his parents back in Hillsboro. A political drumbeat was heard on radio and TV talk shows: if Mustafa's parents had been prevented from entering the United States, Aster Flight 2123 would be a burning hulk in a crater. Speculation swirled around Jen and Chris, still comatose in a Boise hospital. Their blood samples were in a Federal testing laboratory, but the assumption by talking heads was that they had somehow eaten the same tainted food. Maybe E. coli was involved. A scurrilous reporter, seeking career attention, suggested that the pilot and co-pilot could have been overdosing on something in the cockpit behind the sealed door.

Tests showed that their blood had traces of a synthetic chemical that could not be identified. Information was fed out carefully by the National Transportation Safety Board. TV news features spread the life histories of Jennifer Grissom and Christopher McDonald, including interviews with families and friends. News reporters showed up on a family farm near Salina, at a hardware store in Enid, and a neighborhood house in Hillsboro.

Brimstone

An aircraft sliding off the end of a runway or one with a collapsed nose wheel were rare but had happened in the world of commercial aviation. The causes for these relatively minor accidents were numerous; pilot error or equipment failure, or both, usually merited just a brief mention on the TV news of the cities near the airports where they had occurred. But Aster Flight 2123's accident at Boise was much different. The suspected cause unfolded like acrid smoke from unquenchable biblical brimstone. Each news flash stung the senses. TV programs across the nation and around the world were interrupted by somber talking-heads, followed by narrated video of the near disaster from the skies. Electronic media, e-mails, texts and tweets buzzed, followed by old-fashioned hard-copy newspapers read over morning coffees. Moving images looked surreal: a very familiar aircraft shape, down at the nose, milling passengers white with fire-retardant foam, and zoomed-in views of the black tail with the constellation of Orion were peppered with passenger interviews.

†

From a satellite dish on the roof of an abandoned warehouse in Aleppo, news and images flowed down a co-axial cable to the basement room. Hadi raised his remaining hand to calm the jubilant team. Patience was required. He was still very much in charge of the downing of an American airliner. Planning now included capitalizing on the event by taking credit. Two days passed. He carefully watched TV news feeds, especially one where the head of a United States testing laboratory announced that the strange chemical in the pilots' blood was some sort of nerve toxin.

Now was the time. Muhammad Talib moved the computer mouse until the cursor rested over the "Send" icon of Hadi's carefully-prepared short e-mail, "*Jaysh al-Allah* brought down Aster Flight 2123. *Allahu Akbar!*" Hadi pointed and nodded. Muhammad Talib left-clicked the mouse and the untraceable e-mail was unleashed. He shouted, "*Khalaset!*"

The news release spread instantly. He had hesitated with this order. The aircraft was not a smoldering hole in the ground as hoped for. But, they had brought it down; they had gotten past the invincible door. The focus of American news programs and the American public shifted, as did that of those in positions of power, as they had after 9/11.

Self-reflection in the basement was harsh. How could the aircraft be flown without trained pilots? They knew about autopilot, but not so much about autoland. Yet they had succeeded in a prime objective of terrorist action – fear, paralyzing fear.

As the news evolved, announcements were made that officials from the National Transportation Safety Board and Homeland Security would soon be on the scene. Involvement of that latter agency raised some eyebrows. The fact that only the pilot and co-pilot were in critical condition with an uncertain diagnosis added to the worries. That worry spiked when an announcer coldly stated that a new, previously unknown cell, *Jaysh al-Allah*, had taken credit for bringing the plane down. Later e-mails threatened that there would be many more planes falling from the skies over America. References to 9/11, the Transportation Safety Administration, and thinner lines at airports soon infested the news. That news included the rash of airline ticket cancellations. Stock prices tumbled. Fear was working.

†

Kashif also watched and listened. He quickly realized his part in the heretofore unknown plan and smiled, knowing that his 3FT3b-23-2 synthetic toxin had forced the plane down. But the news that the pilots were still in critical condition, not dead, puzzled him. Some news included the fact that passengers and crew members had constantly tried to revive the pilot and co-pilot during descent, with the aid of modern AED devices. He had not been asked, nor had he thought to administer electric shocks to the chests of his test subjects in an attempt to revive them. Kashif remembered the one who had not succumbed to a test toxin, the one Akmal had beheaded alive on the sands of the Rub' al-Kahli. He now suspected that the electric current could have changed the complex molecules before death arrived. He promised himself that this would be part of his future research.

Kashif's father and *mullah* Fahim were in his office in the mosque after the call to midday prayers. They had heard about the downed aircraft, second-hand. Now they watched televised news describing the forced crash landing of an American airliner by *Jaysh al-Allah*. The *mullah* leapt up, raised both hands to the ceiling, "*Allah be praised!*" Kashif's father was more sedate; would force and vengeful wrath be aimed in their direction?

Two workmen in coveralls sat at a coffee shop table in the port city of al-Mukalla. The news of a downed American aircraft came across the screen. Some in the shop cheered. One of the men merely patted the hand of the other on the table. Then they raised their tiny cups of strong spiced coffee and took sips of satisfaction. Now they planned to travel north, back to Aleppo. They had received an inviting text from there, as had Kashif and Fahim.

A young blond American man was changing planes at the airport in Frankfurt. He certainly did not stand out in this part of Europe. Gene was between gates. He watched the news at a bar in the terminal. He let out a small shout when the image came on the big screen of downed Aster Airlines Flight 2123. That caused frowns and hard looks from other travelers at the bar. Realizing his immature error, he downed the last of his beer and quickly left for the gate for his flight to Istanbul to connect with a flight to Aleppo. He had flown this route before.

†

The brimstone burned far deeper in the US, into national agencies charged with aircraft safety and national security. Laboratory analyses of Jen's and Chris's blood revealed the presence of an unknown toxin, its molecules yet to be defined. They had both been poisoned – with the same poison. As they lay in a comatose state, the focus became clear as that news spread, not like brimstone, but like a prairie wildfire in the Midwest. Secret FBI reports were that Jen and Chris were observed often eating together before their flights. Preflight eating habits and the meals themselves would not be merely suggested, but be legally required. Some in the Air Line Pilots Association International publicly balked at what they viewed as regulatory overreach. But the overwhelming public reaction to this was swift and clear: if we have to wait in long lines, empty pockets, throw away liquids, take off shoes, lift carry-on luggage to a conveyor belt, pass through invasive detectors, be patted down in public, then certainly pilots could change how they ate before a flight. Alcohol was already on the "no-no" list, with its bottle-to-throttle minimum time requirements. Now it would be food; what and when it was eaten.

Hellfire

They sat around a heavy conference room table in a windowless room, balding heads and lined faces weathered by years of mental stress. "OK Gunny, tell us what you remember."

"Sir, after I was captured in ar-Raqqah, they drove me and captured Iraqi soldiers west, I think...I'm not sure. I had been advising and training them as part of my assignment. My two-man Iraqi sniper team had been killed when I was taken. The van didn't have any windows. When they took us out, it was in a large open space of a building with small windows near the top of the walls. I remember that it must have been night as the windows were black. Then they took us downstairs to small separate rooms. I was held for many days. There was no way to tell, but I tried to keep track by the number of times I took a crap."

"We're you tortured?"

"No. I was treated reasonably well. But there was one young guard that spit on me when he could, the bastard!"

"Anything else about where you were held?

"Yes – definitely yes. We were loaded into the same van. I could tell by the dents and scratches on one of its interior walls. Well, anyway, as the rear doors were about to be shut, there was the call for the late-afternoon prayer. That distracted the person holding the rear doors; he shut them quickly and went to find his prayer rug. When the van sped off, the rear doors swung open and I caught a glimpse of a tall radio communications tower in the distance. It stuck in my mind that the sun was directly behind the top of the tower. When the driver panic-stopped, the doors swung shut."

Smithy went on and described the trip to the desert site, the few stops along the way, and his brief tussle when he tried to escape, then went on and described the details of his stay in the desert trailers, his escape in a sand storm and stumbling into a Bedouin camp. As Smithy continued, one of the inquisitors in the room laid a big plastic protractor on a large map of the city of Aleppo. Another entered data into a computer application that was used in the Islamic world to determine the precise time of each of the five daily calls to prayer. The inputs were the latitude and longitude of Aleppo, and solar astronomical data including the declination of the sun. The resultant time was entered into another application that output the elevation and azimuth of the sun. The analysts were particularly interested in the solar azimuth. Agents very familiar with Aleppo circled the location of a radio tower, a distinctive feature in that city. With the protractor, a line was drawn eastward from the tower through an industrial area. It crossed over a horizontal, large building. Operatives in Aleppo were soon tasked to clandestinely surveil that building, around the clock, and report.

A seasoned man walked crisply down the long corridor in the bowels of one of the most secure buildings on the planet, in Northern Virginia, close to the nation's capital. Heels of polished shoes *clacked* and echoed on the gleaming floor. He came to a door with a keypad on the wall, flooded with bright light, monitored by a security camera. He held a long roll of old paper under his arm as he entered his set of numbers. He pushed the door open and was greeted by a flashing red light and a buzzer alerting those within of an entry. Conversation ceased and highly classified documents were covered until the man was positively identified, even though he obviously had the access code. The door solidly shut behind him with a reassuring heavy *thunk*. He laid the roll on the cluttered table surrounded by people with deadly serious intent.

He knew them very well, some over his long career. He was in charge. But there were needed outsiders who had been read in. Their security clearances enabled access to the highest levels of compartmented information. A man at the table was dressed comfortably, wearing a well-worn leather jacket. "Hi, Ian. How's it been going in God's country?"

"Not bad, once you get used to the rain." Ian sat there chewing gum, smacking away to the annoyance of others. His jaunty British cap lay on the table before him on a stack of photographs. An older man at the table had a lined face and bushy gray beard. He was not a government employee. He worked for a contractor as the lead engineer for a laser-guided air-to-ground missile, the Hellfire. He had overseen the design of every part of this deadly weapon, including the business end: the warhead.

The room had stark mission-planning ambiance. Large white dry-erase boards were on one wall, covered with facts, actions and dates. On the other walls were mounted large LED screens to view images and recorded video. These were controlled from a laptop computer on the table. Some screens displayed real-time feeds of national and international news programs showing audio-translated text that came from silent voices.

The man with the rolled-up, slightly-yellowed building plans slid a CD into the computer and announced that this would likely be the last meeting before execution of Operation Hellfire. To impress them again, he repeated a few lines in Arabic when he spoke of the target: *Jaysh al-Allah*. He was fluent in this difficult language. As he unrolled the set of building plans, he summarized where and how he had obtained them. The plans had been scanned for presentation on the big screen, their digitized images recorded on the CD, but the actual plans on the table added intentional heft to his presentation.

He pushed a button on the laptop. A high-resolution image from an overhead reconnaissance satellite came up. It showed the streets around a square building. He laid his hand on the paper plans, then advanced their computer images. With mouse-controlled cursor, he pointed to architectural drawings of the building, its plan and side views. One showed the underground area beneath the main floor. While different than in America, he explained that city-planning and property ownership records were similar in Syria. Urban administration crossed cultural lines, and CIA operatives had probed this line of investigation. They had found the original owner of the building who had used it as a warehouse for his business. A meeting with this old, retired

Arab businessman netted important information missing in the plans: materials used for the main floor and roof, and any reinforcing. He expanded the plan of the basement area. He moved the cursor over what had been the office of the owner. "Ladies and gentlemen, this is our target."

He turned the meeting over to the Hellfire engineer. As detailed engineering drawings of the Hellfire missile were shown, he described that they had modified the warheads of two missiles, that they had been delivered to the Navy and were aboard an aircraft carrier now on station in the Eastern Mediterranean. The warheads on these missiles would not be shaped-charges to penetrate heavy armor, but anti-personnel with lethal, razor-edged shrapnel. The blast design of the warhead had been modified to ensure a one-hundred percent kill probability within the dimensions of the basement room shown; the special tungsten shrapnel would also ricochet off the concrete walls. The room would be turned into a hive of high-velocity killing bees. Special hardening had been added around the explosive charge to ensure penetration through the building roof and the concrete main floor. To ensure explosion in that room, not before, not after, precise time delays for the detonator had been incorporated. After it had sensed roof penetration, it integrated the arrival speed of the missile fired from a high-altitude drone. Horizontal aspect angles and vertical penetration angles had been carefully calculated to ensure arrival in the center of the basement room after the missile had been guided to a specific spot on the roof, to be illuminated with a remotely-controlled laser from the same drone. He moved the cursor to the red dot graphically added to the warehouse image from an aerial reconnaissance supersonic overflight.

The old engineer smiled as he brought up the next image. It was of the delivery drone: a large, jet-powered machine, capable of flying at very high altitudes, unseen, unheard. Once armed and launched near its area of operations, with satellite communications links, it could be controlled from an operations center located just about anywhere. But an ops center in Nevada, with hardened and redundant communications, had been selected for Operation Hellfire. They had launched other missiles from this aerial platform before, evaporating unsuspecting terrorists who had thought they were hidden. Everyone in the planning room noted a close up of the tail of the drone. It had been painted jet black. On it were silver dots connected by silver lines in the shape of the constellation of Orion, the Hunter. Next to it was a close-up of the tail of downed Aster Flight 2123. The drone would indeed be the hunter ... and executioner.

"OK, Ian, what have you got?" He stood holding a stack of enlarged color photographs. He spoke with contempt as he threw them down on the table, "This is the sonofabitch that poisoned the flight crew of Aster Flight 2123!" The photographs were spread apart on the table, and the others leaned in to get a better look. He put on his British cap, reached for the laptop and toggled the next images. They showed various views of a young blond-haired man in different parts of the concourse of Portland International Airport. One showed the Route US 66 sign, with him sitting in a booth with two Aster Airline pilots. He tapped a control on the laptop and expanded the image and moved the cursor to his face. "This mission is for that bastard."

The project leader selected the next images, clandestine photographs taken in a wealthy area of Riyadh. "Those folks at NSA did a bang-up data-mining job; intercepted a lot of similar digital texts. Their supercomputers honed in on an overly-frequent use of a single word, *Khalasset,* married to a single number of an apparent sequence that led them to this asshole and the *mullah* at his mosque.

All in the room stared at the close-up image of Kashif and *mullah* Fahim leaving a mosque, easily recognized by his headdress. "Comes from a very wealthy, connected family. He's a fucking genius, actually. Studied snakes and their venom at UCI. Came up with a timed poison. He's under Saudi investigation for killing people in a remote desert location to test the stuff."

Somebody at the table raised his hand, asking, "What the hell does that word mean? I'm not a linguist."

"*Khalasset*; it's Arabic for 'done' or 'it is finished' when completing an important or difficult task. This word was intercepted a number of times, months apart, each with a different number. The recipient of the transmission was likely checking off items on a 'to do' list. Quite a few of these satellite-comm transmissions originated from a remote spot in that big-ass desert in Southern Saudi Arabia, the Empty Quarter, known in that part of the world as the Rub' al-Khali." With a mouse click, text was shown on the screen, "This is our translation of a transmission from that location, probably done in a panic."

American Escape
Kill Ramza
Akmal, I, Bring Chemical Riyadh

"The American is none other than Gunnery Sergeant John Kelly, a Marine special-forces type, a decorated sniper. While advising Kurdish forces in the battle for ar-Raqqah, he was captured and wound up at the desert site, but managed to escape. We've been debriefing him."

Another at the table stood and took to the mouse, a technically-hardened woman, a no-nonsense type from a nearby satellite reconnaissance office. "Gentlemen, we should have picked up on this desert site sooner with our artificial intelligence analysis system that picks up imagery changes. One of our analysts had brought it to my attention, but it looked like any number of other Bedouin tents that dot the desert. Their nomadic movement from place to place triggers our system. We should have paid closer attention to this one. There were no animals near it; camels or goats that our overheads can resolve."

Those around the table stared at the dark square image among obvious sand dunes. She advanced to the next image of the same location, but in an expanded view, and moved the cursor as a pointer. "Those shapes you see there are other tents and camels; the smaller ones are people, goats and camels. Upon further analysis we have concluded that a nearby Bedouin camp has moved in and taken over the place and its tarp-covered trailers. The last overhead pass shows that they are still there."

The project leader stood up. "We have resources on the ground in Aleppo, close to the target. People have been coming and going from the warehouse. The one from Oregon has been identified, as well as the scientist and the *mullah* from Riyadh, but there have been a few others. We suspect that they all had a hand in bringing down Aster Flight 2123 and are there to review what happened and to plan a future attempt, or to otherwise use the special poison. We intercepted a carelessly transmitted text that invited them to the place. Our operatives have a good estimate of the time of day, overnight, when all or most of them will arrive in darkness and will likely be together in the basement room. This will be confirmed on-site in real time, with the go-code transmitted to us, critical to bringing hellfire down on them. If there are unforeseen problems, a no-go-code will be transmitted to abort the mission. Weather, cloud cover, fog or heavy haze, between the drone and the target, have not been forecast, but we'll watch that closely. Those would limit imagery and laser beam transmission. We've got our best weather guessers working on this at a secure facility in Omaha, using all of the world's weather and satellite data and the best super-computer models. Are there any questions?"

There were just a few questions, but all the planning piece-parts were finally in place to execute the mission, directed at the highest level: the President of the United States. "I'll be with the President in the White House Situation Room when the strike is executed."

†

They started to arrive, quietly in the dark of night, to celebrate and plan. They entered with coded slaps on the basement door, met Hadi, then left. Each had arranged temporary living accommodations in other parts of the basement as directed, and to blend in with the populace when required to venture outside for food and water. But that was to be kept to an absolute minimum. Some days later, the day of the full meeting finally arrived. That date had been very well estimated by others in Aleppo and in McLean, Virginia, and given to those sitting in an operations center in Nevada.

Kashif arrived first. His father's wealth had been aimed at the right places in Riyadh, slowing investigators, but not slowing his travel plans. He was not alone. *Mullah* Fahim came in right behind him. Next, two Yemenis entered. These truck drivers were from a lower economic class, and Kashif started to look at them with disdain but caught himself. These, too, were soldiers in *Jaysh al-,Allah,* as was Akmal who entered right behind them. They waited. The last to arrive was late. Finally, with repeated slaps on the door, he

was let in: Gene from America. He had been in
this room a few months earlier and had already
met Hadi and Akmal. With hands placed over
hearts, greetings were made. Then everybody
settled down.

Each part of the plan and their role in it was
revealed and discussed in great detail. What went
right, what went wrong, strengths, weaknesses,
what to do differently. This hot wash-up would
be used to plan the next aircraft downing.

Hadi announced that more people in America
had been flipped, turned to the hard side of
Islam and were ready to help. Below the radar
of Homeland Security investigators, they lived in
Chicago, Dallas and Atlanta. Those large cities
had large airports with large numbers of pilots
flying out of them in two-seat jet liners. Kashif
interrupted with, "New regulations are coming
where the lives of pilots hours before their
flights are now more-strongly dictated, including
eating."

"We know this. But compliance for any
new law is not one hundred percent, especially
for an unpopular one among pilots. We must be
patient. In a year, maybe less, the view of our
threat will fade, as will pilot adherence to how
to eat. Our new brothers in America are watching
for opportunities, when cracks in their defenses
appear. When their guard is down, *Allah* will

guide us."

Hadi leaned over and whispered to Muhammed Talib that he was not feeling well, that maybe it was something he had eaten. The lamb had had a strange taste; maybe it had been left out of the refrigerator. Hadi called over an armed guard and ordered that he be escorted to the roof to get some fresh air.

†

A Marine in full Dress Blues stood next to one of the big cushy leather chairs next to the head of the table where the President would sit. He was squared away, sharp, very fit, hair cut high and tight – a Marine. The project leader from the CIA and heads of security and intelligence agencies had already arrived in the Situation Room. The Secretary of State and Secretary of Defense arrived, followed by the Chairman of the Joint Chiefs of Staff, a Marine four-star general. He strode over to a fellow Marine, John "Smithy" Kelly, gave him a hearty handshake and cuffed him firmly on his shoulder. They spoke about his time in Afghanistan, Iraq, Syria, and in the Rub' al-Kahli. The White House Chief of Staff walked in and announced the President.

She walked to the head of the table, but before sitting spoke to Smithy, loud enough for all to hear, how proud and honored she was to meet him, then shook his hand with a firm grip that surprised him. He replied, "Madam President, it is my distinct honor to meet you."

With that, she sat and motioned for all to sit. The project leader gave a brief overview of what they were about to see. Everyone in the room had seen the highly-classified plan and had received personal briefings. The large LED screen at the far end of the room showed the latest satellite image of the abandoned warehouse in Aleppo, that the go-code had been received. The weather was clear, as forecast. He said that the latest intelligence estimate was that most if not all of the perpetrators were in the building and that the drone would be overhead in twenty minutes. "Madam President, do we have your approval to execute?"

Without hesitation she commanded, "Yes."

The displayed image changed and came to life, showing satellite-relayed, real-time imagery from the drone crossing the Syrian coast. As the ground slid by beneath, fixated eyes were surrounded by muffled chatter. It had been launched from a US aircraft carrier. The same imagery was being monitored at the same time by controllers in the operations center in Nevada, one with his finger on the launch command button, others controlling the camera, the laser designator and the flight of the drone. It was just after midnight in Aleppo, so infrared imagery was seen: black, gray and white dictated by surface temperatures. The imagery moved side to side as the camera was slewed. The room fell silent as the now-familiar outline of the warehouse came into view, moving down from the top of the screen.

The cross-hairs in the center of the image were slewed over a spot near the edge of the warehouse roof. "Madam President, we still have a go-code. Almost all of the terrorists are there."

The launch command had been given. An unseen, infrared laser beam went to where the displayed, now blinking cross-hairs were placed, fixed to the spot. The Hellfire missile was on its way, its locked-on seeker tracking the reflected laser light like it was glued to it. With the video imagery of flashing cross-hairs held steady on the same spot, Smithy knew the missile had left its rail, a large round from a semi-automated sniper in the sky. He took these few seconds of flight to reflect on the Kurdish soldiers he had advised and fought with, his wartime friends that had become test guinea pigs in a trailer in a remote desert. Only one thing could ease his rage.

This was it.

Hadi felt there was enough 3FT3b-23-2 for the next attack missions, to be used in any number of ways, some well beyond flying. He had not learned that a search warrant in Hillsboro, Oregon had changed all that, as well as Saudi police investigators in a Riyadh laboratory.

Mullah Fahim looked up at the low ceiling and announced an encouraging, "*Allahu Akbar!*" As the others in the room repeated this short profession of faith, their world went instantly from brilliant, blinding white to the darkest black, to the Common Eternity. Their prayers would have to be delivered in person. Then they would know.

✝

Two small moving heat images had appeared near the middle of the roof, then a big white glare spread out from the cross-hairs at the roof's edge. The surface wind was as forecast. The erupting smoke cloud drifted away from the cross-hairs. This was followed by another bright flash; the operators in Nevada had unleashed the second Hellfire missile carried by the drone, as planned, just to make sure. The Situation Room did not erupt in applause, but satisfied looks started appearing on slowly nodding heads around the table. Smithy impulsively stood up, raised a clenched fist, and shouted "Ooorah!" then turned. "Excuse me, Ma'am." Then he smartly saluted the President. She didn't hesitate, but stood, returned his salute, gripped his hand and left the room.

Eyes followed this real leader, knowing she had led like a mother lion protecting her cubs, swiping away her enemies with a swift, powerful paw with sharp claws. The post-strike damage assessment would follow her.

†

A different scene unfolded in a different room in a Portland hospital. Two people watched the evening news. They saw the President of the United States standing at a podium in the White House announcing that those responsible for poisoning the pilots of Aster Airlines Flight 2123, that had forced its crash landing, had been struck and killed in Aleppo, Syria by missiles fired from a drone launched from a United States Navy aircraft carrier in the waters of the Eastern Mediterranean Sea.

Dressed in hospital gowns, they looked at each other, then hugged, "They did it, weather guy."

"Yes, captain, they did."

Epilogue

A cluster of men sat in a seaside coffee shop on the Syrian coast in the ancient city of Tartus. Fishing boats tugged at their mooring lines. The heavy aroma of spices was almost intoxicating. They discussed heatedly how the long arm of American air power had reached an old building in Aleppo. They looked up to see a stranger limp in and take a seat on a big floor cushion. They had watched him walk slowly back and forth on the seawall of the harbor, then just stand for some time and stare out at the water. Nothing was said as he ordered spiced coffee. As he reclined, he rubbed his left elbow, as if in pain. They tried not to stare, but could not help it. His left arm was made of wood.